A SNAKE

IN THE

RASPBERRY
PATCH

A SNAKE
IN THE
RASPBERRY
PATCH

A NOVEL BY
JOANNE JACKSON

Stonehouse Publishing
www.stonehousepublishing.ca
Alberta, Canada

Stonehouse Publishing Inc. is an independent
publishing house, incorporated in 2014.

Cover design and layout by Anne Brown.
Printed in Canada

Stonehouse Publishing would like to thank and acknowledge the
support of the Alberta Government funding for the arts, through
the Alberta Media Fund.

Government

National Library of Canada Cataloguing in Publication Data
Joanne Jackson
A Snake in the Raspberry Patch
Novel
ISBN: 978-1-988754-41-3

This book is dedicated to, in order of birth, my mom, Louise, her four sisters, Aunt Irene, Aunt Elsie, Aunt Evelyn, Aunt Beverly, and her one brother, the baby of the family, Uncle Roger.
Love you all.

PROLOGUE - FALL 1949

The store has so much merchandise displayed; employees wouldn't notice if a dozen items were taken, let alone one. Because so few people frequent these shops, it's hard to go unnoticed, but risk is what the boy searches for, revels in. He likes his senses being on high alert, his blood tingling in his veins as he sneaks up on his prey without them suspecting. It's a feeling of being in control, something he doesn't have at home. He picks up a jackknife and rubs the shaft with his thumb.

"Fifteen bucks," the clerk calls from behind the cash register. "Swiss Army Knife. Lots of gadgets inside. Open it if you like."

He's never understood shoplifters who look like thieves. Get some nice clothes, for gosh sakes. Take a bath occasionally. There's a craft to stealing, and looking like a bum only alerts the staff that someone suspicious is in the store.

Today he's wearing a pale green shirt with the emerald cufflinks his mom gave him for his birthday. He has on a beige tie and a brown leather jacket. The last time he was in the city he managed to walk out of a store while wearing the coat with no one the wiser. His pants are pressed, and his shoes are polished. His short hair is clean and slicked off his face and this morning he shaved his soft whiskers before he came into the city. He looks like an innocent youth whose parents have money, which they do. He appears so harmless, there's no way this clerk will suspect him of anything.

Unless this is one of those super-clerks who thinks he's picked him out as a shoplifter the moment he walked in the door. The type of clerk who zeroed in on him as if he's hiding a gun in his shorts. Luckily, most of the people who work in shops like this are employees who don't have a vested interest, so are lackadaisical, especially if you steal on Saturday. Owners don't like to work weekends.

"Yeah?" he says. "From Switzerland?"

"You been there?" the clerk asks.

"Nope. Never left Canada."

Another knife has caught the boy's eyes. Pearl handle, silver inlay. But he doesn't draw attention to it by questioning the clerk. If anyone notices that knife is missing, he wants the employee to tell his boss it was the Swiss Army knife a customer was interested in, not the pearl handled one. *And besides,* the clerk would say, *this clean-cut boy wouldn't have stolen a thing.* Even though he knows shoplifting is a crime, he doesn't like others to think badly of him.

 He ambles to the next shelf and pretends to be interested in the assortment of picture frames cluttering the rack. He picks one up, reads the paper inside the wooden frame that's been painted gold, then puts it back down. "Not the right size," he mutters loud enough for the clerk to hear. He paws through a few more of the frames, never finding the one he wants. He moves up a shelf to the calendars. Why they still have 1949 calendars for sale in September, he doesn't know but he rifles through the pile nonetheless. Anything to make him look like a legitimate customer. He continues in this manner around the shop, picking up this and that, professing the items aren't exactly what he's looking for until he's toured the entire shop.

He glances first at the clerk to ensure he's not being watched, then quickly out the window. His friends are there, waiting for him on the sidewalk, each with their own hands in their pockets fingering what they've managed to steal. As he watches, the father of that square kid, the one he didn't want to join their gang, approaches. The man is shouting at his son, shouting at his friends.

He knows it's now or never, but hesitates, wondering if the employee will realize the commotion outside has to do with him. As the father is dragging his son away and the clerk stops what he's doing to stare out the window, the boy takes his chance. Walking past the shelf with the jackknives, he tucks the pearl handled blade into his palm, then heads towards the exit.

The clerk turns his head. "Thanks for coming in," he calls as the door bangs shut behind the boy with the clean-cut appearance.

CHAPTER ONE

Dad and some men from the neighbourhood have congregated in our living room to toast the birth of my brother with a glass of rye, but mostly the conversation is about the trouble that's happened down the highway at the Tremblay's. It's all anyone has talked about for days. I'm on my front step because Jennifer, my best friend, is walking over from her house a few blocks away. Mr. Pendergrass, her next-door neighbour, is escorting her—kids haven't been allowed to go anywhere alone since the afternoon it happened. Before supper Jen called and said she wanted to come over to talk about high school, so, because grade nine is weighing heavily on my mind, I rushed through dishes. Now she and Mr. Pendergrass are late, and I have to wait outside because our house is full of men.

The inside door is open allowing what little breeze there is on this hot evening to blow through the screened-in front porch, and Dad, not paying as close attention to his daughters as Mom would want, allows the men to talk freely. Deciding to make the most of being stuck out here, I slide behind the dogwood bush where I can hear them without being seen. All I've been able to discern is that the Tremblay family were killed the same day my brother was born, but I know few of the details. I knew Colleen, one of the girls who died, but we weren't best friends. She was a girl who was there when you needed someone to play catch with so you didn't have to spend recess alone. A girl you liked well enough to invite to your birthday party so you could get invited to hers.

I've heard some of the older kids talking outside Fogg's Grocery Store, or while they're gathered at The Park where they can smoke without being seen, but mostly they tell me to get lost before I can hear much. Knowing Dad wouldn't know enough to restrict me, last night after supper I sat down in front of the television to watch the news. I'd made the meal, ground beef casserole with noodles, then washed and dried the dishes by myself. Dad never does dishes, and Rose escaped by saying she had things to do before the sun went down. I figured if I was old enough to be chief cook and bottle washer until Mom came home, I was old enough to sit down and do the same thing my parents do after the supper meal. Lloyd Robertson had just welcomed the viewers to CBC when our phone rang. It was Mom calling from the hospital. She said that *under no circumstances is Elizabeth allowed to watch the news on TV.* I don't know how she knew what I was doing, but she did. She said it was going to be difficult enough at her age to get up with a new baby all night long, let alone a thirteen-year-old having bad dreams. You'd think she'd know I'm made of tougher stuff than that. Perhaps it's being pregnant that's caused her to forget. She's been crabby for the past nine months and I heard her tell Dad that if this turns out to be a boy, she's through. I surely hope her mood has changed when she gets home.

I was resentful about Mom's decree, but I didn't argue even though I'm more intrigued than scared. How could someone walk up to a stranger and shoot him in the head? Or kill a child as he ran away like those high school kids said he did? These things happen in the big city and you cluck your tongue and say *What a shame. That poor family. I'm glad we don't live in a crime-infested place like that.* Here in Willowsbend, in the middle of farmland from horizon to horizon—except for an invasion of gophers, a deluge of hail, or a plague of grasshoppers—nothing ever happens.

I listen as the men's voices go around the coffee-table. Some I can put a face to, some I can't. Mr. Henderson speaks first.

"Marj was sitting on the front porch playing cards with her youngest. Executed her and the little one right there. I don't know which would be worse, shooting Marj first so the daughter sees, or the daughter first for Marj to witness. I can't even imagine." I can picture Mr. Henderson's already long face, drawn even longer as he shakes his head at his own words. His voice pauses before he says, "Don't know what in the world would possess him to take Marj's tongue," and I gasp, pressing the back of my hand over my mouth so Dad won't hear.

"Henry and his oldest boy must have been checking the crops and heard the shots. Drove home to see what the noise was. They didn't have a chance. Found Henry draped across the running board shot in the head, his son sitting in the passenger seat shot clean through the chest, bullet buried in the seat he was slumped against." Mr. Krieger's voice.

"Another boy was found in the hedge that circles the house. Shot in the back. Probably running, trying to get away. Killed the rest of the kids in the backyard. One was sprawled under the net Henry had nailed to the garden shed, basketball wedged under the boy's hand. The oldest girl was lying in the hammock, hole clean through the book she was reading. Only blessing is the shots were dead on, and every one of them died quickly, the coroner said."

"At least he left the children intact," Mr. Krieger says. "If I catch him, I'll tie him up, gouge out his eyes, then cut off his...."

My rubber ball slips out of my hand and bounces down our walkway to the front sidewalk. Instead of slowing down, it picks up momentum as it heads across the street, ending up in the front yard of the Henderson's. I know, at thirteen, I'm getting too old to play with children's toys, but I still like to see how high it will bounce until it's just a black dot in the sky.

The talking stops and the floorboards groan. I scrunch down behind the bush then sit as still as a mouse while Dad steps into the porch; his large frame blocks the screen door. He returns to the living room without seeing me and the conversation resumes.

"Are there any other suspects besides Stanley Drummond?" Mr. Fogg asks.

"The RCMP said Drummond is merely a person of interest. I assume, only because he recently got out of jail, and now he's missing," Mr. Henderson says. "They released him for compassionate reasons after his wife died in childbirth. There's no warrant out for him, at least not yet."

"Can't believe they only gave him five months. Wasn't it the second time he broke into your store, Jim?" Mr. Krieger asks.

"It was," Dad says. "As far as I know, he never steals anything, just ransacks the place. Though it's difficult to keep track of every bolt and nail."

"I don't trust that Drummond family as far as I could throw them," Mr. Henderson says. "Caught one of 'em shoplifting in the drugstore a few days ago. The oldest girl, Gail, I think they call her, was stealing safety pins and talcum powder, of all things. I didn't say anything; let her take what she needed. Paid Neil a bit more when I bought my cigarettes. She's got her hands full with that new baby and now no Mom to look after the wretched thing."

"If Stan did kill Marj," Dad says, "prison must have made him go off the deep end, that's all I can think. I don't know why else he'd do such a thing."

"There is the chance this wasn't a local," Mr. Fogg says. "Could have been anyone driving through town on their way to the city. Just a random shooting."

"I suppose the RCMP have to consider all possibilities," Dad says, "no matter how slim."

In the quiet I hear the chug of liquid being poured.

"When's Patricia coming home?" Mr. Henderson asks.

"Tomorrow," Dad says.

"You finally got your boy, Jim."

Glasses clink as the men toast my brother.

"He's going to have to learn to defend himself, growing up with five sisters," Dad says.

Two months before my second birthday, Rose was born and I quickly came to hate her because Mom didn't pay attention to me anymore. I would reach between the rails of the playpen and pinch my baby sister, then steal her milk and throw it across the room. Mom would find the bottle behind the radio or the couch and say *What a good pitching arm Rose has*, then look at me and smile. Rose is the only one, of the now six kids, who was born at home. Mom has always said *That girl wanted to start living and wouldn't wait another second to be born.*

Hoping for a boy and thinking time might make a difference, Mom didn't give birth for five years, but to no avail; she had another girl and named her Francine. Then I felt sorry for Rose because she was in the same predicament as me. When Fran was three, Robin was born, and we all hated the new baby, though I think Franny was only trying to emulate her older sisters. And when poor little Robin had just passed her first birthday, Alexandra came along, but none of us hated Alex. She's the only one with blue eyes and strawberry blond hair, the rest of us having green eyes and red hair, like Dad. Mom, who has blue eyes and dark hair, calls us her raspberry patch.

For the past few months the whole family has been suggesting names for our new sibling. I liked Marie, which is Mom's middle name. Dad picked Marjorie, but Mom said that's only because it's the name of a girlfriend he had before he met her and she winked at me. My youngest sisters wanted Snow White, but changed to Violet when Mrs. Olyphant took us to see the movie, *Willy Wonka and the Chocolate Factory*, and Rose wanted the more modern name of Kimberly. Mom had picked Janet for a girl's name but unbeknownst to the rest of us who hadn't even considered a boy's name, she'd been saving the name Cole for years, hoping one day she'd have a son to christen.

Dad didn't stay at the hospital with Mom this time. At three in the morning when she went into labour, he helped her into the car while I put a sleepy Alex, Robin, and Franny in the back seat. He dropped the girls off at the Olyphant's farm, took Mom to the city and admitted her into the hospital, then drove straight back home. I guess after having five kids, Mom didn't need her husband to stick around and hold her hand. At eight in the morning when the phone call came, I was prepared to watch his shoulders droop as he found out he had yet another daughter. Instead, he stood tall and gave one of his rare smiles. Now Cole is the sixth in line and the only boy in our little dynasty, and we will always remember his birthday of July twenty-first nineteen seventy-one because it's the day the Tremblay family was massacred down the highway that leads to the city.

"Why are you scrunched down behind the bush?" Rose says in a voice loud enough for Dad to hear. She has her camera around her neck, something she never goes anywhere without. At an early age she showed an interest in photography and Mom gave her a Kodak for her seventh birthday. In the past four years, Rose has become very proficient at getting the right angle and the right lighting and takes candid shots of people all the time. The funny thing is, no one seems to mind. She pops in a flashcube and snaps a shot of me sitting in the shade.

"Shush," I say as I push her hand away, my eyes now blinded.

"Don't tell me to shush," she says. She pulls a notebook out of her pocket and mouths "Eavesdropping," as she writes. She titles all her pictures and has albums full of them stacked in our bedroom. Sometimes we fall asleep looking through the pages and remembering what we were doing at the time the picture was taken. She spends all her allowance on film, developing the film, flashcubes, and albums.

Dad opens the screen door and pokes his head out. "What's going on out here?"

"Waiting on Jen," I say.

"Just taking some pictures of Liz," Rose says.

Dad sighs and I feel his pain. Raising girls is hard on him. He knows tools and nails, paint and shovels, mops and hoses; all the paraphernalia, minutiae, and household items he sells at Murphy's Hardware. Females, he doesn't have a hope in hades of understanding. It's a good thing the three youngest are still at the Olyphant's farm or I'd be babysitting them as well as doing the cooking, cleaning and gardening.

"Wait someplace else, you two," he says. "You don't need to sit there listening to the men talk." He turns to go inside, then spins back to me. "And look after your sister. Don't let her go anywhere alone."

"Yes, Dad."

He allows the screen door to bang shut and returns to the living room. Dad isn't a big talker. That's the most he's said to me since Mom left five days ago.

"I don't need you to look after me," Rose whispers. "I can look after myself. The only reason Dad told you to look after me is because Mom reminded him not to forget about his daughters while she was in the hospital. Anyhow," she says, "I was already alone. I went to look at the Tremblay's house."

"You what?" I drag her to the front sidewalk, which isn't easy as Rose is a stubborn girl.

"Let go of me," she says and digs in her heels.

I let go before Dad hears. "Don't you dare ever do anything like that again. Mom would get mad if she knew," I say.

"And who's going to tell her, you? I'll tell her I saw you sneak out the window in the middle of the night to sit in your treehouse." She puckers up her brow. "Don'tcha want to know what I saw?"

"I guess," I say, my curiosity getting the better of me. I toe the weeds out of the cracks while she talks.

"Well, there's toys and stuff scattered everywhere, like always. Bikes, roller skates, doll carriages, garden tools. Looked so normal I kept thinking the kids were going to come running out of the house. But there's tape, you know the yellow stuff? It's stretched across the front veranda, making it look like a crime scene. And there's a truck parked in the yard with the door wide open. I saw blood on the running board."

"You got close enough to see blood?"

"I wish. Officer Brown came out of the house so I had to hide in the ditch. But it sure looked like blood." She looks at her little instamatic. "I wish Mom would buy me a better camera with a telephoto lens. I could do some real detecting if I had one of those."

"Rose, you have to stop doing stuff like that. What if the killer saw you?"

"Don't be a drip, the killer wouldn't stick around for five days." She fingers the strap on her camera. "Unless he's a glory seeker. I've read about them. They hang around after they've set fire to something just to see how much commotion they caused. Or," she taps her temple. "Maybe he's crazy smart and wants to direct the attention onto some poor schmuck in order to take any possible focus off of him." She dismisses the idea with a wave of her hand. "But he's probably in Mexico lying on a beach drinking some exotic drink with a pineapple and umbrella in it. No one stays around after doing something like that. Not even crazy people."

Footsteps slap the pavement and I put my hand above my eyes to peer down the block. Two figures are approaching and with the setting sun behind them, they look like child renderings of stickmen—all shadows and straight lines, their edges blurred by the glare of the sun. One of the figures races ahead of the other who is moving much slower, his long arms and legs propelling him forward as he tries to keep up. He's calling for Jennifer to slow down and wait for him but she keeps on running, her dark ponytail flying out behind her.

Jen is only five months older than me, but she acts like she's five years older. She bought a tube of pink lipstick at the drugstore and when we go to the movies or out for a Coke, she applies it carefully to her lips while looking at her reflection in a store window; there's no way she could put it on at home, her mother would have a conniption fit. Jen bats her eyes at all the cute boys and is always flipping her ponytail and looking over her shoulder to see if they're watching. But for all her girly ways, she's also a tomboy. She can run faster than any of the boys, and when we have field day in the park, she always wins at long jump. Four years ago, she punched a grade eight girl in the nose for stealing the lunch of a grade two kid. She and the grade eight kid both got detention for a week. Jen told me she'd do it all over again if she had to. The one thing Jen is afraid of, though she'd never admit it to anyone, is heights. I've invited her to sit in my treehouse countless times, but she always has an excuse. Homework, housework, the neighbour's dog needs walking; anything to avoid having to make her way across the roof, which is fine by me. I like having someplace to go where no one else is allowed.

She skids to a stop in front of me, her lips pressed so tightly together, she looks like someone who's bursting to say something but is trying to win a no-talking contest.

"Hi, Mr. Pendergrass," I say as he catches up.

Mr. Pendergrass is a melancholy man. Very seldom have I seen him smile. He's also never been married. I assumed he never married because he's the garbageman and most women don't want to be married to a garbageman, but Jen told me she heard her mom gossiping over the fence with the neighbour who said that Mr. Pendergrass was in love with someone, had been for years. When Mrs. Olsen asked her neighbour who the love of his life was, the neighbour said all she knew was that it was a married woman.

He touches the brim of his cap. "Evening, ladies." He's puffing heavily and pulls a cigarette out of his shirt pocket then pushes it back down and takes out a toothpick. "Trying to quit." He pokes the wooden stick between his teeth. "Stay in the neighbourhood, now, Miss Olsen." He wags a yellowed finger at Jennifer. "Your mom entrusted me with you tonight. That goes for all of you." He looks at each of us in turn.

We nod with sombre faces.

"You're welcome to go inside, Mr. Pendergrass," I say. "The men are in the living room."

He doffs his cap which he wears when he's not working, snaps his suspenders which he wears all the time, and strides across our front yard. When he arrives at the porch, he pauses with his hand on the handle and looks back at us, as if unsure he should enter.

"Go ahead, Mr. Pendergrass," Rose urges. "Dad's expecting you."

He nods and steps into the porch. He gently closes the screen door then looks back one last time before entering the house.

When he's out of sight, Jen explodes. "I saw him," she whispers as she grabs my shoulders.

"Who?" I say.

"The man who, you know," she makes a slicing motion across her throat with her fingers.

"No, you didn't," Rose says. "Quit being so melodramatic."

"And you," Jen pokes a finger at Rose without touching her because Rose would poke back, "quit using words that are bigger than you."

Rose narrows her eyes at my friend. "I only use big words because I know what they mean, unlike you who has to speak in two syllable words because you're illiterate."

"C'mon," I say to Jen, pulling her away from my sister. "What was so urgent you had to tell me?"

She glares daggers at Rose before allowing me to pull her away.

"Well," her tone is conspiratorial, "you know how when we were in grade eight all the boys seemed young?"

"Actually, everyone in my class is thirteen or fourteen. Except for Billy McDougal. I'm sure he'll keep redoing grade eight until he's twenty years old. This year was his second try and still he failed. He can barely fit into the...."

"No, not the same age, the same *age*, you know, mentally. Remember when I learnt in health class that girls mature much faster than boys?"

Being as how in the Catholic faith, where abstinence is expected until after marriage, sex education is not included in the curriculum like it is in the public-school system. So, Jen, who goes to the public school, passes any information she learns from her health classes on to me. When the day came that Mom decided I was old enough to tell me the facts of life, I didn't let on I already knew.

"But in high school, because we're the youngest, we'll have our choice of boys older than us, boys closer to our maturity level. No more stupid little-boy pranks like locking us in the bathroom or panty raids while we're in the shower after gym class. No more panting as we walk past them in the hall or jokes about what size our boulder-holders are. The boys in high school will be so much more mature."

From a distance, we hear Rose say, "Boy crazy."

"Baby," Jen says. "You don't know anything."

"I know you didn't see the murderer on your way over here, that's what I know," Rose says.

"Did too!" Jen says. "When Mr. Pendergrass and I were walking over here I saw someone skulking down an alley. He had the hood of his bunnyhug pulled up and kept looking around as if he was worried someone would see him. I'll bet he was the murderer and he's going to ask the priest for, what do you call it, asylum."

"Father Mackinnon is harbouring a criminal? I doubt that," I say.

"No, no. I didn't actually see him talking to the priest, he was in an alley, heading in that direction. So, I can't say for sure where he was going, but he sure looked suspicious."

"Did Mr. Pendergrass see him too?" I ask.

"Are you kidding? He was so busy scrutinizing everyone's front yard for weeds and broken fence pickets, he didn't see anything else. He's a bit of a fusspot, if you ask me which is kind of weird considering he empties garbage cans for a living."

"What did he look like?" I ask.

"Who? Mr. Pendergrass?"

I scowl at her.

"Oh. You mean," again she slices her throat. "It was hard to tell. His hair looked tangled and greasy, blowing out the edges of his hood, and his clothes didn't fit right, kind of baggy like they didn't belong to him, or maybe like he'd lost weight. He looked like your basic run of the mill murderer."

"Like a murderer," Rose guffaws. "And how do you, a girl who's never left the Canadian prairies, know what a murderer looks like?"

"You'll find out if you don't watch your mouth." Jen steps towards my sister. They're both hot-heads and have never got along.

I swing Jennifer around. "Stop it, you two; you're going to get us all in trouble."

Mrs. Henderson's front door opens and she sticks out her head. "Show some respect, you three. A family is dead. You should be in your rooms praying for their souls, not arguing in the street about who gets to use the skipping rope first." She points at her petunia patch. "And who's rubber ball is that?"

"Sorry, Mrs. Henderson. That's mine," I say. "I'll get it."

She glowers at us before closing the door.

"Who gets to use the skipping rope first? How old does she think I am?" Jen says. "I'm fourteen, for God's sake," she yells at Mrs. Henderson who's pulled aside her living room curtains and is standing at the window watching us. "I haven't used a skipping rope in two years!"

The woman lets the drapes drop, veiling the sour look on her face.

"Busybody," Jennifer says under her breath. She flips Mrs. Henderson the bird.

I slap her hand. "Don't do that. She'll probably tell her husband who will tell Dad. I don't want to be grounded for the next week. You know how my dad is about not embarrassing our family."

"Yeah, Jennifer, shut your trap," Rose says. She turns to me. "But the woman is a busybody. You have to agree with that, Liz."

Jen points at the ball in my hand. "If you'd quit playing with toys, maybe she wouldn't think we're still children."

I feel my face heat up and toss the ball onto my front yard. "Let's get away from everyone watching us standing in the middle of the road," I say.

Then, even though I know we shouldn't be venturing so far from the house, the three of us walk to the end of the block and turn west into the sun that will set in less than an hour.

I put my hand to my eyes and look at Saint Mary's church in the distance. The cross on the steeple glints in the sun this time of the day, sending rays shooting across the sky. I follow the shafts of light with my eyes as they point towards the grain elevators to the south that have poked through the horizon for fifty years, and the seniors complex to the north, which was built last summer. Along with my family, I attended the grand opening. We sat in folding chairs on the front lawn and listened as our mayor made a speech. He said this building is a modern addition to our great community and he knows it will be used for generations to come. Then he cut the ropes holding the wrapping in place and unveiled the sign. Instead of reading Willowsbend Home for Seniors, it read Willowsbend Cemetery. The town council had decided to have two signs made because they received a better price. The delivery people didn't check which went where, just plopped one on the grass and left. At first everyone gasped, but soon laughter rippled across the crowd when they realized the cemetery got the Home for Seniors sign.

Saint Mary's Church is across the street from Saint Mary's Catholic Elementary School that I've just graduated from, and Willowsbend Public Elementary School Jen graduated from. A playground separates the two schools. It's what we call, The Park. If you ever want to meet anyone, say you'll meet them at The Park and they'll know where to go.

Willowsbend High school sits in the far corner of The Park, separated from the elementary schools by a ball diamond. Enrollment at that school is large for a small town; it's the only high school for miles around and is attended by both Catholic and non-Catholic students. Jen and I will be starting there in just a few, all too short, weeks.

I know of town kids whose parents are staunch Catholics and have billeted out their sons and daughters to friends or relatives in the city for grades nine to twelve just so they could continue to attend a Catholic school. Many of the kids from my grade eight class are leaving for the city in the next couple of weeks. Thank God Mom won't be doing that. She said by the time her child has finished grade eight, if she hasn't learned good morals and Christian values, then she probably isn't going to learn them and no amount of Catechism classes will help.

The playground is empty, not even the high school kids are gathered here smoking tonight, and Rose races ahead to nab the best swing. She lays her camera on the grass beside the swing's frame, then sits on the leather seat and pumps her legs so hard and fast, soon she's parallel to the ground. Whatever Rose does, she does with all her might. I take the swing to the right of her and drag my feet in the rut where a thousand kids have dragged their feet before me. Jen climbs the ladder to the top of the slide then sits there.

"I wonder what it felt like," Jen says.

"What, what felt like?" I ask.

"Being shot. I wonder what it felt like. Do you feel the bullet enter your body? Do you know you're going to die? How bad does it hurt?"

"I doubt you have time to take assessment of the pain." The wind from Rose's swing blows my hair across my face.

"You must feel something. Are you surprised? Do you wonder what happened?"

"I think you get shot and you die." I pull an elastic out of my pocket and tie my hair back. "You don't have time to think of anything. At least not the Tremblays. I heard the men talking tonight and one of them said that they died fast."

"That's good. I hate to think of the kids suffering." Jen lies back; her legs dangle down the metal ramp.

"What was it like?" I ask. "At the funerals? Dad didn't say much when he got home."

The funerals were held yesterday and because Mom didn't want Fran, Robin or Alex to see the people crying and carrying-on, she asked the Olyphants to drop them off at our house and then pick them up on their way home. Rose and I had to stay home and babysit. Jen was able to attend because it's only her and her mom in their family. There are times when I'm jealous of her not having siblings, but there's also times when I know she's lonely.

"It was what you'd expect, I guess, only more because, you know, there was seven of them at the same time." She pauses. "I've never seen a child's coffin before; so tiny."

A robin sings announcing to the world it's dusk.

"Mr. Tremblay's brother spoke about what a good man his brother was. Then one of the aunties talked. Said she knew her niece was in heaven playing with her sisters. That brought a gush of tears from everyone. Father Mackinnon said they were a good Christian family, and it was a horrific way to lose friends and neighbours, but the town had to find it in their hearts to forgive whoever did this monstrous act. Saw lots of people shake their heads when he said that. If it had been announced that the killer had been found right then, there would have been a lynch mob in the street. Say," she sits up, "I've never been to a Catholic service before. There was lots of sitting and standing and chanting and amen-ing. Is that what you do every Sunday?"

"Pretty much."

The three of us are quiet for a while until Jen breaks the silence.

"Do you think you go directly to heaven or hell when you die, or do you go someplace where they decide if you've been a good enough or bad enough person? Like a jury or something."

Rose has stopped swinging and picked up her camera. She has it pressed to her eye as she pretends it has the telephoto lens that she covets and watches Jen on the slide. "Listen to you, an atheist asking about heaven and hell," she says.

"I'm not an atheist, you little twerp. I just don't go to church ten times a week like you do. I still believe in," she waves her hands in the air, "something."

Rose snaps Jen's picture then takes out her notebook.

"The Catholic Church believes in purgatory," I say, "where you have to atone for you sins. I guess if you're really repentant, you get to go to heaven."

"Would you look at that." Rose has shifted her attention from my friend, to the back doors of Jen's school.

I put my hand above my eyes. "What?"

"Someone's in the atheist's school."

"I told you, I'm not...."

"Probably the janitor," I say cutting Jen off. "They like to strip the wax off the floors then re-wax in the summer when the place is empty." I laugh. "Last September the vice-principal took a header and slid on his stomach all the way down the hall. The nuns had to wrestle him up off the floor."

"Unless the janitor has taken to wearing skirts, that's not him," Rose says.

We peer towards Jen's school. A girl has pushed open a window and is climbing out. When she lays her eyes on the three of us, she takes off around the other side of the one-storey building.

Even though Jen had to slide down before she could begin running, she soon passes Rose and me then disappears around the corner of the school. Rose reaches the building next and turns in the opposite direction. I stop running and sit on the bars of the bicycle rack, waiting for them to circle the building and come back to me. Until I remember we're not supposed to be alone.

CHAPTER TWO

"Rose, come back," I shout as I stand up. "We're not supposed to separate, remember?" I race to the front of the building without passing either of them. My panic turns to anger when I see the two of them in the distance, a couple of blocks from the school. Rose has her camera to her face and Jen is gesticulating with her arms for me to catch up.

"You guys scared me to death!" I say as I run up to them. "Don't ever do that again. I thought the murderer had got you!"

Jen's pointing with one hand towards an avenue that runs along the edge of town, while holding a green sweater with the other. "You should have seen her go, Liz. Thought I was going to catch her, but she took off like the devil was chasing her. I think it was Gail Drummond and she was stealing clothes from the lost and found."

Gail graduated grade twelve a year ago and has younger siblings still attending St. Mary's Elementary. One of them, Stevie, is in Rose's grade. I used to see the family at church, but not since her dad was put in jail, and her mom died having a baby.

Jen holds out the sweater. "Picked this up off the ground. She dropped it while she was running. Belongs to Jimmy Hutchinson. Hand-me-down from his sister. Always complained about having to wear it. Must have put it in the lost-and-found then told his mom he lost it. I should take it to his house, tell his mom. Serve him right for teasing me about being so skinny. Can I help it if I take after my dad?"

I've seen pictures of Jen's dad and she's right; she does look like him.

Rose walks to the end of the block as she pretends to look at flower beds, and birds. She peers down the road then turns and waves at us.

I lift my palms. "What?" I say.

"Get over here," she hisses.

Jen and I drag our feet towards my sister. With her back to the road Rose says quietly, "She's stopped at her house. I need to get closer. I think she might be talking to someone." She turns and inconspicuously snaps a picture before turning back. "Seems to be telling him to go inside. She's shooing him, you know, like this." She waves her hand by her hip. "When I develop the film, I might be able to see him with my magnifying glass."

"Maybe it's the man I saw behind the church?" Jen says. Her eyes go wide. "Maybe her dad is the murderer and that's who she's telling to go inside."

"Probably shooing a dog away from the road," I say.

Gail disappears behind the trees on her property and Rose turns and takes a few steps forward.

"Where do you think you're going?" I ask.

"To see what's going on, of course."

"Rose, you are not going to the Drummond's. Whatever Gail was doing, she's on her own property now. If she stole clothes from the lost and found, they must need them badly. We aren't going any further. We shouldn't even be this far from home."

"I'd hide in the bushes and use my camera, no one would know I was there. I just want to see. We'd be like, you know, Nancy Drew searching for clues. We could call it, *The Green Sweater Murders*, or something like that."

"That's ridiculous. The three of us are not going to search for a murderer. And this is not like someone stole a hammer from the hardware store, this is serious. Mom put me in charge until she gets home and you are not leaving my side any more tonight."

Rose continues to stare towards the Drummond's, but she doesn't disobey me.

"We'd better get back," I say. "It'll be dark soon."

We cut through The Park. Rose runs under a swing, pushing it high in the air before letting it drop behind her. Me and Jen bring up the rear.

"Do you think Mr. Drummond is the murderer?" I ask.

"I don't know. I was just trying to get Rose's goat. Could be anyone. Could be your neighbour, my neighbour. It could be Mr. Pendergrass for all we know. I'd sure go crazy if I had his job. Smelling garbage all day long; I can't even imagine." She shivers in disgust. "But I think the most likely scenario is, it's a complete stranger."

"I heard the men saying tonight that Mr. Drummond is a suspect."

"Well, I for one would be happy if it is him. Then they can make an arrest. It's going to be a long rest of the summer if we can't go anywhere or do anything."

"I hope Mom doesn't have any more babies," I say. "I don't want her to die like Mrs. Drummond so I'd have to raise my sisters by myself."

"You have your dad to help, you wouldn't be raising them by yourself. And anyhow, your mom isn't going to die. She's had six babies and managed to survive giving birth to all of them. Even," she points at Rose running ahead, "that sister of yours, and she was born at home. If she didn't have red hair like the rest of you, I'd swear she was adopted. I thought you told me your mom isn't going to have any more babies now that she has a boy?"

"Yeah," I say. "Hey, do you want to go swimming tomorrow? Dad might let me take the girls to the pool while he goes to the city to pick up Mom and Cole. We'd be safe around all those people, even without an adult with us."

"Sounds like a plan," Jen says.

A police car drives slowly past and the officer opens the window. "Time to go home, girls. You shouldn't be out here by yourselves after dark."

"Yes, sir," we say.

Dad and the men are mingling on the street and we weave our way between them as they each head to their own houses. Dad hasn't noticed we were missing.

"Liz, take Rose and go inside. Mr. Pendergrass will walk Jennifer home."

"I'll call you later," Jen says. "Talk to you more about you know what." She pumps her hand over her heart.

"All that girl thinks about is boys," Rose says as the screen door bangs behind her.

Dad and I join her inside. "I'm bringing your sisters home tomorrow," Dad says. "You'll look after them while I pick up your mom and brother at the hospital." Dad isn't one to ask favours of his children; he tells them.

I ask about swimming. "Can I take the girls to the pool tomorrow? While you pick up Mom, I mean?"

He nods without speaking, then sits in his chair and shakes open the newspaper.

CHAPTER THREE

Traffic is minimal and Dad easily parks his truck in front of the Willowsbend Municipal Pool. Mr. Pendergrass has walked Jen over and she's waiting under the tree with Mr. and Mrs. Olyphant and my sisters. Their land is a mile from the Tremblay's on the other side of the highway. Too far away for them to have seen anything, but close enough to be worried.

My sisters each hold a grocery bag with their bathing suits and towels inside. They took their suits with them to the farm because unlike most small-town folks who plant every square inch of their yards to produce, Mrs. Olyphant has a back lawn and always has the sprinkler set up someplace. The day our brother was born, Dad dropped me and Rose off to join our sisters running through the spray while he went into the city to see his son. With the Tremblays' bodies not yet discovered, we laughed and played all afternoon, worries about school and having a new sibling in the house pushed to the backs of our minds for three carefree hours. I still shudder when I think of them lying there dead, while we drank lemonade and ate cookies only a mile down the road. By the time Dad arrived to pick us up, Mrs. Olyphant had already put the little ones to bed and Rose and I, tired of waiting on the front porch for his return, were about to walk home. He said he stayed longer at the hospital than he'd planned because Mom didn't want him to leave. I suppose post-baby blues can strike even the most stalwart of women.

Alex runs to me and hugs my legs. At only two years old, I'm sure she misses Mom the most. I pick her up and give her a kiss on the cheek.

"Is Daddy bringing Mommy home from the hospital today?"

she asks.

Alex is a child with a vocabulary that belies her age. With four older sisters always yakking about something or other, she learned early on that in this family, you have to speak up or be forgotten about. I've often wondered if there'd be as much conversation in our household if we were all boys. From my experience with Dad, I'm inclined to think not.

My youngest sister pinches my cheeks with her chubby fingers.

"He is," I say. "Mom will be home when we get back from the swimming pool. Is that ok?"

Alex nods her head; her strawberry-blond curls bounce.

"And you'll get to meet our new baby brother," I say.

"I don't want a baby brother." She sticks out her bottom lip, something she does to get her way.

I press her close. "It'll be fun, you'll see. Mom still loves you. She loves all of us. Maybe she'll let you feed him. You'd like that, wouldn't you?"

"Yes," she says but there are tears in her blue eyes.

Lois hands Jen a picnic basket. "Made some sandwiches. Egg salad for you and Rose," she says to Jennifer. "Tomato with mayonnaise for Liz, and peanut butter and honey for the little ones. Jug filled with lemonade in there as well."

"Thanks, Mrs. Olyphant," Jen says.

"Mom and I will be home by two this afternoon," Dad says to me. "I'll pick you up at three, don't be late. You hear me?" He hands me five dollars, our admission fee.

"Yes," I say, then add, "Thanks for letting us go swimming today, Dad."

Dad, not being an effusive man, leaves without acknowledging my gratitude.

Mrs. Olyphant puts her arm around my shoulders. "Keep an eye on your sisters and if your dad hasn't arrived when you're ready to leave, you stay right here, no walking home alone." She watches Dad walk away.

"We won't," I say.

"I'm still not sure if this is a good idea, leaving you girls here on your own." She glances at Dad's retreating truck. "I'm glad your mom's coming home today." She nods her head in Dad's direction. "He seems more distracted than usual."

"We'll be fine." I've heard Lois tell Mom that she thinks Dad isn't as involved with his family as he should be. "Dad's got a lot on his mind. He talked to me this morning," I say. "He told me to be careful."

Lois gives my shoulders a squeeze then she and Mr. Olyphant get into their car and drive away. Jen takes Robin's hand and leads her and Fran towards the building.

"He told you nothing of the sort and you know it," Rose says quietly. "As long as Mom didn't find out, we could have come here every day she's been in the hospital and he wouldn't have noticed. Not that I'm complaining."

Keeping Alex in my arms, we walk up to the turnstile. I give the lady the money, which she counts, then counts our heads, gives me fifty cents change, six keys with safety pins, and motions us through. We enter the locker room and I strip Alex, Rose helps Robin, and Franny manages to put on her yellow suit by herself. We enter the pool area.

Even though the temperature is pushing into the high eighties, the place is eerily quiet. Normally you can't hear yourself speak for the noise of laughter and splashing, transistor radios and the lifeguard's whistle, but today, only the very young chase each other across the grass and the adults, who've been elected to chaperone the kids, speak quietly as if talking too loudly is disrespectful of the dead. The children in line at the concession stand, instead of punching each other in the shoulder or snapping each other with their towels, are quiet as they exchange their nickels and dimes for licorice whips and paper bags filled with gummy strawberries.

Jen points out a group of girls who were in her grade eight class. The three of them are stretched out on the lawn, their exposed skin glistening with baby oil. Jen whispers in my ear about one of them. "Her name is Holly Black. Her dad owns the Twin-plex Theatre. Get in good with her and grade nine will be a breeze."

We spread out our blanket and Rose begins taking candid shots of the people around her. "This is crazy, heh?" she says. "He's got everyone too afraid to move, exactly what he was hoping for, I imagine. He could be right here, watching us, laughing at us."

"I thought you said he's lying on a beach in Mexico?" I say.

"And I also said he could be sticking around to see if his actions have changed our behaviour." She snaps the shutter. "And from the number of people here today, I'd say he's done just that." She surveys the sparse crowd through her camera. "See that guy standing over near the fence? See how he's sneaking looks at people? Sort of like he doesn't want anyone to notice him? He could be the killer."

"Or he could just be ogling the girls in bikinis," I say.

She turns to the left. "Or that woman. Why is she all alone at the swimming pool instead of supervising kids? Maybe she hates children and that's why she killed the Tremblays."

"That's Mrs. Kennedy," Jen says. "I've babysat her kids. They're brats. She probably has the afternoon off and doesn't want to have anything to do with kids for a few hours."

"There's Mr. Johansson," Rose points. "He's totally the killer, dressed in his street clothes at a swimming pool. Who does that?"

"You know he never wears a bathing suit. He's self-conscious of his prosthetic leg," I say. "He only comes here to look after his grandkids. I think, Rose, that you could point that camera of yours at anyone and come up with something suspicious."

"Maybe," she says. "I wish I had some clues. I could figure this out if I had some clues."

Jen laughs. "You don't need any clues. The police are going to figure this out, not you."

Rose glares at her. "I'm totally going to solve this, just wait and see."

Silence spreads across the grass when one by one, heads turn towards the entrance. Gail Drummond, a child's hand in each of hers, has walked into the pool area. Stevie is following behind pushing a baby carriage. In the stillness, the words, *their dad's the killer,* echo across the compound. Gail comes to a stop on the cement apron surrounding the pool. She squares her shoulders then continues to tug her siblings towards the grass. While we watch, a rock flies through the air and hits one of the little girls on the shoulder. The child begins to cry.

"Who threw that?" Gail yells. "Who threw a rock at my sister?" Gail scans the people watching her. No one claims responsibility nor, to my shame, do we look away, transfixed by what we're witnessing. Even the lifeguard, who, with so few people here likely saw the rock thrower from her perch eight feet in the air, says nothing.

"Shame on you," Gail shouts as she puts her arm around her sister. "What did this child do to you?" She finds a spot to spread her blanket. Gradually eyes look away, though some continue to sneak glances and whisper.

"Well," Rose says as she stands. "I don't know about the rest of you, but I didn't come here to watch small-town melodrama." She tucks her camera into the lunch basket, then runs to the edge of the pool and jumps in. Being a timid girl, Fran is afraid of the water and stays behind with me and Alex on the blanket. Jen has agreed to supervise Robin and they wade into the shallow end together.

I grab Alex's and Fran's hands. "Time to cool off."

"Why did someone throw a rock at that girl?" Fran asks, pulling her hand out of mine.

"I don't know," I say.

"But Mommy says we shouldn't throw rocks. Was that little girl bad? Is that why someone threw a rock at her."

"No, she wasn't bad. Mom's right; you shouldn't throw rocks." I attempt to lead my sisters towards the pool.

"But why did someone say their dad was a murderer?" Fran continues. "Did their daddy kill those people?"

I've tried my best to keep the facts of the murders from the girls, as I know Mom wouldn't want them to hear anything, but Fran has overheard conversations she shouldn't have and being a bright girl, has figured out that a bad man killed some people. Luckily Alex and Robin are still in the dark.

"No, their dad did not kill the Tremblays," I say, my voice lowered as Alex skips along beside me. "The person who said that was wrong."

"But...."

"Fran," I say. "Enough questions. Come on, it's hot in the sun; we came here to swim."

"I don't wanna," she says. "I'm afraid."

I squeeze her hand already wishing we'd stayed home. "There's nothing to be afraid of. Just get your toes wet. You don't have to duck your head under."

I pick Alex up, carry her to the pool and sit her on the edge of the cement. Fran sits beside her and the two of them dangle their toes in the water. I sit, sandwiching Alex in the middle of our trio, my feet also submerged. Rose, who's been doing laps, swims towards us then begins blowing bubbles at the little girls' feet. I turn my head; a pair of legs is standing by my side. They slip into the water and Stevie Drummond sits beside me.

"Want to know what my dad says about your dad?" he says so only Rose and I can hear.

"Not particularly," Rose says as she continues to blow bubbles.

"He says your dad thinks he's above the law. Says he was like that in school and nothing's changed in twenty years."

"What are you talking about?" Rose says. "Don'tcha know what everyone's saying about your dad?"

"Rose," I say, "Be quiet."

"Well, it's true," she says. "It's his dad everyone's talking about, not ours."

"My dad says your dad thinks, because he's got lots of money, he can do whatever he wants and get away with it, just like when they were kids. Says people would be shocked if they knew what he got away with when he was younger." He wipes his nose with the back of his hand.

Rose's face has turned as red as the paint on her three-speed bike. "You be quiet, Stevie Drummond, or I'll tell your teacher that you cheated on your arithmetic test last year," she says.

"Ah, you don't know anything," he waves his hand at Rose. "You're just a girl."

"Everyone knows you cheat. That it's the only way you can pass a grade."

"Do not!" Stevie shouts.

"Do too," Rose yells back. "And you don't know anything about my dad. He's an important person in this town. Your dad is nothing but a...."

Stevie's little sister, the one who was hit with a rock, runs up to our group, stopping Rose from finishing her sentence. The girl absently scratches the red welt blossoming on her shoulder while she speaks to her brother. "Mama says you're to come to our blanket and have a sandwich."

"Olive," Stevie says. "Gail is not our mother. She's our sister. Mom's dead."

His voice catches in his throat and my heart goes out to this kid who's trying to be tough.

"I know that," Olive says. "I just like to call her Mama."

Fran, seeing her chance to question the person who had the rock thrown at her, jumps to her feet. "Were you bad?" she asks before I can tell her to sit back down. "Did someone throw a rock at you because you were bad?"

"No, I'm not bad. My mama told me I'm a good girl. She's gone to heaven."

"My mommy's coming home today with my new baby brother. His name is Cole. I'm starting grade one pretty soon. I'm going to St. Mary's."

"Me too," Olive says. "We can be friends."

"You can't be friends with these people," Stevie says.

"Why not?" the little girl asks.

"Because they think they're better than us, that's why."

Rose's short fuse has burnt to the end and she pushes a wave of water out of the pool so large that it soaks not only Stevie, but Fran, Olive, me and Alex. The boy jumps into the water and soon he and Rose are trying to dunk each other while Fran cries about being wet and Olive and Alex cheer on their respective sibling.

The lifeguard blows her whistle. "You two," she points at Rose and Stevie, "out of the pool, now!" The young woman climbs down the ladder and marches over to the two of them then talks quietly while they hang their heads.

Rose slouches away from the pool's edge and stands in front of me.

"Well," I say. "What did she say? Are we kicked out?"

Rose shakes her head. She looks angry. "She said we both have to stay out of the water for the afternoon. We don't have to leave the grounds, just stay out of the pool."

"Ok, then. I'll meet you at the blanket in a few minutes and we'll have some lunch."

"But I shouldn't have been kicked out of the water!" she says. "He started it. Did you hear what he said about Dad?"

"Since when do you defend Dad? You're usually the first one to criticize him."

She toes the grass. "Yeah, well, our dad might be an uninvolved father," she looks across the lawn and says a bit too loudly, "but at least he's not a drunk and an ex-con who everyone thinks killed seven innocent people!"

"Hush," I say. I put my hand on her shoulder. "Go and have a sandwich, I'll be right there."

Rose pushes my hand off. "I told you, I don't need any help." She stomps away in a huff towards our spot of grass.

I sigh, then picking up Alex and grabbing Fran by the hand, I take them to the shallow end where Fran, now that she's soaked, manages to lie down in the water and blow some bubbles. When we're cooled off, we head back to our blanket, passing the group of girls Jen pointed out to me.

"Gail Drummond has some nerve coming here today," Holly says to her friends. "My dad wants to go to their place and roust her dad out himself."

I turn. "Do you know that people in our country are innocent until proven guilty?"

The girls look surprised I'm talking to them. "Did you say something?" Holly asks. "Oh, I know you. You're that Catholic girl who's starting high school with us. And your best friend is Jennifer Olsen? Someone should tell her that no matter how much you shorten the skirt or re-dye the blouse, your mother's old clothes still look like your mother's old clothes." The four of them laugh with their hands pressed over their painted lips.

When I arrive at our blanket, Jen says, "You were talking to them? Did one of them ask about me?"

"No." I draw out the word. "And I don't know why you want to be friends with them. They're nothing but snobs."

My voice has risen and a few people look our way probably hoping for more theatrics from the Murphy clan. I pick up a sandwich and take a bite before I realize its peanut butter and honey.

I hear a click. Rose has taken my picture. I wash down the goop with a gulp of lemonade then wipe my face on my towel. "Time to go home," I say. "We can wait in the shade on the front lawn for Dad to pick us up. I've had enough of being stared at."

"Aw, but we just got here," Fran says. "I wanna stay."

"You don't even like the water. Do as you're told or I'll tell Mom."

I jam everything into Mrs. Olyphant's basket, Rose hangs her camera around her neck, and we eat our lunch in the shade of the elm tree at the front of the building while waiting for Dad.

CHAPTER FOUR

My sisters and I are standing at the end of our front walk, the anger about leaving the pool early eclipsed by the worry of meeting our baby brother. Dad has gone inside to make sure Mom's ok with a noisy troop of kids in the house.

"Come on," I say. "It'll be fine. It's just a baby. How hard can it be?"

"Mom'll like Cole better than me," Alex wails then sticks out her lip.

"What about me?" Fran complains. "You're two, I'm six. She'll ignore me even more than she'll ignore you."

"For heaven's sake, you two!" I say. "Mom won't ignore any of us. And you don't even know what ignore means."

Fran stomps her foot. "Do too! It means to pay no attention to."

"How do you know...." I look at Rose who has a smirk on her face.

"Mommy and Daddy always wanted a boy. They're gonna love him more," Robin whines.

"Don't be silly," I say but secretly hold that same fear.

Rose, who's gotten over the scuffle at the pool, says, "Get your head out of the sand, Liz. Mom's going to be too busy to look after us, and we already know how much attention Dad pays to his family. We're on our own from now on."

"We are not." I scowl at her. "You're scaring the little ones."

"Just facing reality," Rose says. "I can't wait to be independent. I'll be able to do whatever I want. There's too many damn restrictions in this household."

"You'd better watch your language when we go inside," I say. "I can tell you right now, you are not going to be allowed to be independent at eleven years old. And with the," I whisper, "murders, your independence this summer will be curtailed even more." I look at her bare feet. "Put your sandals on, you know Dad doesn't like you to walk around bare foot in the house."

"I've told him time and time again that chilblains only happen in the winter," she argues. "Telling me to wear shoes is just his stab at parenting. Same as telling us to turn out the lights when we leave a room, or to not stand with the fridge door open."

"Whatever the reason, he doesn't want you barefoot. You only do it to make him mad."

She smiles and shrugs.

Rose is stepping into her sandals when Dad opens the door.

"Mom wants you to meet Cole," he says. Then, picking up Alex, he leads the way to the office.

The office is a room off the kitchen. Stairs that lead to the second floor are in one corner of this tiny space and in the other, the desk Rose and I share when doing homework. It's also the room where Mom pays the bills and where Mom and Dad have quiet talks while Dad sits in the straight back chair and Mom sits in her rocking chair. And whenever Mom has a baby, this is the room you'll find her in when the house is quiet, the baby pressed to her shoulder as she rocks the new infant and whispers into its ear. That's exactly what she's doing when we walk into the room.

"Hi, Mom." I step closer and give her a kiss on her cheek.

"Would you like to hold him?" she asks.

Tired of having the responsibility of being the oldest, but wanting to show my sisters, especially the little ones, that everything will be fine, I nod. Mom removes Cole's blanket revealing his blue sleeper, and I gingerly take my brother from her arms. His skin is so soft it's difficult to feel his cheek under my finger, and he has the beginnings of dark hair sprouting over his ears and on top of his bald head. He opens his eyes; they're blue like Alex's but I know a baby's eyes can change from blue to green, to brown within the first few months of life. I kneel down to give my sisters a better view.

Rose and I have seen our share of babies before—I personally have held each of my sisters as newborns—so we aren't surprised at our brother's size or the pinched look of his face. But Fran and Robin, who thought he'd look like the pictures of the baby on the outside of the baby food jars, hang back and hold onto my leg. Robin is the bravest and steps forward first.

"He's so tiny," she whispers as she strokes his face.

"He's bigger than you were when you were born," Mom says. "He weighs seven pounds nine ounces, and you, princess, weighed six pounds five ounces."

Fran jumps up and down. "How much did I weigh, Mom?"

"You, Francine weighed seven pounds three ounces."

"Me next," Alex says as Dad puts her on the floor.

"And you, sweetie, were seven pounds one ounce."

"I was the biggest, I was the biggest," Alex sings.

"No you weren't," Rose says. "Fran weighed two ounces more than you. And anyhow, it doesn't matter. Babies that are ten pounds can grow up to be the smallest in the family. Right, Mom?"

"That's right, Rose. You were my only eight-pound baby and you're probably not going to be as tall as Franny."

"How do you know?"

"Because the last time we marked your heights on the basement wall, she was already taller than you were at six."

"Can we mark Cole's?" Robin asks.

Mom ruffles her daughter's hair. "I think he's a bit young yet. I'll write in his baby book how long he is and how much he weighs, but until he's one, we won't stand him up against the wall and measure his height."

"What does he eat?" Robin asks.

"Milk for now. Soon I'll be mushing up banana with rice cereal and he'll gobble that down. He's going to change a lot in a couple of months. You'll see, he'll be smiling and cooing at the five of you before you know it. He's lucky to have so many sisters."

"Mom, can I take his picture, or will that be hard on his eyes?" Rose asks.

"That's a fine idea, Rose. Why don't you let Dad take the picture and then you can be in it with the rest of us? Would that be alright, Jim?"

Dad doesn't respond and the six of us turn to look at him. His chin is on his chest and his body is slumped into the doorframe. His eyes are closed and he's breathing deeply as if asleep. He has bags under his eyes and the shirt is the same one he was wearing yesterday; something he never does. He lifts his head when he feels us staring.

"Jim," Mom repeats. "Could you take our picture?"

Dad pushes himself off the wall and takes the camera from Rose.

"All you have to do is look through here and push this button," Rose points as she pops in a flashcube.

Dad holds his tongue at the instructions for use as Rose stages us around the rocking chair. Robin and Fran stand on one side of Mom who's holding Cole, and Rose, me, and Alex, on the other.

"Say cheese." We do as we're told and Dad snaps the shutter.

"I'd better go and see about supper," I say as everyone traipses out of the office.

"Now that I'm home you don't have to do that, Liz."

"I can manage one more day. I was going to make sausages and scalloped potatoes." I blush, "Or is there something you'd rather have, or something you'd rather not have?" I know after Alex was born certain foods gave Mom heartburn.

"Sausages and scalloped potatoes sound heavenly." Mom squeezes my hand. "I couldn't ask for a better eldest daughter. Because of the murders, I wanted to be discharged early, but the doctor said absolutely not; the birth wasn't as easy this time." She touches my arm. "Are you being careful, Liz? I want you to take care of your sisters until the police find the person who killed the Tremblays."

"We're being careful, Mom," I say.

"I know Rose can be difficult to reign in," she continues. "She might be smart about a lot of things but she's fiercely independent, like you, only you have a more level head on your shoulders. Rose's temper runs hot. Takes after your Aunt Frieda. That woman can pick a fight with anyone about anything." She strokes Cole's head, lost in thought about Dad's sister. The woman never married, and I've heard Dad say that she could never find the man who would tolerate her independence. "Until I'm feeling more up to it, try your best to keep Rose safe, please."

"I will, Mom." I lower my eyes. "I'm sorry you're sad," I say.

"Sad?" Mom says.

"When Dad went to the city to visit you and Cole, he was late picking Rose and me up at the Olyphant's. He said you didn't want him to leave. Thought you must have that thing some women get after they have a baby when they get sad."

"No, I'm not sad. Dad left the hospital in plenty of time to pick you up. Perhaps he had some errands to do or stopped at the hardware store. That man is a workaholic," she says as an excuse for Dad's tardiness. "And now with another mouth to feed, he's probably concerned about money."

"There was a bit of trouble at the pool today," I say. "Stevie Drummond was there and he and Rose got into a fight. The lifeguard kicked both her and Stevie out of the water for the afternoon."

"That family has had its troubles. Maybe I'll give Father Mackinnon a call, see if he has any ideas how we can help."

CHAPTER FIVE

Supper is a success until Rose swears at the table. She says, *These are the best damn scalloped potatoes I've ever had*. Dad, probably thinking we're all under a bit of stress and he should give his second oldest a bit of slack, only tells Rose to watch her language. But when Rose says, *Take a chill-pill, Daddio*, it's more than he can swallow and sends her to her room with no dessert.

Mom and I finish doing the dishes, then I smuggle two cookies up to Rose. She sits on the floor of our shared bedroom to eat them with one of her photo albums on her lap. There are two old nail boxes sitting on top of our dresser and Rose keeps used rolls of film in one until she has enough money to send them in for developing, and unused in the other, which she buys in multiples when there's a two-for-one-sale. The film from today has already been taken out of her camera, dated, then placed in the designated box.

I open the window and pop out the screen. "I'm going to my treehouse," I say. "And you can't tell Mom how long I stay because I brought you cookies."

"Liz, I'd never tell Mom that you wait until you think I'm asleep, then climb out the window and into your treehouse every night all summer long and stay out there until three in the morning when you're supposed to be in bed by midnight. I also will never tell that you and Jen talk about boys all the time, or that you have a pack of cigarettes in the bottom drawer of the dresser. What do you think I am, a snitch?"

"You went in my drawer?"

She shrugs. "I wanted to borrow that green shirt I like."

"The cigarettes aren't mine. They're Jen's. She can't keep them at home because her Mom would find them." I add, "And quit going in my dresser."

"I'll quit going in your dresser when you quit thinking you're the boss of me. I might be twenty-two and a half months younger than you but that does not make me less mature. As a matter of fact, I think I'm old for my age and if we could measure our maturity on some sort of scale, I'd probably be older than you."

"Just because you skipped a grade does not mean you're as mature as me. You may be smart and you may be independent, but you're not more mature. And I'm only the boss of you when Mom tells me to look after you, which will be a lot this summer with the murders and a new baby in the house, so get used to it!"

We turn our backs to each other while we cool down.

When Rose was in grade two, she started acting out—not wanting to go to school, being mean to the other kids, disobeying everything Mom or Dad told her to do. At the suggestion of her teacher, Mom took her daughter to get tested for everything from vocabulary, to cognitive ability, to mathematic equations, to analytical thinking and memory. At the end of the day the tests concluded that Rose had an IQ measuring 140 and she was especially gifted in vocabulary, analytical thinking, and memory.

Rose speaks first. "I've read scientific reports that say cigarettes are a major cause of lung cancer. You should tell your friend."

"Jen thinks smoking will make her look older. I doubt telling her it's bad for her health would make a difference."

Rose raises her palms. "Only telling you what I've read. What the surgeon general should do is have pictures of lungs that look like Swiss cheese, or cancerous growths in mouths and throats on the packages; that might make people think twice. Pictures have more of an impact than words."

Not only does Rose read books on photography and every murder mystery paperback she can buy at Woolworths, but she reads all sorts of magazines as well as the newspaper every day, leaving it in disarray, much to Dad's chagrin. She loves facts and information, remembers them forever, and loves regurgitating them back to us when a subject of her expertise arises. She has told me on more than one occasion that, like the pictures she takes, she has a photographic memory, and I believe her. She remembers things from years gone by that have long since been forgotten by everyone else.

"Reminding Jen that smoking causes cancer wouldn't be enough to stop her. She's probably not as mature as you and me." I put one foot out the window. "But if you want to tell her, be my guest. Just be ready to get out of the way when she tries to punch you."

I duck the rest of my body outside and walk across the roof of the mud room to my treehouse. The structure sits in the tree growing by the steps which lead to the mud room on the back of our house. There are two porches in our house; one in front which is screened in, and one in back that we call the mud room and is where we keep our coats, boots and shoes. A deck, the only modern addition to the house, extends from the top of the steps, and along the back wall of the house. Mom and Dad quite often sit there on warm summer evenings to talk.

Thirteen years ago, in the hopes I was going to be a boy, Dad constructed the five by five shelter while Mom was pregnant with me. When I turned out to be a girl, he said the treehouse would have to wait to be used until Mom gave birth to a son. When Rose was born, he still didn't give in, saying treehouses were for boys not girls.

Finally, when Fran was born, Dad said he was tired of waiting for a boy and didn't want to have wasted his time building the thing if it wasn't going to be used. So, he supposed, even though it went against his principles, his eldest daughter could claim the treehouse as her own.

Mom, who hadn't had to protest before, decided it was time to air her views and said she didn't want any child of hers climbing so high on a ladder. Dad reminded Mom that I didn't have to climb the ladder because the treehouse was accessible from the window of my bedroom. All I had to do was cross the roof of the mud room. Mom said there was no way she was going to allow any child of hers to climb out a window as tiny as that and walk across the roof of a hundred and thirty-year-old house, especially one with such a steep pitch. Dad said the window may be too small for him to fit through, as he's a large man, but a child, or small adult would have no problem. And, he'd argued, he could easily rebuild the roof, flattening the very top of the peak by turning it into a catwalk with a wooden floor, pickets, and handrails. He ended his argument by telling Mom that crossing the roof would be as safe as walking down a sidewalk. Mom had no choice but to agree.

Even at the tender age of seven I understood that Dad wasn't arguing because he was eager to have his daughter use the treehouse. He was arguing because he didn't like being told what to do, especially by a woman. Now that I've been coming out here for six years, Mom has grown accustomed to me crossing the roof, though using the treehouse in rain or snow is strictly forbidden.

Our house began its long-lived life on this very spot as a tool shed. My Great-Grandma and Great-Grandpa Murphy, after immigrating to Canada from Ireland, secured their own one-hundred and sixty acres outside of Willowsbend, the name chosen because of the grove of willow trees on the edge of town. The grove is still there, growing in the ditch that separates the old road from the wider highway which was built twenty years ago.

Great-Grandpa didn't know how he was going to build a house in time to keep himself, his two children, and his wife, pregnant with their third baby, warm for the quickly approaching winter. A resident of Willowsbend, seeing the family's plight, charged Great-Grandpa fifty dollars for a plot of land he owned in town which housed a dilapidated shack that was being used as a tool shed. The man wasn't sure if Great-Grandpa would accept, but Great-Grandpa said thank you, and after clearing out the tools, moved his family into the shed.

The family survived their first prairie winter through the generosity of neighbours who provided them with food, beds and blankets, a wood stove, and access to enough wood from land a farmer was clearing. Great-Grandpa bought a wagon to haul the dead-fall in and a draught horse to pull the wagon, and kept that stove lit twenty-four hours a day, getting up at all hours of the night to stoke the fire. Come spring, Great-Grandpa began adding on to the building, renovating the existing structure from a one-room shack, into a two-storey, five-bedroom house. Great-Grandpa and Great-Grandma raised their family in that house, filling the five bedrooms with two more children.

Witnessing firsthand the everyday struggles of a farmer, the older siblings became uninterested in the meagre amount of money the land generated, and when they were grown, moved to the city, leaving my grandpa, the baby of the family, to work the farm. He embraced the challenge. In conjunction with the agriculture department at the provincial university, Grandpa started planting experimental crops suitable for the short growing season this province offered. In doing so, he made the land far more profitable than it had ever been. He began buying up the acres around him until he became the largest single-owner farm in the area. Because he had been so busy working the farm and making money, he married late in life. But he and Grandma managed to have a family, albeit Grandma was already in her forties when she had Aunt Frieda and Dad. Aunt Frieda moved away at a young age, but Dad stayed behind to help on the farm. Within four years, Grandma fell frail and died, and Grandpa followed a few months later. After the death of his parents, Dad quit farming, sold the land, then opened Murphy's Hardware in town. The house that had been his boyhood home, became his. Along came Mom and eventually all of us to fill it up. Rose and I sleep in the same bedroom our grandpa and our dad slept in when they were boys.

Rose complains that she wishes we had a modern house like the houses in the newer neighbourhoods. She likes the built-in ovens and air-conditioning, the wall-to-wall carpet and floor-to-ceiling drapes, but I love the creaks and moans our floor gives when I walk across the wide wooden planks. I love lying on the kitchen floor in the sweltering summers when we open the doors to let a breeze blow through. And I love the idea of living with all these ghosts. Even with its advanced age, there's life yet to be lived within these old walls.

The sun sets around nine this late in July and from this high up, it's a golden orb on the horizon with no houses or grain elevators to block my view. I've always been partial to the nighttime when everything becomes peaceful, with no sisters to bug me, no chores to do, and fewer cars on the highway as they race through our town towards the lights of the city.

I pick up my binoculars and press them to my eyes. I ordered the field glasses through Eaton's Catalogue a couple years ago. I'd baby-sat as much as I was able—which, with four younger sisters to look after, for which I don't get paid, wasn't as much as I wanted—and by the end of the summer, I had fifty dollars in my wallet. The binoculars cost fifty-nine ninety-five and Dad gave me the remaining money in exchange for sweeping and mopping the hardware store every Saturday for a month. He says he has never believed in getting something for nothing and gives us our allowance only if we've done our chores.

I bought the binoculars so I could see the stars but soon discovered they were also good for looking at the town from up here. I turn in a circle. Mrs. Krieger is standing in her raspberry patch on the other side of our shared caragana hedge. She says this is the best time to pick the fruit because the snakes have gone home to bed and aren't coiled at the edge of the patch, soaking up the heat. That's the only thing I hate about raspberry patches; the garter snakes. And, she says, because the house is cooling off, she can make raspberry jam into the wee small hours of the morning without getting too hot.

I move my head to the south. There's Mr. Pendergrass a few blocks away, kneeling in his yard digging up weeds. He's probably doing the chore at dusk so no one will know that he too has dandelions. He likes to complain about his neighbours' lawns, and I've heard Dad say to Mom that Mr. Pendergrass has his head up his ass.

I look to the east towards Main Street, Willowsbend's business district, and see Murphy's Hardware. The front of the shop faces the other direction, but the alley and the back door are easily visible from my treehouse. Sometimes I spy on Dad as he's locking up and loping his way home. He always looks serious but I'm sure he's glad to have a house bustling with life to come home to.

Movement catches my eye and I turn north. A shadow is darting back and forth across the alley. It stops at Mrs. Seamer's at the end of our block, the last house before the highway that passes by the Tremblay's. Mrs. Seamer's back gate opens and the person, still in the shadows, enters her backyard. Wondering if I've spotted the killer, and perhaps I should go and tell Mom and Dad, I focus my lens on the face of the trespasser and recognize the person as Gail Drummond. She steps to the apple tree and begins plucking fruit off the branches then dropping them into a pocket in her coat. I let out the breath I've been holding.

Satisfied I haven't found the killer, I lift the bench lid and put my binoculars inside. I remove a blanket, then using it as a pillow, lie on the floor and fall asleep watching the sky change from orange, to dark blue, to black. I wake up at three in the morning with dreams of swimming to rescue Fran in the deep end of the pool while Stevie Drummond holds her head underwater. I climb back through the window and crawl into bed beside Rose, who's fallen asleep with a photo album over her chest.

* * *

Our kitchen is filled with a gaggle of women all clucking and milling around as they prepare our breakfast. This happens in Willowsbend every time someone dies, or a baby is born—the neighbourhood women show up with cakes and breads, baskets heaping with homemade muffins and bowls overflowing with fruit. My sisters are gathered around the kitchen table being fussed over, with Rose objecting to each kiss on the cheek and hand smoothing down her unruly hair.

Mrs. Krieger lifts the lid off a pot and, even though it's hot enough to fry an egg on the sidewalk, begins plopping large spoonfuls of oatmeal porridge into bowls. "Liz," she says. "Your mom wants to talk to you. You're to go right to her bedroom the moment you get up. There'll be a bowl of porridge waiting for you when you're done," she calls as I'm leaving the kitchen.

Mom and Dad have the only bedroom situated on the main floor, the room which used to be the original tool shed. It's to the side of the living room and is right below Rose's and my bedroom. There's good and bad to this setup. The good: I can hear them talking in the night as their voices drift up the register. The bad: our voices drift down. Today, before I came downstairs, Rose and I heard Dad rummaging through dresser drawers and grumbling about losing a cufflink. Even though he owns a hardware store and deals with farmers who dress in blue jeans and grease stained t-shirts, Dad has always been one to dress well.

I pass him in the hall and the look on his face is one of trepidation. He slows his gait and pauses on the threshold between the living room and the kitchen, hesitant to enter a room filled with females. My dad is afraid of women. Not in the same way Mrs. Ernst's husband is, who won't say boo to his wife even when she's reprimanding him in public; but rather, Dad is uncomfortable around women who speak their minds. I've witnessed him squirm when a woman laughs too loud or gives an opinion on a subject that he deems only men should be able to discuss. Perhaps his mom was overbearing and strong women bring back memories he's trying to forget. Aunt Frieda certainly is opinionated, and Rose is turning out to be just like her. I'm sure there will be a lot of head-butting when she grows into those rebellious years.

Mrs. Krieger motions for Dad to sit at the table, but he rushes out the back door without stopping for his prerequisite bowl of porridge.

I enter their bedroom; Mom's sitting up in bed and Cole's asleep in his bassinet. He'll stay here for a few months, then Dad will set the crib up in the last bedroom upstairs at the end of the hall, the smallest room in the house.

Robin and Alex share a room, as do Rose and I, and Fran has her own room across the hall from them, which isn't much bigger than Cole's. Mom's asked her many times if she wants to switch with

Robin and share with Alex, but she insists she likes having her own space, even if it is tiny. She's a loner and in her self-imposed seclusion has already taught herself to read. She begins grade one in the fall and I'm worried she might have trouble fitting in.

"Hi, Mom."

"Liz. How long did you stay in your treehouse last night?"

I blush. She must have heard Rose and me talking before bed. "Not long. Was in bed by midnight, I think."

Mom looks like she doesn't believe me.

"I saw Gail Drummond stealing apples from Mrs. Seamer's tree last night," I say to take the focus off me.

"That's what I want to talk to you about. I've called Father Mackinnon to talk to him about the Drummond family. He's gathered some clothes from the donations box, and I've pulled some hand-me-down clothes and toys from the boxes in the basement. There's also a box of rice cereal for the new baby, a bag of buns, and a bottle of whole milk. Father's coming by and I want you to help him take everything to their house."

"Ah, Mom, I looked after the girls all day yesterday. And I've made supper for a whole week!" I finish my rant with, "And what if Mr. Drummond is the murderer? You don't want me to get murdered, do you?"

"Mr. Drummond is the murderer? For heaven's sake, Liz, that's not something I'd expect to hear from you. You know as well as I that you can't convict someone on hearsay. Even your sister knows better than that."

Since I have four, I want to ask her which sister she means, though I already know the answer. On cue Rose sticks her head into the bedroom.

"The priest is here, Mom. Are we going to pray or something?"

"No, Rose. He's here for Liz. Where did you leave the good Father?"

"I sat him down at my place at the table. He's eating Dad's bowl of porridge since Dad already left."

"Go and tell him that Liz will be right there, please." Rose leaves.

"The boxes are in the mud room," Mom says to me. "Put them in Fran's wagon then you and Father can walk out there."

"I have to walk? In this heat?"

"You know Father doesn't own a car. The exercise will do you good." She shoos her hand at me. "And make sure you wear a hat."

Rose meets me in the living room. "What'd you do that you have to see the priest?"

"Didn't do anything. Have to take some stuff to the Drummond's."

"Mom's sending you to the Drummond's? Cool. Can I come?"

"No, you can't come," I say in my best big sister voice, which sounds more worried than authoritative.

She lifts her camera and snaps a close-up of my face. "I'm titling this one, Scaredsville."

"Quit that. I'm not afraid." I push her camera away.

"You sure look scared. I wouldn't be scared. If something happened, I'd take a picture, catch him red-handed. A camera is so quick, I could catch anyone doing anything."

"Quit saying that, nothing's going to happen," I shout as we arrive in the kitchen.

"What's not going to happen?" Father Mackinnon asks.

"Nothing, Father. Just Rose being a poop-head."

"Ah, yes," he says. "I remember having spats with my siblings too. I believe instead of poop-head we called each other bone-heads, though it's been too many years to remember."

The women giggle and pour Father another cup of coffee.

"I'll meet you outside, Father. I have to drag the boxes from the mud room and stack them into the wagon." I make it sound like it's more of a chore than it is.

As Father is about to say something, Dad walks into the kitchen, saving me from what I assume would have been a sermon about graciously giving alms to the poor.

"Forgot my glasses," Dad says. "Too much commotion going on around this place this morning. I'd forget my head if it weren't screwed...." He sees the priest. "Oh, morning, Father. Didn't see you there."

"Jim," Father says. "Congratulations on your son. Will we see you in church for the christening?"

The only time Dad sets foot in a church is for a funeral or a wedding. He says he can pray just as easily at home without having to kneel and stand like all the other sheep in the congregation. Last year Rose tried to stay home by saying she didn't want to be a sheep either; that she was as independent as the next person. All that got her was a thwack on the ear and Dad telling her to hurry up and get her butt out the door before he personally escorted her.

Dad rushes into the living room, picks up his glasses from the end-table, then to avoid having to talk to Father, he leaves by the front door. I go to the backyard and begin loading the boxes into the wagon.

Dad rounds the corner of the house. "Where are you going with all this?" he says.

"Me and Father are taking some clothes and stuff to the Drummond's."

He frowns, looks at the wagon, at the house, then back at the wagon. I'm sure he's wondering whether he should go and talk to Mom about me going to the house of a possible murderer; or if his daughter walking to the Drummond's is less hazardous than him going back inside and having to face the priest.

Deciding to throw me under the bus, he says, "Be careful," then opening the gate, he leaves the backyard and strides down the alley on his long legs.

Dad doesn't take his truck to work, not even in the winter, preferring to walk the eight blocks in the heat or in the cold. He views being healthy as something you should incorporate into your everyday life, not something you should strive to achieve by negating poor habits with exercise. Other than special occasions, he has only one glass of rye on Saturday evening, and a beer with Mr. Olyphant when we go to their farm. He eats tons of vegetables, and except for the occasional homemade cinnamon bun, he never eats sweets. And he's never been a smoker like many of his peers. I've often thought of my dad as a man ahead of his time.

"Liz, are you ready for me?" Father calls out the screen door just as Dad disappears around the corner at the end of the alley.

I want to say, *Not in a gazillion years,* but instead I say, "Yes, Father."

And so, while Rose, Fran, Alex and Robin press their noses to the screen door, Father and I begin our trek towards the Drummond's on the other side of town. I look back once when Rose takes our picture.

CHAPTER SIX

I'm dragging my feet, taking my anger at being forced to accompany Father, out on the bottoms of my shoes, when Father says, "You're awful quiet. Liz. I've heard the words *sullen teenager* bandied about lately."

Not being allowed to marry and have a family, I assumed priests didn't know much about the younger generation and he takes me off guard with the comment.

He taps his stubby fingers to his forehead. "I remember having growing pains. You're stuck somewhere between being a child and being a grownup. It may seem hard and perhaps unfair, but those were good years that went by so fast, before I knew it, I'd become an adult. Enjoy this time in your life. You'll never get it back. As a matter of fact," he continues, "I did my share of standing on the corner watching the girls go by. Then I discovered God and that changed my entire life."

"Oh, yeah," I mumble, uncomfortable talking to him without a sliding screen between us.

We pass the Henderson's then turn the corner at the end of the block. I bump the wagon down the curb on one side of the road, then over the curb and into The Park on the other side. It's difficult to talk as we rattle along so Father, thankfully, is unable to continue talking about God. We pass between the two elementary schools, cross the yard in front, then walk down the street, stopping on the sidewalk Jen and Rose chased Gail down a couple of evenings ago. Father and I are quiet as we stand in the heat and stare at the avenue that leads to the Drummond's. He asks no questions as to why I've stopped and stands peacefully beside me enjoying the day. Suddenly, privacy screen or no privacy screen, I feel the need to talk to someone who won't tell me to not worry about it, it's not any of my concern, or I'm too young.

"Why do you think he did it, Father?"

"Who?"

"The murderer. Why do you think he killed them all, even the children?"

"I suppose it's because he needs help."

"You mean, mentally?"

"Not everyone finds their path. People get confused."

"Do you think he believes in God?" I ask.

"I don't know. He might. People who believe in God can get lost just as easily as those who don't."

"Did he really do that thing I've heard people say?" I can't bring myself to say *cut out her tongue*, as the thought of even speaking those words makes me gag.

Father hesitates, but to his credit, tells me the truth. "He did, Liz, I'm sorry to say. But I'm sure he regrets what he did. If not now, eventually. Everyone sees the light sooner or later. You have to have faith."

"Do you think we should forgive him?"

"Certainly, I do."

"But he killed seven people! How can you forgive him?"

"All souls can be saved. If you were to look into his eyes, you'd realize he's as human as you and I and you'd say, *if you understand what you did was wrong and repent, God will forgive you.* God forgives all who repent, no matter the sin." He waves his hand. "And the souls of the Tremblay family are in heaven and at peace now. No sense worrying about them. Their time on this earth is over. It's the people left behind who are suffering."

"People say what he's done doesn't deserve forgiveness, that all he deserves is our hate."

"But if you keep hate in your heart, then you're no better than he is. He needs our understanding, not our hate. Everyone deserves to be listened to, no matter who they are or what they've done."

A dust eddy swirls around us then disappears into the distance.

"Some people say he's not human; the murderer, I mean. They think he's the devil. Do you think people can be possessed?"

"I suppose there's that too," Father says. "I've never witnessed it personally, but I've known of priests who've encountered it. A priest who taught me philosophy at seminary college told the story of exorcising a demon from a young woman who was talking in tongues. Said he saw the beast with his own eyes as it left the woman. Said he never wants to witness something like that again. But I doubt that's what this was about. I believe this is a confused person who needs help. I don't believe he's possessed."

I shiver in the heat. "I think," I say, "it's someone who's mixed up and has done a very bad thing. I don't know if I'd ever be able to forgive him, but I'd try to understand him."

"You're a wise girl, Liz. Your Mom and Dad must be proud of you."

The sun beats down on us and I feel the heat through my shoes as we wait on the cement. I don't know how Father can manage to wear his black suit and high white collar, but he doesn't even appear to be sweating. Perhaps his faith is keeping him dry. I forgot my hat and mop my brow with my arm, then Father and I step off the sidewalk and begin down the road that leads to the Drummond's.

* * *

It's a narrow avenue, bare of sidewalks, and is the last street before the highway on the west side of Willowsbend. If you leave town using this road, you will be on your way to the next province, not heading towards the city as you are when you use the highway that passes the Tremblay's. There are houses on one side of this avenue, and farmland on the other where the town ends. The ditch on the side next to the houses is deep and overgrown with thistles, and sunflowers; I can just imagine the tangle of snakes squirming in its depths. The barbed-wire fence on the farmland side is high, as if keeping the people who live in the houses, at bay. The wheat on the other side of the fence grows tall; I see combines in the distance waiting to be put to work.

This side of town has a reputation for being the place to buy alcohol if you're underage. Jen has joked about coming here, but I'm pretty sure she never has, at least she's never told me if she has. And I certainly haven't. Dad would blow a gasket if he found out I'd bought beer and more importantly, if anyone had recognized me buying beer.

The houses are rundown, and dirt roads that lead to the houses, cross the ditch at intervals. We turn down the third driveway, stopping at the end of this rutted path that would barely fit a truck, to stare at a house.

The shingles are sparse and only one window has glass; the rest, boarded over with scrap pieces of wood. The screen door gently bangs in the little bit of breeze that's able to pass through this yard isolated by trees and bush where barely a beam of sunlight can penetrate. I don't know how the occupants of the house survive when it's thirty below and the leaves are gone; the wind must blow right through the thin walls. A trail of smoke wafts out of the chimney even on this hot day and I wonder if it's to keep the dank and the damp from rotting the place into the ground. A tricycle with one wheel is half buried in the dirt beside the step and a deflated basketball slumps against a tree that's struggling to survive. A rope is strung between two of these half-dead trees and the dirty twine sags under the weight of a row of limp diapers. No one comes out to meet us and Father walks up to the door. I reach for his arm to stop him, but quickly pull my hand away, wondering if it's a sin to touch a priest.

The door creaks open. Gail Drummond stands on the other side with a baby in her arms. The baby is crying. She sticks her finger in the infant's mouth and the whimpering stops.

"Gail," Father says. "I'm so sorry about your mom. I tried calling but your phone doesn't seem to be working. Wanted to give my condolences, offer some comfort."

"Thank you, Father," Gail says. "Phone was disconnected last month."

"Is it a boy or a girl?" Father asks.

"A girl."

"And the name?"

"Debra."

"Lovely name. Bring her by the church, I'll baptize her for you."

Gail points her chin at me as she pats the baby's bottom. "Why'd you bring her if you're here to offer us sympathy?"

Father turns to me. "Miss Murphy and I have brought you some things." He holds up his hand. "Now, I know you're fine on your own, but sometimes a little bit of help isn't so bad."

"Dad says we don't accept charity."

"Is your dad around?" Father says peering past Gail and through the screen door. "I'd like to say how sorry I am for the loss of his wife, for the loss of your mother."

"No," she says quickly. "I haven't seen him since the day of—since he got out of jail."

"Well, then, you certainly could use some help. If I was cold, I'd take the first sweater that was handed to me and not consider it charity. Just one human being kind to another. Let us show you what we brought. Would that be ok?"

Gail pauses, then steps to the ground. As she approaches, I can see how pretty she is. Her eyes are green like mine and her thick blond hair shines like the moon. She reaches out and takes a green sweater from one of the boxes.

"That was mine," I say. "A few years ago. I've grown...."

Her eyes flick to the hedge and she throws the sweater back down. "Kids don't need anything."

"Surely the children could use a pair of boots, mittens, a winter coat? It's going to be awfully cold in just a few short weeks. There's cereal for the baby and homemade buns for the kids. And believe me," he says as he pats his round belly, "Mrs. Murphy is the best bread maker around." Father picks up the bag of buns and offers them to her. "Give the kids a treat."

"Charity is charity, and pity is pity," Gail says. "Dad said we're not to take anything from anyone." Her gaze falls on me as she steps backwards. "Especially from them."

"I don't pity you or your family, Gail. That, my dear girl is the last thing I feel. I think your father is a man who struggles with his demons and tries his best to look after his family after a terrible tragedy." Father pulls the wagon closer to Gail.

Once again, she looks to the bushes. I squint into the gloom but see nothing.

"The kids are hungry." Father's voice pleads.

Gail snatches the buns from Father and the milk from the wagon then returns to the house. For the first time I see her siblings standing inside the door, Stevie and Olive among them. All but Olive follow their sister deeper into the house. The little girl jumps over the rotting wooden step and lifts up a small cloth bag to show me.

"This is my marble collection," she says as she holds out the purple bag. "Wanna see? Mama sewed me the bag before she went to heaven."

I approach her. "Sure," I say.

"Olive," Gail appears behind the screened in door. "Come and have a bun and a glass of milk." She steps outside and puts her hand on the girl's shoulder then nudges her into the house. She turns to Father and me. "You've done what you came here to do, now go," she says.

"We'll just leave the wagon for you to look through and see if there's anything you can use," Father says.

"But Father, it's Fran's ...." I say. He shushes me.

"Perhaps Miss Murphy can come back and pick it up at a later date? Her sister's wagon, you see."

"It'll be by the gate," Gail says.

As Father and I walk out of the yard, a curl of cigarette smoke wafts out of the brambles.

CHAPTER SEVEN

"Where's my wagon?" Fran wails. "I want my wagon. Bring it back."

I'm outside after lunch, waving goodbye to Mr. and Mrs. Krieger as they head to the city, when Fran notices her wagon isn't in its usual place under the tree. Even though she hasn't played with it all summer, she's decided that just because the toy isn't here, she needs to play with it this afternoon.

"Well, you can't have it. I had to use it. I'll go next week and pick it up," I say.

Mom calls out the back door. "I'm pushing the carriage to the store. I need you to watch the girls for a couple of hours, Liz. Your dad's behind on his books."

I sit on the stairs and pout. "But, Mom, I helped you this morning, Can't I have the rest of the day off?"

"You can have all day tomorrow to yourself. I promised your dad a couple of hours this afternoon." Mom bends over and rubs my shoulder. "Thank you for walking to the Drummond's with Father this morning. He said you were great company and a very intelligent young lady. Don't let me down now."

Mom is good at manipulation, that's how she became Dad's bookkeeper. Before she and Dad were married, Mom kept books for Donaldson Law Office in the city. Dad, having been told that a co-worker of Mom's was wanting to move to the country, arrived at the office to offer the woman a job. Good salary, her own office, shorter hours, and lots of nice apartments for rent at a fraction of what they cost in the city.

Mom wondered how this man could be so misinformed as she knew her co-worker had no desire to live in the country. Mom, however, had confessed many times that she didn't like the fast pace or the high cost of city life, and if the right proposition came along, she'd move to the country in a heartbeat.

After Dad told Mom why he was there, Mom proceeded to answer the phone, take dictation, and type a hundred and seventy-five words a minute on her Underwood Electric Typewriter. By the time she was finished demonstrating her skills, instead of waiting to ask her co-worker if she wanted to move to the country, Dad, so impressed by her work, asked Mom. Mom agreed and packed her bags that night. Eight months later they were married.

The first time I heard this story, I told Mom I thought the entire account of Dad wanting to hire her co-worker sounded like a ruse and it was she whom Dad had really come to see. Mom said nonsense, there's no way she could be fooled that easily.

"Rose is lying on the couch," Mom says. "She's not feeling well. Check on her and take her a glass of Canada Dry. I don't think it's too serious. Growing pains, I imagine."

I don't tell her that Rose stayed up until midnight looking at her photo albums and that she ate the two cookies I gave her as well as snuck downstairs and stole two more. Or that she hates helping me babysit and will do anything to get out of the chore.

"It's garbage pick-up day. Make sure the girls are inside when Mr. Pendergrass arrives."

When Mom was young, a neighbourhood child climbed onto the bumper of a garbage truck, and unbeknownst to the driver, fell inside and was killed. Because of that, Mom wants her youngest children in the house on garbage day.

"Mrs. Henderson prepared the girls an afternoon snack; watermelon and raspberries," Mom says. "They are to have none of the cookies or muffins the neighbours dropped off. And make sure they have their snack no later than three. The potatoes are peeled and sitting in water on the stove. The roast is cooking on low. Just baste it once in a while, please. And could you snap the ends off the green beans? Mrs. Krieger, God bless her soul, picked them this morning but ran out of time to prepare them. I'll cook them when I get home. Your dad likes them crispy anyhow. There are two half-pint sealers of homemade pickles and crab-apple jelly on the counter that Mrs. Fogg brought up from the basement. Make sure Mr. Pendergrass gets them." She ends her instructions with, "And no leaving the yard."

Mad that I had to accompany Father this morning, and now I'm saddled with my sisters all afternoon, I say, "Maybe you should stay home if you're going to worry so much."

"Elizabeth, did you hear what I said or are you too busy thinking about how to get out of helping me?"

"Yes, Mom. I heard you."

"Call only if it's an emergency, but otherwise, I'll see you around four." Then pretending she doesn't see me pouting, she pushes the carriage with my brother tucked inside, out the gate, down the alley and into the sunshine.

"I wanna go in your treehouse," Fran says the moment Mom disappears around the corner. She's jumping in the hopscotch squares and bends forward to pick up her rubber ring and toss it to the next square.

"You're too young to go up there; you already know that."

"Am not too young."

"Are too."

"Daddy let you use the treehouse when you were seven. I'm just about seven."

"I don't care. If you want to go in a treehouse, ask Dad to build you one. You're not going in mine. Play hopscotch if you want something to do."

Alex begins hopping on two legs up and down the hopscotch squares. "I'll play with you, Fran," she says when she comes to a stop. "See, I know how to hopscotch." She bends her little legs and jumps to the next square.

"No you don't," Fran says. "That's not how you do it."

"Is to," Alex says. "I can play as good as you."

With her arms crossed, Fran stands in the next square, preventing Alex from jumping any further. Alex plops to the ground.

"I'm bored," Robin says. "What can we do, Liz?"

"What about a playhouse in the front porch? I can spread a blanket between the chairs and the couch with some clothespins."

"Yay," Alex shouts, her attention easily swayed. "I wanna playhouse."

"With some real tea and snacks. Not pretend stuff," Robin says.

"I don't want to play house," Fran says. "That's for babies."

"You can read then. As long as you stay in the porch."

The garbage truck turns down the alley and stops behind the neighbours three doors away. Mr. Pendergrass's lanky frame unfolds from behind the wheel. He stays by the truck.

"Hi, Mr. Pendergrass," I call. "How are you today?"

He shifts his toothpick from one side of his mouth to the other. "Can't complain," he says. "I'll be by to collect your garbage soon as I've done these houses."

"I have to get the girls to the front porch. Don't leave when you're done, Mom has something for you."

He nods and chews on his toothpick.

I shoo the girls ahead of me while Fran plods behind, protesting her annoyance at having to stay in the porch with a two-year old and a three-year old.

A wicker couch sits against the back wall of the porch, and two chairs line the front. I turn the furniture around, pull the blanket off the back of the couch, then spread the hand-knitted coverlet between them. After significant fiddling, I finally get it tight enough so the girls can't complain the roof is sagging, and fix it taut with clothespins. Alex and Robin climb underneath and begin to giggle as they ask each other if they'd like a cup of tea in the British accents Rose taught them. Fran sits in one of the chairs, lost in Charlotte's Web.

"Stay here. I'll get your snacks," I say. "Fran, watch the kids for a sec, ok?"

She nods from behind her book.

I step into the living room. Rose is on the couch, a photo album open across her lap. When she sees me, she slams the book shut and slides it under the couch, then lies down and crooks her elbow over her face.

"You don't look very sick to me," I say. "You just wanted to get out of babysitting."

"That's not true." She coughs.

"Faker," I say. "You were ok this morning when I walked to the Drummond's. You even asked to go along."

"I'm not faking, you don't know how I feel. I didn't feel sick this morning. It just came on suddenly."

"Yeah, suddenly, like when you heard you had to help me."

"Doesn't mean I'm faking. I'm a very stoic person. I try not to burden others with my problems. So, tell me," she says changing the subject, "what did you see at the Drummond's? Any clues as to who the murderer might be?"

"Of course not," I say. "I only saw Gail and the kids. Her dad might have been hiding in the bushes, but if he was, he didn't show his face. And I, for one, am glad he didn't."

"I wish I could have been there. The fact that he's hiding is a clue to his guilt, although he could be hiding out of fear. Maybe he knows who the real killer is and he's afraid he's going to be next." She lifts a finger in the air. "That's not bad. I need to write that down." She pulls her notepad out and jots down her thoughts.

"I need you to go to the porch and watch the girls while I get them their snack."

"Too sick. Need to stay on the couch," she says as she slides her notepad back into her pocket.

"Rose, it's right through that door!" I point to the front porch. "You can lie on the couch out there as easily as you can in here."

"Fran's there, she can watch them. And anyhow, surely they can be by themselves for a few minutes?"

"Fran has her head buried in a book. You know Mom doesn't like Alex and Robin to be alone even for a few minutes when Mr. Pendergrass has the garbage truck running."

"So, because Fran's a bookworm, I have to get up out of my sickbed?"

I put my hands on my hips. "If you have enough strength to look at your photo album and write things down in that blasted notebook of yours, you can watch the girls for a few minutes."

Rose stands and limps to the porch with one hand on her stomach, the other on her forehead. "If I get sick and die, it's all your fault." She drags her bare feet across the threshold and into the porch.

In the kitchen I begin to get the girls snacks together on a tray. I'm pouring a splash of tea into the play teapot which I've already filled with milk, when Robin runs into the room. "Have you seen Fran? We want her to be a guest at our tea party, but we can't find her."

"Maybe she went to the bathroom?"

The little girl scampers into the office and up the stairs. I listen as her footsteps sprint to one end of the hall, back again, and down the stairs.

"She's not in her room and the bathroom door is wide open."

"Then you just missed her somewhere. She's probably on the couch beside Rose, reading her book."

"She's not. And Rose is sleeping. She's sick."

"What?" I stomp through the living room to the front porch. Rose is curled up on the couch, sound asleep. "Rose," I shout. "What are you doing?"

She opens her eyes. "I told you, I'm sick," she says.

"Fran is missing. Where is she?"

"I don't know. I don't feel good."

"Oh, come on, Rose. You're not sick."

"Am too," she says. "I have a terrible stomach-ache and my head feels like it's going to explode." She stands and takes a step towards the house then throws up all over the porch floor.

"Eww, yuck," Alex and Robin say.

Rose runs inside, her fingers pressed to her lips as she bolts through the house.

"I'm not eating out here," Robin says. She pinches her nose. "It smells funny."

"Well," I say, "you're going to have to wait until I get this mess cleaned up before you get your snack now, anyhow." I look at the footprints Rose left in her wake as she ran up the stairs. "And it could take a while," I say.

"We still haven't found Fran," Robin says.

"I don't know where she is," I say.

"She's disappeared." Robin throws her hands in the air and says, "Poof."

I'm on my way to retrieve the mop and pail when it dawns on me. "The garbage truck," I whisper. "I forgot about the garbage truck." I run through the house with Robin and Alex on my heels.

Rose slaps her just washed feet down the stairs. "What's all the commotion?" she says.

"You lost Fran," I say.

"Did not! I told you I was sick."

I race out the back door, the girls follow. Mr. Pendergrass has finished emptying our cans and is about to start the mechanism that chews up the garbage. "Don't do that," I yell. "My sister, my sister is in there."

"What?" he says. "Your sister is in there? You mean in the back?"

"Don't turn the motor on, Mr. Pendergrass. My sister is in there."

"In there?" he says as he again points his thumb towards the back of the beast.

"Turn off the truck," I scream.

He turns off the ignition and climbs out of his vehicle. Sensing the fear in my voice, the little girls cower on the deck, while Rose and I run behind the truck. I step onto the back bumper, then steeling myself against the smell, I stick my head inside. "Fran, where are you? Are you ok? Did you fall in?"

Mr. Pendergrass peers inside along with me. "There's no one in there, Miss. I would have seen if someone climbed in."

"Were you here the whole time?"

"Well," he rubs his hand through his hair, "I guess I had a smoke." He points across the alley, away from the yard. "Over there while I was waiting for you." He shakes his head. "Can't seem to stop."

I call again. "Fran, answer me. Are you ok?"

A small voice answers me. "I'm ok, Liz. Just scared."

"Oh my God, Fran. Where are you? I can't see a thing, there's too much yuck."

"I'm here, Liz, up here."

"Up here? What do you mean? Are you standing on something?"

"There's nothing to stand on down there, Miss," Mr. Pendergrass says. "Nothing but metal walls, grinders, and garbage."

"You have to get her out before Mom and Dad get home!" I lean inside and call. "Can you climb out, Fran? Are you able to climb through the garbage and get yourself out?"

"I'm not in there, Liz. I'm up here."

"You're up here? What do you mean, up here?" My voice is muffled by mounds of crushed cereal boxes, rotten vegetable peelings, eggshells and coffee grounds.

"Up, Liz. In your tree."

Robin and Alex have climbed down the deck steps and now wander towards us. Mr. Pendergrass, Robin, Alex, Rose, and I turn our backs to the truck and crane our heads in the air. Fran is halfway up the tree, about a foot below the floor of the treehouse. She's climbed the branches on one side, then reached around to get hold of what's left of the ladder Dad took down when Mom said she didn't want me climbing the tree. Most of the pickets are broken or missing and I don't know how she's made it as high as she has.

"Don't be mad at me, Liz."

My legs become weak as relief floods through my body. "I thought you fell in the truck, Fran. I thought you were buried in the garbage. Get down here right now!"

"I can't. I'm stuck."

"What do you mean, you're stuck? Just come back down the same way you got up there."

"I'm too scared."

"Then go up. You can climb over the railing into the treehouse then cross the roof."

"I can't, Liz. I just can't."

"Well, there's no other way. If you don't come down or climb up, you'll have to spend the rest of your life in the tree. And I'll be in trouble for a very long time."

She begins to cry. "I'm sorry, Liz. Do you think this is a 'mergency like Mom said?"

"I think she was talking about the murders, not you getting stuck in the tree. It's ok. I'm coming up to get you."

Mr. Pendergrass speaks up. "Pardon me for saying so, Miss, but dead weight is a lot heavier than you think it's going to be, even if it's only one sixty-pound girl. Once you get up to her, she's going to hang on to you for dear life. You're not strong enough to carry your sister down."

"What else can I do? She can't stay up there. Do you have a ladder in your truck?"

"No ladder, never had a use for one. Garbage cans are on the ground, not in the air." The man strokes his chin. "I haven't climbed a tree in thirty years." He pulls his pants up higher on his thin waist and snaps the suspenders on his narrow shoulders. "But I suppose you never know what you can do until you try." And with those words, he pushes the toothpick he has clamped between his teeth, out of his mouth with his tongue, then spits on his hands and grabs the lowest branch of the tree.

With much effort, he swings his legs and pulls his weight up and onto that branch; it bends but doesn't break. He kneels and reaches for the next branch, then the next, and the next, finally arriving below Fran.

"Ok, little girl, set your feet on my shoulders."

"I'm afraid," she says into the leaves and branches swaying over her head.

"Nothing to be afraid of. I won't let you fall. And if you do, I'll let go and you'll have me to land on when we both hit the ground. I'm bigger than you so I'll fall faster; it's basic physics. You won't hurt yourself if you fall on me, I guarantee it."

"Fran," I call with my head craned back and my hands cupped around my mouth, "do as Mr. Pendergrass says because if Dad comes home and sees you there, he'll chop the damn tree down to rescue you! Then we'll all be grounded for the rest of our lives."

Fran puts her feet on the tall man's shoulders.

"Now slide your legs down and put your arms around my neck, Missy," Mr. Pendergrass says. "I may be skinny, but I've been lifting garbage cans for more than twenty years. I'm strong enough to carry both of us down the tree." Fran obeys, then Mr. Pendergrass, with Franny's little arms wrapped around his scrawny neck, descends the tree.

"There you go," he says, placing my sister on the ground. "You're braver than me, little girl, climbing up there." Mr. Pendergrass ruffles Fran's hair then pulls a toothpick out of his shirt pocket, poking it between his lips.

The other girls, now that the drama is over, head to the house and Fran follows to tell them about her ordeal, I'm sure making it sound scarier than it was.

"Thanks, Mr. Pendergrass," I say.

Mr. Pendergrass, with a spring in his step, opens the gate, and stops at his truck. He turns. "Hold on, Miss Murphy," he says.

"Yes, Mr. Pendergrass?"

"Your sister, the one with the camera? She's a loner, isn't she? Likes to wander around by herself taking pictures, writing things down?"

"I guess," I say. Then quickly add, in case Mr. Pendergrass tells Mom that her daughter is disobeying the rules, "Before the police said kids can't go places alone, she did."

"And she's smart? Tries to come up with theories, figure things out?"

I nod.

"Has she told anyone what she thinks?"

"About what?"

"The murders. Has she told anyone her thoughts about the murders?"

"No, well, just me."

"What did she say?"

"She said Mr. Drummond might be hiding because he's afraid he's going to be murdered next." I shrug my shoulders. "But she's a kid, Mr. Pendergrass. I wouldn't take anything she says seriously."

"Tell her to be careful about who she tells her thoughts to. Tell her no one is to be trusted no matter who they are. Some people aren't what they seem. Do you understand?"

"I suppose."

"I'm serious. Trust no one," he says and climbs into his truck. As he rumbles to the next house, he opens his window and shouts, "I'll keep a lookout, too," and I wonder if the murders have made Mr. Pendergrass weirder than usual.

I join my sisters. The girls have gathered around Franny's wagon parked at the bottom of the steps. A purple bag filled with marbles is on the ground beside the wheel.

CHAPTER EIGHT

The first two weeks of August are hot with no rain in the forecast. The farmer's crops grow tall in the heat and the possibility of a bumper crop are words whispered but never spoken aloud. The good news helps to buffer the gloom that has settled over the town, although the murders are still the first thing on our minds when we wake up and the last thing we think of when we go to bed.

No one told Mom and Dad about Fran getting stuck in the tree, not even Mr. Pendergrass, and I'm grateful for that. Every time he sees me now, he winks and shifts the toothpick he always has in his mouth, from one side to the other. Not knowing what to do with the marbles, I threw the bag in my dresser alongside the cigarettes I'm hiding, with hopes that I'll get the nerve to take them back to the Drummond's, though I can't see that happening any time soon.

Because the RCMP are saying the possibility that the murderer is still in Willowsbend is slim to none, the restrictions not allowing kids to go places unescorted have been lifted during daytime hours. Once the sun goes down, however, they're recommending children not wander the streets alone. Since Mom knows that Rose likes to roam, she's being allowed to continue her photographic endeavours unhindered by the confines of her own backyard. The rules are, she has to be home by supper, and she's to stick to the busy streets, no straying down back alleys or through parks. And, Mom said, she's not to go any further than the town limits without an adult by her side. Though—and I assume I'm the only one who knows how far she actually travels—rules haven't restricted her in the past.

It's eight at night and my three youngest sisters have been tucked into bed. Rose did the dishes, then because Mom doesn't like to waste anything, dumped the dishwater on the rhubarb and is now in the front yard taking pictures of anyone who passes and is willing to pose for her. I laughed when I saw her snap a picture of Sister Veronica biking down the road, her habit sailing out behind her as if she had wings. I watched as Mr. Pendergrass stood completely still, his hat in his hands, not a smile on his face as Rose took his picture. I'm thinking she will title that photo, *The Walking Dead*. I left her taking pictures of birds, butterflies, and the odd gopher that was brave enough to run through Mom's flower beds, to go to my treehouse.

Mom is having the ladies over, and Dad has gone into town where the men gather in the backyard of the community hall on warm summer evenings to have a beer or cup of coffee and discuss business, though I imagine the talk this summer is about the murders. Cole is asleep in his carriage beside the deck, a mosquito net stretched tight over the top of the pram, and I'm on the floor of my treehouse reading a book with a hot water bottle pressed to my tummy.

It was my turn to do the dishes tonight, but I had a stomach-ache and whispered to Mom before supper to ask if I could be excused from my chore. She said Rose would cover for me if I filled in for her at some point this summer. Rose wasn't happy and bartered for two of her turns.

Through the cracks in the floorboards, I look below as Mrs. Henderson, punctual as usual, walks down the flagstone path that connects our front yard with the back. She peeks at Cole, climbs the back steps, and knocks on the door.

"Elva," Mom says. "Come, take the rocking chair. I'm just bringing out the cookies and iced tea."

As Elva rocks, the back gate opens again, this time allowing Mrs. Olyphant and Mrs. Dickenson to enter. The Dickensons live a couple of miles further down the highway from the Olyphants, and Mildred likely picked Lois up in her car. Mr. and Mrs. Dickenson have three young children and, in the winter, if the school bus isn't running, Mr. Dickenson brings his, and the neighbour kids to school on a horse drawn sleigh.

The two women are having a laugh about something then stop to look at Mom's vegetable garden, before they, too, climb the steps to the deck. In the next ten minutes, Mrs. Krieger and Mrs. Fogg also enter our yard. I put my book down and settle back to listen to the gossip.

"You're looking well," Mrs. Dickenson says to Mom.

"Thanks, Mildred. I'm feeling good, not one hundred percent but better than I was. Don't know what I'd have done without all of you that first week. After six, you'd think I'd bounce back quickly. Seemed to have worked the opposite this time."

"It certainly doesn't get any easier, does it?" Mrs. Olyphant says. "The more babies we have, the faster we pop them out, but the toll being pregnant takes on our bodies gets tougher and tougher to get over."

"I wanted to have you all here so I could say thanks for your help. You're good friends." I peek as Mom pours and passes out glasses of iced tea.

"So, is this the last?" Mrs. Olyphant asks.

"I suppose one never knows," Mom says. "But if I have my way, Cole is the last."

"Jim always did want a boy. At least there's that," Elva Henderson says. Mrs. Henderson is a pessimist and has something negative to say even when she's trying to put a positive spin on things. I remember one time complaining I had to babysit my sisters and she said *I should be grateful to be the oldest because I'll have someone to look after me when I'm old and gray.* Unlike her, she told me, who has no siblings or children and if she outlives her husband, she'll likely die alone in her bed with no family to mourn her loss.

"That he did, Elva," Mom says. "Cole's in for a rough ride with five older sisters. At least he should grow up understanding women better than most men I know."

They all laugh.

"What are they doing with the Tremblay's property?" Mrs. Krieger asks.

"I heard it's being put up for sale by Henry's brother," Mom says. "Money will go towards paying off the funerals."

"When I buried Mom five years ago, it cost a thousand dollars," Mrs. Henderson says. "Can't imagine seven all at once. Dying isn't cheap, but then, neither is living."

"That was good of Liz to go to the Drummond's," Mrs. Olyphant says.

"She didn't want to," Mom says.

"Not sure I'd want to either." Evelyn Fogg is a timid pale faced woman who speaks so softly I have to press my ear to the floor to hear her. Her husband owns the grocery store where she's a cashier and sometimes I see the two of them walking hand in hand down the sidewalk on their way to work. I've always been surprised at this show of tenderness, especially at their advanced ages, as Mom and Dad never display their feelings for each other in public. "I know Jim and Stan are friends," she says, "and I shouldn't speak badly of the man, but everyone is saying that he's the most likely suspect."

"They were friends in high school," Mom says. "Not any more."

"Did Liz and Father see Stanley?"

"No, but Liz said Gail kept looking in the bushes at the side of the house as if he was hiding there. Said she seemed hesitant to take the clothes and food, like she was afraid he'd be angry. But he stayed where he was, if it was him."

"He doesn't seem the type," Mrs. Fogg says. "He's always been a gentleman when he's come into the store."

"Jim did say that prison can change a man. Turn him into something he wasn't before he spent time surrounded by hardened criminals."

"I find this all so stressful," Mrs. Fogg continues. "I've been keeping my doors locked, even during the day."

"Haven't we all," Mrs. Olyphant says.

Robin has gotten out of bed and now opens the back door to ask for a glass of water. Mom stands and takes her daughter inside. I lie on the floor of the treehouse and can hear their footsteps as Mom escorts Robin back to bed. Mom seems to be walking slower than usual.

"And it's the people living in the country who are most on edge," Mom says when she returns to the deck. "At least in town we have each other close by."

"George has begun sleeping with a gun under his pillow. I don't like the idea but what else can we do? I wouldn't hesitate for a second to shoot someone threatening my family." Mrs. Dickenson takes a bite of cookie. "Although there are times I find it quite inconvenient," she says through a mouthful of crumbs. "Sometimes I have to tell George to put the damn thing under the bed before we're found dead in some compromising position."

All the ladies, even Mrs. Fogg, laugh so hard, tears run down their cheeks.

"It doesn't make any sense," Mrs. Henderson says as she dabs at her eyes with a handkerchief. "Why haven't the RCMP found anyone yet? Do they expect us to live in fear the rest of our lives?"

"These things take time," Mrs. Olyphant says.

"I've seen more police driving up and down the road these past few weeks than I've seen in the past ten years," Mrs. Henderson continues. "All it takes is the murder of a family for them to get their asses in gear." She presses her fingers to her lips. "This has got me so upset I'm beginning to sound like my mother. That woman criticized everything." She dunks her cookie in her glass and shakes her head.

"Perhaps this is the beginning of how life is going to be from now on. Locking our doors all the time, everyone owning a gun, being wary of strangers," Mom says. "I don't like it, but this might be our new normal."

The ladies are quiet as they ponder Mom's words. When they begin talking again, the subject is how bountiful the gardens are turning out to be this year. According to Mrs. Dickenson, she has zucchini coming out her ears.

When the iced tea pitcher is empty, Mom brings out a bottle of Mrs. Krieger's raspberry wine. Last Christmas, much to Mrs. Krieger's dismay, Mr. Krieger gave me an inch of the red liquid in a juice glass. My mouth waters as I remember how sweet and tart it tasted. Mom pours all the ladies a drink.

"To Cole," Mrs. Olyphant says.

"To Cole," they respond as they take dainty sips.

Mrs. Fogg raises her glass. "Let's pray the murderer is found sooner rather than later."

They all lift their glasses.

"To the Tremblays," Mrs. Dickenson says. "May they rest in peace."

"To the Tremblays," everyone murmurs.

When they've finished their wine, Mom summons Rose to the backyard. The ladies stand and smooth the wrinkles out of their dresses, tuck wisps of hair behind their ears, and dab the shine off their foreheads with tissues they've pulled from various cleavages, pockets, and sleeves. With their arms around one another, in the waning hours of daylight, Rose takes their picture.

CHAPTER NINE

The train tracks lie as straight as a ruler on this flat land and I run my eyes down the metal rails that disappear into the horizon and beyond.

Jen lies on the ground with an ear to one of these rails. She lifts her head. "Nothing," she says then puts her ear back to the beam. "Not a rattle, not a hum. Nothing." She stands and brushes the tumbleweeds off her shorts.

"Good. We can go home," I say.

"Don't be so juvenile. Your mom gave you a day to yourself. If you go home, you'll be made to babysit, pull weeds, or wash the floors. And I'll have to help."

"I'm not being juvenile, I'm being smart. We aren't supposed to leave town, let alone play chicken with a train."

"And just because you, Miss Goody Two Shoes, always does everything she's told, doesn't mean I have to. Besides, we can see Spooky's house from here. It's not like we're two miles down the tracks."

Mrs. Witherspoon, or, Spooky, as we call her, is the town eccentric whom everyone tolerates because *every town must have someone they can talk about without feeling badly,* or so I've heard Mrs. Henderson say. Mrs. Witherspoon likes to paint, and draw, sculpt and *create*, as she's told me. She recycles broken and used articles that people, instead of taking them to the dump, haul to her yard, and turns them into her gizmos, and artwork. Her large triple-sized lot is full of whimsical renderings of cats and dogs with big eyes made from hubcaps, and bushy tails made from worn out brooms. Lions have manes constructed from hundreds of forks with missing tines, which rattle on a windy day, and giraffes have necks made from garden hoses and bodies from rain barrels. Mazes, which meander around every corner, have all manner of articles blocking one's view; from refrigerators with the doors removed, to cars with their doors welded open and you have to crawl through to get to the next path. There's even a windmill in the far corner of the lot made from fan blades and lawnmowers, which powers a fountain made from a bird bath and an elephant statue.

Besides being an artist, Mrs. Witherspoon is also a baker of cookies. Oatmeal rounds, refrigerator crisps, chocolate chip, sugar cookies, and peanut butter are some of the many offerings she has in her repertoire. At every christening, wedding, funeral, or event where food is served, you can count on her to bring a tray brimming with the sweet treats, and you always know where they are on the buffet table as it's where the crowd has gathered.

Her final hobby is being a clairvoyant, hence the name, Spooky. One would think that in this conventional farming community she wouldn't garner a single customer, but that isn't the case. In the far corner of her backyard, next to the gate off the alley, there's a small stone house where she tells people their fortunes. A double hedgerow leads to a secluded archway over the door of this little building, so unless you're watching every minute of the day, no one can see you enter or exit. She has a flag to raise once you're inside, alerting her a client is waiting and more often than not, that flag is flying high. It costs five dollars a visit no matter what you're wanting to see her about.

Last spring Mrs. Witherspoon set up a booth at our carnival night and the lineup to see her was all the way down the hall and out the front door all night long. Jen, Rose, and I stood in that line behind Mr. Pendergrass for nearly an hour. When I got inside her booth, she told me I was going to do well in my arithmetic exam the next day, and I did. She told Rose there was going to be one picture she'd take in her lifetime that would make her famous. When Rose asked what picture, Mrs. Witherspoon said it hadn't been taken yet. She told Jennifer that she'd find a dollar bill by her front step sometime within the next week, and sure enough, there was a dollar bill tucked between the branches of the rose bush by the front door when Jen got home from school the next day. She told Mr. Pendergrass he was going to become famous, though not until he was dead.

As a result of her hobbies, the woman doesn't get much housework done and is always soliciting kids who venture too near, to come in and do her a favour, which means, clean her house. Anyone in the know, which is practically every kid in town, steers clear for fear she'll drag them inside.

Jen holds out her hand. "Pass me my smokes. May as well do something while we wait."

I pull the crumpled package of Players Filter Tip that Jen purchased at The Noodle House, from my pocket. Jen taps a cigarette out, lights it, and takes a deep breath, then leans her head back and blows smoke rings in the air. "Ah, that's more like it," she says as she holds out the pack to me.

I shake my head. "Rose told me she's read that cigarettes can be dangerous to your health. They say they might cause cancer."

"Then explain to me why the companies who make these things would want us to die? They'd lose all their customers. And considering the number of people who smoke and pay fifty-two cents a pack, those companies must be making money hand over fist." She takes another puff. "Anyhow," she says through the cloud of smoke, "I'm only having three or four a week, not like some people who smoke an entire pack a day. I can quit any time I want to. I just don't want to yet." She sits on the track and sucks in another lung-full.

I sit beside her; the rail is hot. "Some day Mr. Wong is going to find out your mom doesn't smoke and realize you're writing those notes yourself, you know."

"No way. Mom orders Chinese food on Friday and by then she's so tired from cleaning houses all week, she can barely move when she gets home. I always suggest she rest while I walk over and pick the food up. She's never set foot inside The Noodle House, and if I have my way, she never will."

"Dad won't let us order Chinese food," I say. "He says there's something in it called MSG that isn't good for you. I wish he would, I kind of like the taste when I've had it at your place."

Jen shrugs. Even though she never says so, I know she thinks my dad is a smart man and I wonder what it would be like to grow up without a father.

"Are you worried about starting high school?" I ask.

"Nah."

"I am."

A lone pelican swoops low overhead then lands on the slough behind us. Mr. Pendergrass told me that the males who failed to mate are ostracized and forced to live alone.

"Ok, ok." She holds the cigarette out and clumsily taps the ashes off. "If we're being totally honest here, maybe just a little. Scared, I mean." She throws her arm around my shoulder. "But we have each other, it'll be good."

"You know more of the grade nine kids than I do." I pull a blade of grass from between the wooden ties. "Most of my class is going to the Catholic school in the city."

"You know some of the kids I graduated with, don't you? This is a small town."

"I suppose, but you know them better."

"Do you wish you were going to the city?"

"No. I just want everything to stay the same." I peel the blade down to the tender stalk then put it between my teeth.

"We're growing up, Lizzie, and starting high school is part of it." She takes another puff. "Then it's teacher's college, nursing school, or secretarial school. Then work, then marriage, or both. Then kids, grandkids, old age and death."

"Look who's suddenly serious."

"It's this town, this summer. We've all grown up; have been forced to grow up."

"We're not innocent anymore, are we?" I say. "We know people who've been murdered!"

Jen pushes the smouldering stub of the cigarette into the dirt with the toe of her tennis shoe, then tugs the pack out from under her sleeve.

"You're having another one?"

"C'mon, I get enough grief at home. That mother of mine is afraid I'm going to get pregnant or something."

"Don't come running to me when you get cancer."

"I promise I won't come running to you." The cigarette dangles between her lips. "Are you going to date in grade nine?" She flicks the match.

"No. I told you, Mom said I can't date until I'm sixteen."

"That's over two years away!" she says between puffs; the end of the cigarette glows hot. "I'm not waiting that long. I just need Holly Black to introduce me to some boys."

A tingling runs up my spine.

"Train's coming." Jen stands and tugs a handful of pennies from the pocket of her shorts, then hands me a couple.

"Seems like a waste," I say as I hold the pennies out on my palm. "This could buy me a gummy strawberry or a piece of sponge toffy. Now it's going to be squished flat."

"Sure don't have to worry about you growing up too fast," Jen says. "You seem stuck on staying a kid. C'mon girl, we've got to get some cred, you know? We can't start high school without lying pennies on the tracks. It's a rite of passage."

We see the train in the distance.

"That's your rail," she points. "This one is mine."

I take a deep breath, then step over the tracks and straddle the rail on my side. I lie my coins on the warm iron beam; they glint in the sun. Jen does the same.

"And you can't jump off until I say so," Jen says.

"Why do you get to say?"

"Because I brought the pennies," she shouts as the train gets closer.

I frown.

"That's the rules, Liz. It's the way it's been done for decades. Ask anyone."

I'm sure she's making these rules up on the fly, but this is not the time to argue. I look at Jen; her face is lit up with excitement. With a shaking hand, I rub the sweat from my eyes.

The train whistle screeches. I lift a foot, ready to dash.

Jen grabs my arm and screams, "Not yet," her words blown away in the wind and the noise.

I can see the conductor at the window. "Jen," I shout, "let go!"

"Now," she yells.

I jump, but in the noise and confusion, I can't tell if Jen does. I land in a clump of weeds knocking the wind out of my lungs then crawl to my knees, gasping for air. I put my head down to try and look underneath the cars, but the train is moving so fast, all I get is gravel blowing into my face as the blurred wheels rattle past. Snakes being the furthest thing from my mind, I back into the ditch and look to the horizon; the cars extend as far as I can see. For three minutes I wait for the train to go by, not knowing if my friend is alive or dead. When the caboose finally passes, I see Jen standing in the ditch on the other side. She's jumping up and down.

"Woohoo," she screams as the noise of the train fades. "Woohoo, that was something!" She runs to the tracks and peels the shiny copper discs off the rail. They've been flattened to twice their normal size. She drops one into my palm—it's warm—then lifts her eyes to mine. "What's the matter with you?"

"I thought you were dead!" I push her away and turn my back. "Don't ever do that to me again." I rub tears from my eyes.

"I wanted to see how long I could last." She pats her body then touches my arm. "See, I'm in one piece. I jumped a split second after you. Faster than that even. A split, split second."

I don't turn around, embarrassed by my tears.

"I'm sorry, Liz." She touches my shoulder. "I didn't mean to scare you."

"I'm not scared," I say blinking back my tears. "I was worried. I thought you'd been hit by the train. I couldn't see, I couldn't hear. You're the only friend I have to start high school with. It's bad enough you smoke and might get cancer," I say, "and we're out here in the wilderness with a murderer wandering around. The last thing I need is for you to get splattered all over the countryside!" I face my friend.

"Well, when you put it that way." She punches my shoulder when she sees I'm not joking. "Hey, I'm not going anywhere. It's ok."

I swipe at my cheeks.

"Do you want to do it again?" she asks.

"Do I...."

"Just kidding. Besides," she says, trying to make light of my reaction, "if I got killed, you'd be the one who got in trouble. And best friends don't abandon best friends."

* * *

I'm so grateful we didn't get killed, and Jen is so pumped from dodging the train, that both of us forget to take the long way around past Mrs. Witherspoon's house. The woman, plump from eating too many of her home-baked cookies, sticks her head out her front door.

"Girls, can you come here for a minute?"

"Crap," Jen mutters. "Sorry, Mrs. Witherspoon, gotta head home. You know, killer on the loose." We begin to walk fast in the opposite direction.

"I'm going to have to insist, I'm afraid," Mrs. Witherspoon says. "I need a favour and now you both owe me."

Jen skids to a stop. "We owe you?" she says over her shoulder.

"I've been in my backyard all afternoon building a display for Christmas. You should come and see. My vision is for Santa and his reindeer to travel on a roller coaster track. So far, I've built a loop-de-loop, a corkscrew, and now I'm trying to figure out how to build a ramp where Santa sails over an empty span of track then lands on the other side."

She pauses and Jen and I attempt to sneak away. She starts talking again.

"When I heard the train sound its horn I peeked over the fence. Imagine my surprise when I saw the two of you straddling the rails."

She puts her fingers to her chin. "Unless it was two other young ladies, one with red hair and one with dark hair who happen to be walking past my house after a train has gone by on this fine summer's day. But I'm quite sure it was Liz Murphy and Jennifer Olsen." Her eyes twinkle. "It's not like I didn't do that kind of thing when I was your age. Playing chicken with trains has been going on for as long as there've been trains. Still, it's a dangerous game which I'm quite sure your parents wouldn't approve of you doing." She winks at us. "I could use a hand today and what's better than two girls just blossoming into womanhood to lighten an old lady's heart and make her feel young again."

Reluctantly, I move towards Mrs. Witherspoon's house. Jen stubbornly keeps her feet glued to the road.

"C'mon, Jen," I say. "We can't have Mom finding out about this."

Jen shakes her head. "I'm not going in there," she says. "She's bluffing."

"I assure you, Miss Olsen, I am no more bluffing about phoning your mom and telling her how you spent your afternoon, than you are about going on dates, or smoking one of those cancer sticks you have tucked in the sleeve of your shirt." She crosses her meaty arms around her bulging middle.

"Dodging the train was your idea, you have to," I hiss. "You can't let me go in there alone. You just said best friends don't abandon best friends."

Realizing that Mrs. Witherspoon not only has us on playing chicken, but she can also rat on her plans to go on a date, Jen scuffs her feet across the road and up the sidewalk. We both stop on the bottom step.

Mrs. Witherspoon's face lights up. "Come on," she says as she motions us inside. "Don't be shy."

Over the next two hours Jen and I clean the fridge and the bathroom, change her sheets, scrub the kitchen sink and wash the floors. I'm putting the mop and pail in the broom closet while Jen already has one foot out the front door.

"Just a minute, Jennifer," Mrs. Witherspoon says. "Elizabeth, you too."

We stop while Mrs. Witherspoon retrieves her cookie jar from the kitchen. She removes the lid and extends the peach shaped canister towards us.

"I don't want to see the two of you out there alone again, you hear me? Getting hit by a train is the least of your worries this summer. I'll have to call your parents next time."

"We hear you, Mrs. Witherspoon," I say. "We won't do it again."

"You're looking after your sisters, Elizabeth? Not letting them stray too far on their own? I know Rose is quite independent."

"I guess," I say between bites.

She nods.

"If it's the killer you're worried about, Mrs. Witherspoon, he's long gone," Jen says as she pops the last of her cookie into her mouth then reaches into the jar for another. "Everyone says so."

"Then everyone is wrong," Mrs. Witherspoon says. "The killer walks among us, girls. He walks among us every single day."

CHAPTER TEN

"May I please be excused," I ask.

"You may," Mom says. "Dish yourself out some raspberries and you can eat them on the back step. Liz and Jennifer cleaned Mrs. Witherspoon's house today," she tells Dad.

Dad nods, then wipes his mouth and places his napkin on his empty plate. He never leaves any food behind. And he expects the same from his children. He says there's too many people in the world who go hungry and we'd be better off donating money to the poor than filling our plates with food we aren't going to eat. Once Rose said she'd like to donate her liver and onions to the poor. That got her sent to her room for the night.

"But," Rose says, "it's Liz's turn to do the dishes."

Mom glances at the schedule above the sink. "It says Rose, dear."

"But," Rose says again. "I...."

"I know you did lots today too, Rose. Helping Mrs. Krieger pick all those raspberries. And thank you for that. But we can't argue with the schedule."

I've dished out my raspberries and am stretched out at the bottom of the steps, savouring the last of the sweet fruit, when suddenly I'm dripping in cold slimy water. "What the hell," I shout.

Rose is standing on the top step with the empty dishpan in her hands. "You knew it was your turn, you just didn't want to do anymore housework. Poor Liz had to clean Mrs. Witherspoon's house. Well, I had to listen to—" she looks towards our neighbour's house and whispers, "—Mrs. Krieger's stories all blasted afternoon. Do you know how boring that gets?" She lifts one palm in the air. "*The squash isn't as good as it was last year*, and, *The daisies have taken over the flower bed.* I could have been taking pictures of things I'm interested in, not digging potatoes or deadheading petunias."

I gag as I pull tomato off my face and pick bits of cauliflower out of my hair. "It says your name on the schedule. How dare you throw this crap on me!" I toss a slimy piece of porkchop fat at her head.

"You traded with me because you were having your period. You purposely forgot to change it on the schedule. You knew I couldn't argue with you at the supper table because we can't talk about those things in front of Dad. And what's so special about having your period anyway? I'm not going to be such a baby when I have my period, you can bet your sweet ass!"

Every time she says the word period, she pounces on it, drawing it out in a sing-song voice loud enough for the entire neighbourhood to hear. The backdoor opens.

"What's going on out here?" Dad says. "My two oldest daughters are yelling at each other in public about things that I certainly don't want to hear about and I'm sure the neighbours don't either! And swearing as well!" He looks at the brown water with food floating in it coating the steps. "What's this mess?" He doesn't allow us to explain. "Clean this up then go to your room. And don't say another word to each other!"

"I'm not cleaning this up," I whisper when the door closes. "I didn't throw the dishwater."

"It's your fault whether you threw the water or not, so you'd better help or I'll tell Dad."

"I forgot I traded with you, Rose. I'm sorry. Jeez. Quit making mountains out of molehills. And you can bet your sweet ass," I continue to whisper, "that you will also be a baby when you start your period."

I stomp into the mud room, my shoes squishing with each step, and grab the mop. Rose goes to the garden and gets the hose.

* * *

An hour later we're in our room, a perfectly good summer's evening wasted. Voices drift up to the open window from our sisters enjoying the end of the day without us.

Rose is sitting on the floor thumbing through a photography magazine, and stops to look at a picture of a camera. "Boy, I wish I could afford one of these." She slides her finger down the list of features. "Single lens reflex, 35-millimetre, interchangeable lenses." She sighs. "Guess I'll have to wait until I'm rich and famous." She drops the magazine then looks up at me brushing out my just-washed hair. "I wish I'd taken your picture," she says. "You looked like the monster from the black lagoon."

"That's because you threw disgusting dishwater at me."

"Yeah, well, sorry about that. Guess I need to learn to control my temper."

"Ya think?"

She picks up a photo album and flips open a page. "Did you and Jen flatten pennies today?"

My brush stops mid-stroke. "You know we're not supposed to do that."

"And you know I'm not stupid. Why else would you be anywhere near Spooky Witherspoon's house? You avoid that neighbourhood like the plague, just like every kid in town. Last time Mom dragged me there, I didn't eat for a week."

I should have known I can't fool Rose. Three years ago, when she was eight, Mom asked me to pick the peas. Because of the spiders that cling to those plants, I didn't want to, so I told Rose that sometimes there's a golden pea in one of the pods and it's worth a thousand dollars. She said I might have believed that when I was her age, but she wasn't as easily fooled, and I should save that tale for someone more gullible than her.

"Do you think Mom guessed?" I ask.

"Normally I'd say yes, but she hasn't been the same since Cole was born. Did I tell you I found her in the laundry room the other day and she couldn't remember how to turn the washing machine on? I had to show her. And it didn't even seem to faze her. Just laughed it off as getting old. I suppose she is thirty-nine now. So, no, maybe she didn't realize what you were doing if she's still in the throws of that post-pregnancy thing." She puts down the album and takes another off the stack. "Did Mrs. Witherspoon tell you your fortune?"

"No."

She looks up from the book. "You're not telling me something. I can hear it in your voice."

"She said the killer is still here. In Willowsbend. She said he never left, that he walks among us everyday."

"She is loony tunes, you know that, right?"

"I know. But the way she said it, I kind of believed her."

"She did tell me I'm going to take an award-winning picture some day," Rose says. "And she predicted Jen would find that dollar bill."

"Yes, but she also said Mr. Pendergrass was going to become famous after he died. That man's so meek and mild he has trouble making people remember him from one day to the next, let alone after he's dead."

"Like I said, loony tunes." She flips a page. "Hey, look at this." She has her magnifying glass to her face and is peering at a picture.

I sit on the floor beside her. "What?"

She taps the photograph. "Remember when we chased Gail Drummond across the schoolyard? I got a shot of the person she was shooing off the road. I can see him in the shadows." She looks at me through the heavy lens; her green eyes are as big as saucers.

I take the magnifying glass from her and hold it in front of the picture. "He's barely in the shot, but there's definitely someone standing there. Someone scruffy."

"I know, hey? I hate to agree with your friend, but this might be the same guy she saw behind the church."

"This doesn't prove anything. It might be the same guy. Doesn't mean he's the murderer."

"I didn't say he's the murderer, that's what Jen said. All I was agreeing with was the description is the same." She flips to the next page to insert the pictures she picked up today. She peers at the one she took of Mr. Pendergrass in front of our house. "I thought I saw someone in the background," she says. "But when I took my camera from my face, he was gone."

I take the picture from her and hold it behind the glass. "It looks like the same guy that's in the other picture. And he's staring at you, our house, or Mr. Pendergrass, can't say for sure." I look again. "We should show an adult." I say.

"I don't want to show anyone. I know I can figure this out on my own. I read enough mysteries."

"This isn't fiction, Rose. We need to show Dad."

Rose closes one eye at me. "I think Dad is the last person I should show," she says.

"You think he's involved?"

"No, of course not. I just think if I were to show anyone it should be a third party, someone with no history in this town. It's the only way to get an objective opinion."

"Mr. Pendergrass told me that anyone could be a suspect."

She thinks for a moment. "The man may be weird, but he's right. How do we know Dad isn't involved? How do we know Mr. Pendergrass isn't involved and he's telling us to be careful to throw us off his track? Both of them knew the Tremblays, both have lived here all their lives. They could be as involved as Mr. Drummond."

"I doubt Dad is involved," I say.

"Just tossing out ideas. That's something you have to do when you're trying to solve a murder; look at all sides. There's always more than one possibility, more than one suspect. You have to narrow it down to the right one."

"You're not trying to solve a murder, you're eleven years old, for heaven's sake."

"Actually, there's documented cases where children have solved crimes. I've read about them in magazines. I don't see any reason why I can't figure this out as easily as an adult, easier even. My brain isn't cluttered with useless information. The trouble is, what do I have?" She counts off on her fingers. "The same guy who's in two of my pictures who may or may not be the murderer. The people who have already decided Mr. Drummond is guilty because he's an ex-con and is missing, and a clairvoyant who says the killer walks among us. I need more than that before I can figure this out. Hey, do you think this is the picture Mrs. Witherspoon said would make me famous?"

"Doesn't seem like it would be the one," I say. "Do you want to sit in the treehouse with me?"

"You want me to sit in your treehouse? You never want me there. As a matter of fact, you told me you'll never allow any of your sisters in there because it's the only place in this house where you get peace and quiet."

"Well, Jen said today we're growing up. Maybe we are."

"That's probably the only profound thing I've heard that girl say," Rose says.

* * *

We've made our way across the roof without Mom and Dad hearing or pretending they didn't hear as they sit on the deck below. We lay on the floor, whispering and watching the sky until the sun sets and Mom and Dad go inside to watch the late-night news. A breeze, still warm from the days heat, blows through the wooden walls of the treehouse.

I hand Rose my binoculars. "I see the big dipper," Rose whispers.

"Oh yeah. Me too. And I see Venus." I say.

"Dad doesn't like me much," Rose says, the lens pressed to her eyes. "He's always finding something to get mad at me about."

"Rose, you dumped an entire pan of dishwater on me! And talking about having your period outside for everyone to hear! What did you think he'd do?"

"Yeah, well, I guess I shouldn't have done that. But he of all people should forgive me for my short fuse; I get it from his side of the family. You never get in trouble. Everything I do he finds fault with."

"That's not true."

She waves the binoculars through the air. "Swearing, giving my opinion, reading the paper, talking back. Taking too many pictures, wearing overalls, going barefoot, losing my temper. You're the first born. The first born is always the favourite. And you're more like Mom; quieter, more thoughtful, willing to take advice from others. Fran too. She's shy, Dad loves that about her, though I'm sure it's because she doesn't argue with him. And Robin and Alex are hard to resist, at least while they're toddlers. Cole, he doesn't have to do anything but be a boy. I'm not as cute as the rest of you. My hair is redder and I'm not as sweet. Last year my teacher told me I was too outspoken."

"Mrs. Clemmons was just threatened because you're smarter than her son. That boy of hers is duller than a hammer. And anyhow, Mom loves your brains and your honesty. She never has to guess what you're thinking."

"Nu-uh. *Children should be seen and not heard,* that's what Mrs. Clemmons said. And I think we both know Dad's opinion of me. He thinks I'm too much like his sister. That's my worst offense."

"Whether Dad admits it or not, he likes us to be self-sufficient, then he doesn't have to coddle us. You're already independent before you're even twelve years old. Franny is going to have to work at it. We'll have to help her at school this fall."

"She'll be ok. She's like me, not afraid to be alone."

I point at another constellation. "There's Orion's belt."

Rose aims the binoculars in the direction I pointed, looking for the row of three stars. "Do you know what I did today while you were at Mrs. Witherspoon's?" she asks from behind the eyepieces.

"Other than going to Mrs. Krieger's?"

"I walked to the Tremblay's place. Went right up to the house."

"Rose!" I whisper. "You're not supposed to go out of town, Mom said."

"You can't say anything, you went to the railway tracks. Anyway, nothing happened. I walked around the house and went into the backyard, that's all. Not much to see. Toys have all been taken away and the hammock isn't there anymore. That's what I was really looking for. Wasn't going to lie in it or anything, that would be gross. Wanted to see what it looked like; I remember swinging in it with Kylie. Mom took me to their house once to drop off some buns when Mrs. Tremblay had a baby. There's a For Sale sign in the front yard. Truck's gone."

"You shouldn't have gone there, Rose."

"It's not a crime scene anymore. Cops have cleared out, not even yellow tape across the porch. Either they think the killer has left town, or they suspect who it is and are gathering evidence. Didn't see anybody on the way there and only Mr. Pendergrass on the way back. He said before the murders he walked that road every day for exercise and he needed to get back to his old routine. I know what he means. I feel like nothing's the same anymore, like the town and everyone in it has changed." She stands and stretches. "I'm going to bed. Lots to do tomorrow."

* * *

At two in the morning I follow Rose to bed. Mom, who was likely feeding Cole, and Dad who's a light sleeper and probably woke up when Mom got out of bed to heat the bottle, are talking quietly. Their voices drift up the register.

"Gail Drummond came around the store today driving that beat up truck her dad used to drive," Dad says. "Said she had to cover the gaps in the windows of their house before winter and asked what she could buy for ten dollars. Gave her some plywood and nails, no charge. I offered to help with the repairs, but she declined. I guess taking the supplies from me was as far as she'd go."

"Have the police searched their place for Stanley?" Mom asks.

"They've gone to the house, but the family's either hiding him or he's left town. As soon as the RCMP have enough evidence, I assume they'll issue a Canada wide warrant for him."

"So, you think he's guilty?" Mom asks.

Dad hesitates. "He certainly had the opportunity. No one even knew he was out of jail. He could have gone to the Tremblay's undetected and killed them all."

"But why?" Mom says. "What's the motive? He got out of jail early because his kids needed him. Why would he run back here, then kill an entire family? He's of no help to his kids hiding from the police. It makes no sense."

"Who knows what went on in his brain? Prison can do strange things to men. And remember, he's an alcoholic. He'd have had no access to liquor in prison, maybe he went on a bender as soon as he got out."

"Lots of people think the same as you. People are convicting him for the simple reason he's disappeared. If he came forward to defend himself, it would be better. I think he's hiding because he's scared."

"Or he's hiding because he's guilty," Dad says. "As far as I can see, it's either a random killing done by a total stranger, or Stan. And to me, Stan is the most likely."

Cole makes a mewling sound and Mom says, "Shush now."

"Somewhere along the way, he got angry," Dad says. "I don't think he's said two words to me since graduation. He married Abigale right out of school, then holed up in that house and drank his life away."

"I wish I knew how to help his kids without it seeming like charity," Mom says. "Gail told Liz and Father that her dad won't allow them to take anything. Barely took the buns and clothes I sent. I don't know how they're managing without a parent to help."

Rose sits up and our bed springs squeak, echoing through the floorboards. She mumbles something in her sleep about getting the focus right then throws herself back down. Mom and Dad stop talking.

Sleep tugs at my brain and I close my eyes wondering what Mr. Drummond is angry at Dad about. Cole whimpers and the floorboards creak as Mom walks around the bedroom singing the song she's sung to each of us as babies: "To-Ra-loo-ra-loo-ral, to-ra-loo-ra-li. To-ra-loo-ra-loo-ral, hush now, don't you cry. To-ra-loo-ra-loo-ral, to-ra-loo-ra-li. To-ra-loo-ra-loo-ral, that's an Irish lullaby."

CHAPTER ELEVEN

I left the window open last night to let whatever cool breeze there may have been, waft into the bedroom, and this morning, I'm awakened by the piercing screams of two little girls. I jump out of bed still half asleep, but Rose, sound sleeper that she is, flings her arms onto my pillow and pulls it over her head. On legs wobbly from being jarred from my sleep, I stand and look out the window. Robin and Alex have abandoned their swing set and are in the middle of the backyard, mouths open wide, fingers pointing towards something I can't see. As I watch, Mom races out the back door, her apron strings flying while my sisters run and hide behind her legs.

"Can I help you?" Mom asks the person who's standing directly under my treehouse. A boy, a few years older than me, steps into my line of sight. I press my forehead to the screen to get a better view. He has a hat in his hands, his hair tied in a ponytail at the nape of his neck, and a guitar strapped across his back.

"Sorry, didn't mean to scare the little ones. Was walking down the alley last night and saw this patch of grass under the tree." He waves behind him. "Came into the yard to sleep. I'll be on my way." He begins to stride towards the back gate.

"No, wait," Mom says.

"He stops. "Yes, Mrs.?"

"Where are you from?"

"Out east, Halifax. Spending the summer hitchhiking across the country. No better way to see the world than to walk down its highways."

"Are you hungry? I was just taking some biscuits out of the oven. And I've a fresh pot of coffee perking."

"My stomach is grumbling." He rubs his narrow waist. "Guess I could use a bite to eat."

"Robin, Alex, you come inside and have your breakfast," Mom says as she prods my sisters up the steps and into the mud room.

I dress, run past Fran reading in bed, stop in the bathroom to comb my hair and pinch my cheeks, then sprint down the stairs. "Morning, Mom," I say. "Going outside to get some fresh air."

"And to meet the cute young man you saw from your bedroom window, I imagine," she says as she places bowls of Cheerios in front of Robin and Alex.

"Oh, is there someone out there?"

"Here," she passes me a cup of coffee. "You can take him this."

I take the coffee and exit the back door, letting the screen door bang behind me. He's sitting in a chair on the deck and turns to look at me.

"Hi," he says. "Is that for me?"

"Oh, uh, yes," I say and push the cup towards him.

"My name is Mac. Actually, it's Jamison Macpherson the third. But mostly people call me Mac."

"Hi," I say.

"And what do they call you?" he asks.

"Elizabeth," I say. "You can call me Liz."

"Cool." He takes a sip of his coffee.

Mom exits the house with a plate of biscuits and the pot of coffee in her hands. "Liz, could you bring out the tray I've left on the counter by the fridge?"

I return to the kitchen as Rose descends the stairs.

"Who's out there?" she asks rubbing sleep from her eyes. Her uncombed hair is sticking out in all directions.

"Someone hitchhiking across the country."

"Cool." She walks towards the back door.

I grab her arm. "You can't go out there," I say. "Have you looked in a mirror yet today?"

"Why would I want to look in a mirror?"

"Just look out the window. Tell me what he's doing."

She gawks out the window.

"Don't stare," I say.

"How am I supposed to see what he's doing if I can't stare?"

"I want you to peek or he'll think I asked you to look at him."

"Well you did."

"But I don't want him to know."

"Why not?"

"Just because! God, are you that young?"

"Look who's got a crush on a boy," she says.

"I do not!"

Robin and Alex are watching us as they spoon cereal into their mouths. They begin to giggle. Whispering, I threaten Rose that if she comes outside and embarrasses me in any way shape or form, I'll tell Mom how far she ventures outside the town limits to take her pictures. I take another cup from the cupboard, pick up the tray then exit the house. Mac is grinning and I realize that our voices were heard through the open window.

"How long have you been in our province?" I ask, trying to sound older than thirteen. I set the tray on the table then half fill my cup with milk before topping it up with coffee and two spoons of sugar. I open a lawn chair and plunk it down opposite him.

"This is my third day," he says as he takes a napkin and a biscuit from the tray Mom's offering him and looks around. "It's a beautiful place, this prairie. Flat, but beautiful."

"Yes," I say. "But not as flat as many assume. There's valleys and rivers around this area, and further north, there's forests. To the south there's even a desert. I've lived here all my life. I love it." I take a sip of my weak coffee and try not to wince at the taste. I'm about to ask him where he's going next when Dad steps outside.

"Who's this?" he asks.

"His name is Mac." I stand. "He slept under the tree last night. We're giving him some breakfast. He's hitchhiking across Canada."

"Is he now?"

Mac swallows the last of his biscuit and holds out his hand to Dad. "Jamison Macpherson the third." He does not tell Dad to call him Mac.

I back away, keeping my gaze on Mac and notice that his face has changed from joyful to wary. I glance at the back door; Rose peers out at me from the mud room, her face crisscrossed in shadow from the mesh screen. She has her notebook and pencil in her hand.

"You're lucky, young man, that my wife found you before I did. Do you know that seven people were killed here this summer? People are on edge, suspicious of strangers. Someone is just as likely to chase you off their property with a rifle as to give you a cup of coffee."

"You're right, sir." He looks at Mom. "I apologize."

Dad sits in my chair and I know my chance for asking our guest any more questions, is over. "So, you're hitchhiking, are you? Never had time for such things when I was your age. Worked on my dad's farm until I was twenty-two then opened my own store."

"I suppose we all lead different lives," Mac says as he helps himself to another biscuit.

The corners of Dad's mouth lift in a patronizing smile. "Do your parents know what you're doing?"

"Jim," Mom scolds as she pours Dad a cup of coffee. "Leave the young man alone. It's none of your business."

"It's ok, Mrs., I don't mind answering," Mac says. "Yes, my folks encouraged me to do this. I graduated from Teacher's College this past spring. This is my last chance to indulge in my wanderlust before I begin my new job in a few weeks. There's lots of kids out here travelling across the country. I've met hitchhikers from as far away as the North West Territories."

"Hitchhikers don't usually stop in our town. Not much around here the young people are anxious to see. What drew you here this summer?"

"Actually, sir, the murders. That's what's drawn many of us here. Everyone wants to see the infamous Willowsbend."

"Is that right? The murders drew you here?" The tone of Dad's voice has become arrogant, almost proud and Mom lifts her eyes to her husband. "The murderer hasn't been found," Dad says. "I'd be careful if I were you."

"After a while you learn how to read people," Mac says.

Dad peers at Mac over the edge of his cup. "I suppose one hones that skill the more people they meet." He blows on his coffee. "Just remember that some people are really good at hiding who they are."

Mac becomes quiet.

"I don't think it's something I would ever allow my children do," Dad continues. "But I guess every parent has different ideas on how to raise a family."

"Jim," Mom scolds again.

Dad turns to her. "Would you let your eldest daughter hitch-hike? Or Cole?"

"Being as how Cole is only one month old and Liz is thirteen, no, I wouldn't let them hitchhike," Mom says. "But Mac is at least twenty."

"Twenty-one," Mac says.

"He's made it all the way from Halifax," I say, wishing Mom hadn't divulged my age.

Dad looks over his glasses at me standing outside the back door. I stop talking. He addresses Mac. "I think hitchhiking should be frowned upon. Lots of crazy people out there."

"But still," Mom says, "are you trying to scare the boy?"

"No. Merely pointing out that the murderer has not been found and he should be careful who he associates with."

"I appreciate your concern," Mac says.

Dad washes down a bite of biscuit with a drink of coffee. "Just curious," he says. "What are you and all your hitchhiking friends saying as you stand out there with your thumbs out? There must be lots of notions about who you think might have done such a heinous act."

Mac meets Dad's eyes. "Being as how I don't live here; I don't know if I should say."

"Go ahead, son. Everyone's entitled to an opinion," Dad says.

Mac swallows hard; his Adam's Apple bobs. "Of the people I've spoken to," he says, "most are of the opinion that it was a random killing. A crazy man who heard a voice in his head telling him to stop at their house. It's happened before so there is a precedent. But, as I'm sure you already know, there is another possibility."

"And that would be....?" Dad says.

Mac sets his third biscuit on the napkin draped over his knee. "It was someone the family knew so he was able to get close without suspicion. A friend, a neighbour, someone the family trusted."

Dad is quiet for a few moments, appearing to think about what Mac has said. Finally, he asks, "What are you leaning towards? Neighbour or stranger?"

Mac pauses. Dad smiles his encouragement.

"Well," Mac says, "the theory that it was a stranger is enticing, then it would be cut and dried, wouldn't it? No mess of accusing a resident of Willowsbend. No hard feelings between neighbours when innocent people are suspected. Just some crazy bum passing through town. But to my way of thinking, the most likely scenario is, it was someone they knew, someone who was very angry. What would cause a perfect stranger to take someone's tongue?" He shakes his head, his ponytail slides across his back. "No, whatever it was, it wasn't random."

"Then he was good at covering his tracks," Dad says. "It's been over a month with no leads. It's the perfect crime."

"There's no such a thing," Mac says. "Sooner or later something will turn up to incriminate him, something left behind at the crime scene, something he forgot to do, some loose end he didn't tie up." He lifts his biscuit then sets it back down without taking a bite. "No one is that good at hiding what they did." He lifts the biscuit and finishes it in two bites.

I glance at Rose behind the screen door; she's scribbling in her notebook.

"I think you've missed your calling," Dad says, tugging at the cuff of his shirt. "You should have become a police officer instead of a teacher." He ponders Mac. "If you believe the killer is a local then he might be someone who's fed you or given you a ride. What you and the others are doing is nothing but a foolish adventure. I would never be that irresponsible with my well-being."

"I think this young man is capable of looking after himself, Jim. You're too cautious," Mom says. "You have to live your life, not be afraid of it, right, Mac?"

"That's what I'm trying to do." Mac nods at Dad. "But your husband has good advice. I need to be more careful about who I take rides and meals from." Mac stands and hands his cup with the napkin stuffed inside, to Mom. He picks up his guitar and lifts the strap over his head, resting the instrument across his back. "Thanks for the food. I'd better be on my way." As he's leaving his eyes meet mine. He looks uneasy.

CHAPTER TWELVE

The fire roars high when Mr. Olyphant throws another log into the flames causing sparks to crackle and pop into the air, then twinkle back to the ground. Lois and Marvin have invited us to their farm for an end to summer, beginning of school wiener and corn roast, and my stomach is rumbling for the treats.

Dad is in the bushes that serve as a windbreak beside their farm-house, whittling green twigs into wiener sticks. He pokes his head out. "How many sticks do we need?" he calls.

"Ten, Jim. Can't you count?" Mom shouts through the open kitchen window.

"I thought there were eleven of us," Dad says.

"If you can get Cole to eat a wiener, by all means, whittle him a stick too."

Dad pauses, then re-enters the hedge; his hand grips his jack-knife, the polished silver glinting in the sun.

Lois places the hotdog buns and corn-on-the-cob wrapped in tinfoil on the table while Mom walks out the backdoor with a stack of paper plates in her hands. She fusses with the cups and cutlery until Mrs. Olyphant scolds her and tells her to sit down and rest.

"Fire will take about twenty minutes for it to burn down to the embers," Mr. Olyphant says as he lays the cobs on the coals at the edge of the pit. "Corn'll be done by the time the fire's ready for the wieners." He prods one of the tinfoil wrapped packages with his stick, pushing it further into the flames.

"Can Jen and I go for a walk?" I ask Mom.

"No. I need to be able to see you and I'm busy with Cole and helping Lois."

"Aw, Mom. We're not going to go anywhere near the Tremblay's. We only want to walk down the road. Please?"

"They'll be fine, Pat." Lois says. "We're done bringing everything out so we'll be able to see them the whole time. Young girls need to get away from the adults for a while."

"Alright," Mom says. "But not too far." She wags a finger at me. "Stay on the old road, no crossing to the highway. And don't go gallivanting off into the field. You hear me?"

"I hear you," I say.

She finishes with, "If you see anyone, I don't care who it is, you run straight back here."

Jen, who has been taking a step closer to the old road with each of Mom's cautionary words, says, "God almighty, give it a rest."

I prod her in the ribs with my elbow, then she and I scuff down the gravel driveway. Rose follows. Fran skips behind.

"Where do you think you're going?" I ask.

"With you, of course," Rose says.

"We don't need kids tagging along."

"Mom," Rose wails. "Liz won't let Fran and me go with them."

"Either you all go, or none of you go," Mom says.

Rose crosses her arms and lifts her chin.

"And look after your sisters," Mom calls.

"Ok," I say to Rose with clenched teeth. "But don't eavesdrop. You're going into grade eight, which in reality should be grade seven. We're going into high school and we need to talk." Fran runs in front as the four of us step onto the road.

"Like you two have such important things to say. Solving the world hunger problem?" Rose mocks. "Coming up with a plan for peace? All you want to talk about is boys. At least I have more important things to think about."

"I mean it, Rose. If you listen to one word we say." I stop walking and look her in the face, ready to threaten her with telling Mom that she was at the Tremblay's house. Her green eyes meet mine. "Never mind," I say.

Jen throws her hands in the air. "What's this? You're suddenly full of sisterly love?"

"For God's sake, let's go," I say a bit too loudly.

"Liz," Mom warns. "Quit swearing."

We look down the crumbling asphalt towards Willowsbend. The air above the blacktop ripples in the heat, distorting the outline of Gas-n-Go visible on the horizon. The Gas-n-Go Café sits at the edge of town, the town-limit sign stuck in the dirt at the end of their driveway. The café is attached to the gas station hence the name has been shortened to simply Gas-n-Go. Rose, of course, always makes a joke about farting, and Dad never fails to frown at her. The restaurant, which is popular with the locals, borders the old road, as does the Olyphant's farm. If you cross the old road, climb through the ditch, then cross the new highway, about halfway in between the Olyphant's and Gas-n-Go, is the Tremblay's farm.

Mr. Olyphant's fields are tall with golden stalks of wheat and they bend in the wind that never stops blowing. I've often wondered why Dad wasn't interested in farming. To me, there's nothing nicer than being out here in the country. I can't imagine being raised anywhere else.

A head bobs above the stalks and Rose looks through her camera. "A deer," she says. "Probably the fawn is in there too. Just can't see it above the wheat. This time of the year they've grown big enough to follow their mamas around, but aren't big enough to live on their own. When they're newborns, their mom leaves them alone for up to an entire day while she forages for food. The spots on the baby's fur camouflages them so they can't be seen by predators."

"Ok," Jen says. "Enough of Hinterland already."

"Just trying to educate you," Rose says.

Jen leans in close to me. "I saw Holly Black talking to some boys outside her dad's movie theatre yesterday. I walked by and she nodded and smiled at me."

"Do you have your school supplies yet?" I ask.

"School supplies! Is that all you can think of? Didn't you hear what I said? Holly Black smiled at me."

"You think she wants to be your friend because she smiled at you?"

"What else could it be? She's very selective about who she associates with. Maybe she can introduce me to some of the boys she knows."

"What are you two whispering about?" Rose says.

"Nothing that concerns you."

I hear Mom's voice. "That's far enough, girls."

"Jeez. Your Mom treats us like kids," Jen says.

"I hate to break this to you, Olsen, but you're only fourteen," Rose says. "You're not officially considered an adult in this province until you're nineteen."

"Bullocks," Jen says. "Anyhow, I've always been old for my age. I have a cousin in the city who's fifteen and I swear she acts younger than Fran." Fran is kneeling on the road stacking stones into a pile then throwing them into the ditch. "Always asking if I want to play Barbie Dolls or colour in her colouring book." She pulls a crumpled cigarette out of her jeans pocket.

"What the heck," I whisper. "You can't smoke here."

"Ok, ok." She massages the cigarette back into her pocket.

"One day, you're going to get yourself into real trouble thinking you're older than you are." I don't add—and neither does Rose—that last week she and I coloured together in the front porch for an entire afternoon.

Rose points her camera back to the field of wheat. "Something else is out there," she says.

"Probably another deer."

"I don't think so. The head isn't bobbing up and down like a deer's head does. Did you know the nickname for deer in our province is jumpers? Because they jump when they run."

This time Jen doesn't complain about the biology lesson as the four of us look in the direction Rose's camera is pointed. A head and shoulders are moving quickly through the wheat towards Gas-n-Go.

"Could be a bird," Jen says.

Rose looks at her. "Are you blind?"

"Ok, so it's not a bird. What about, uh, a..."

"You got nothing."

"Tumbleweed. It could be a tumbleweed."

Again, Rose looks at Jennifer as if she's just said the most stupid thing in the world.

"Ok, so I got nothing," Jen says.

"It's a person and I'm going to find out who it is." Rose takes a step towards the ditch.

"I'm not going in that ditch," I say. "There's snakes in there. Besides, we aren't supposed to leave the road."

"I'm not afraid of snakes," Rose says. "And they're all so gaga over Cole, I guarantee you they won't notice if we're gone for a couple minutes. Mr. Olyphant will probably bring out the beer and then they'll notice our absence even less. Besides, even if they'd never say it to our faces, they enjoy time spent without all the kids hanging around." With those words she takes off running down into the ditch and up the other side. Soon she's disappeared into the stalks of wheat.

I look at the side of the house where Mom and Mrs. Olyphant are sitting in the shade. Lois has Cole on her knee, Alex is sitting on the blanket in front of Mom, pounding the bingo bed, and Robin furiously turns the knobs on the Etch-a-Sketch. Mom and Mrs. Olyphant busily talk—I can see their hands waving in the air—I'm sure about gardens and school beginning and how Fran will have to learn to not be so shy. Mr. Olyphant is exiting the house with a six-pack of beer, and Dad must still be in the bush because I can't see him.

Jennifer lifts her eyes to me, a mischievous look on her face. "Race ya," she says as she charges into the ditch behind Rose.

I throw my hands in the air, then shooing Fran ahead of me, the two of us take off after the two of them, with me praying that Rose and Jen have scared the snakes away. As we're chasing each other through the field, I forget about how much trouble we're going to get into and instead enjoy the feeling of being free.

The summer after Rose was born, Mrs. Olyphant, to give Mom

a break, brought me to their farm. I have a distant memory of Lois, her daughter Alison who was eleven, and me, making sandwiches and lemonade, though at three years old I imagine I wasn't much help. We packed the food into the Coleman Cooler then drove out to the field in search of the men; I have no idea how she knew where they were but she did. When they were done eating, I hid in the wheat while Mrs. Olyphant packed everything away. I saw my first garter snake while I was hiding in that field. I screamed and shot out between the stalks so fast you'd think the snake was chasing me. The men laughed and I blushed. Mr. Olyphant then lifted me into the back of the truck and sat me on top of a huge pile of freshly harvested kernels and I chewed a wheaty handful until it was like gum in my mouth.

Twenty feet ahead, Rose's red hair is in stark contrast to the golden colour of the wheat, and Jen, with hair as dark as night, makes both girls easy to follow. When the two of them finally stop at the edge of the field where the wheat ends and the summer fallow begins, Fran and I are able catch up. Rose turns around and puts her fingers to her lips. I look to the right; the person we've been chasing has left the field and descended into the ditch.

"Rose," I say, recognizing who it is.

"Shhh," she says, recognizing him as well.

Dad has pushed his way through the willow trees that separate the old highway from the new, and is now climbing the other side of the ditch. He crosses the road then kicks and scuffs at the gravel as he walks up the Tremblay's driveway, appearing to look for something among the rocks. When he reaches the corner of the house, as if sensing he's being watched, he turns. Jen, Rose, and I instinctively duck into the wheat, but Fran, excited to see her daddy, steps out of the stalks to say hi.

Luckily, this morning Mom was too busy packing her contribution for todays lunch as well as getting Cole, Robin, and Alex ready for the picnic, to have time to dress her third eldest, and she let the little girl dress herself. Consequently, Fran's wearing yellow from head to toe and the pants and t-shirt blend into the backdrop perfectly. Rose grabs her sister by the bright-coloured top and pulls her into the stalks of wheat, slapping her hand over Fran's mouth. None of us move, and after a few moments of looking our way, Dad leaves, cutting across the ditch further up the road then into the field towards the Olyphant's.

Fran shakes herself free of Rose's hand. "Why didn't you let me say hi to Daddy?" she says as she wipes her mouth.

"I don't think he wanted to be disturbed," Rose says.

"What was he doing?" Fran asks.

"Apparently he wanted to see the house where the Tremblays were murdered."

"But why did he want to see the house where those people were murdered?" the little girl asks. "And why was he kicking at the driveway?"

"Could be he was looking for clues," Jen says. "Cops are offering a reward."

"I doubt Dad is looking for clues," I say. "It's probably the first time he's been out here since the day the murders happened. He went to school with Mrs. Tremblay. He wanted to pay his respects."

"Maybe he wanted to be away from the adults too." Fran says.

"That's a very good observation," Rose says.

"Come on," I nudge Fran's shoulder, "we need to get back. Don't tell Dad we saw him," I say as we walk down the dusty road. "Mom said we weren't supposed to go into the field, we'll get in trouble if she finds out where we were."

We step into the farmyard. Dad ponders us for a moment before returning to his conversation with Mr. Olyphant.

"Girls, you're back," Mrs. Olyphant says as she sips at her half glass of beer. "Grab a stick and a wiener. The corn is in the dish on the table. Did you have a good chin-wag?"

I kneel in front of the fire roasting my hotdog and wonder if Rose is right and we are destined for independence, as it appears Dad is the only one who noticed we were out of sight.

CHAPTER THIRTEEN

"I want overalls," Rose says. "With lots of pockets for my film and stuff."

"You know the nuns won't let you wear pants to school," Mom says.

"They're too old fashioned. I've heard of nuns who don't even wear habits anymore. Change with the times, I say. How is the world supposed to progress if we're always stuck in the past?"

"You're welcome to wear all the overalls you want at home, but at school, until the nuns say otherwise, you have to wear a dress." Mom lifts Cole out of the carriage. "And I don't want to hear any arguing in the shop either. I'll have enough to do looking after your brother and shopping for the five of you." She hands Cole to me. "I think, Liz, because your school is no longer a Catholic school, you're allowed to wear pants."

"No fair!" Rose shouts.

"Your turn will come," Mom says. "Just one more year. And Franny, we need to buy you something special for your first day of school." She pushes the empty carriage towards her station wagon which she's backed out of the garage and parked in the alley behind the gate.

"Maybe a sailor dress?" Fran says as she squints at Mom. Her eyes have suffered from reading with a flashlight under the covers at night and I wonder if Mom notices, being so busy with the new baby.

"I'm sure we can find you a sailor dress," Mom says.

Dad steps out the back door. "Heading to work," he says, stopping beside the car.

Out of the blue Rose says, "Dad, maybe you could look after Cole while Mom takes us shopping?"

Everyone is shocked into silence.

"No, Rose," Mom finally says. "Don't bother your dad. Looking after a new baby is challenging. I can manage."

Dad, seemingly annoyed his wife thinks he's incompetent, but not realizing that his arguing might backfire on him, says, "You don't think I'm capable of looking after my own son, Patricia?"

"No, no," Mom says. "It's not that."

"Sure sounds like it to me," Dad says.

"No," she says again as she slowly pries her fingers from the handle of the carriage. "That isn't what I meant. You're right, he's your son too. You can look after him if you want to. I suppose I am going to have my hands full shopping with five girls." She takes Cole from my arms and places him back in the carriage, pushing it towards Dad.

"Actually," Dad says without taking the handle, "I did have something else to do this afternoon."

"Don't you go down to the hotel coffee shop on Wednesday afternoons?" Rose says. "You could put that note up on the shop door that tells your customers where you are. I'm sure your friends would love to meet your son. Just the other day, Mr. Fogg stopped me on the sidewalk to ask when he could see the new baby."

Again, we're quiet. Rose has painted him into a corner. If Dad says yes, he's saddled with a baby all afternoon. If he says no, he looks like a father who isn't proud of his new son. And for as long as I can remember, Dad has worried about what others think of him.

"You go for coffee, Jim," Mom says. "I'll be fine."

Rose lifts her camera up to take Dad's picture, then, perhaps thinking she's pressed her luck far enough, lowers it to her side. Dad, after a few more moments of hesitation, grabs the carriage handle from Mom and the last we see of him he's rounding the corner at the end of the alley, heading in the direction of the store.

"Well," Mom says as if what just happened wasn't extraordinary, "Let's go and see what's new in girl's clothing."

We pile into her car and with Mom at the wheel, drive to Hampton's Women and Girls Clothing Store. The shop has been around for decades, although the original owner, Mrs. Tremblay's dad, sold the shop many years ago. When the new owner bought the business, because everyone knew the place as Hampton's, he kept the same name.

Mom parks in front and we clamber inside. Delores Billings, the owner's daughter, approaches. "Good morning, Mrs. Murphy. How are you today? And how's that new son of yours?"

"He's well, Delores. Thank you for asking."

"I'm sure you're a mess with the," she puts her hand beside her mouth and whispers, "murders happening so close to you. I'd be crazy with worry if I had so many kids to look after."

"It is a worry, Delores, but we're managing. Thank you."

Delores Billings is an unmarried woman who went to school with Dad. She's also a gossip. "Poor Jim," she says. "He must be distraught, having been serious with Marj in school. First Abigale dies then Marjorie." She shakes her head. "Give him my well-wishes, would you?"

Mom pauses. "Certainly, Delores."

"Did you hear about Marj's tongue....?"

Mom cuts the woman off. "Sorry, Delores. I left Jim looking after Cole. Kind of in a rush. We're here for school clothes. Ages thirteen, eleven, and six. As well as some play clothes for a three-year-old and a two-year-old."

Rose has zeroed in on her preferences. "I like these, Mom." She holds up a pair of orange overalls. "Aren't they great?"

"They are indeed great, Rose. But you can't wear those to school. Pick out a couple of dresses please."

"I bet if I wore them under a dress the nuns wouldn't even notice."

"Rose, I do not have the patience to debate whether or not you can wear pants to school. If you argue with me one more time on this subject, I will escort you out of the store and you'll have to wait until your sisters are done for your turn."

Very seldom does Mom get angry with us and we are astounded by her abruptness.

"Ok, already," Rose says. "No need to go ape on me," she mumbles.

Without another word, Mom pinches Rose's shoulder and ushers her out of the store. While the rest of us watch, she sits my sister down on the bench outside the front door, wags her finger in her daughter's face, then returns to the shop.

"Now then, where were we?" Mom says.

When the four of us are done picking out new clothes, I wait on the bench with my sisters while Mom takes Rose inside. Rose, who's like a dog with a bone, begins to bargain for the overalls in exchange for something we can't hear, then Mom and her stand at the cash register while Delores, who has a big smile on her face, adds everything up. Dressed in her new orange overalls, Rose leads the way outside with the rest of her bundles and Mom's arm around her second eldest's shoulders.

"Can we go to Gas-n-Go for supper?" Rose asks after we're all in the car.

Robin and Alex bounce on the front seat and chant, "Out for supper, out for supper."

Mom hesitates. "I don't know, Rose. Your dad wasn't very pleased about being left with Cole. Maybe I should make supper tonight. Although I didn't get that pot of stew cooking like I'd planned."

"He'll be fine," Rose persists. "You've had us all afternoon." She looks at her watch. "And it's already five-thirty. Do you really want to start making supper when we get home? It's the perfect excuse for a night off."

Mom looks in the rear-view mirror at Rose and me in the back seat. "Ok, I'll ask," she says. "I am kind of tired." She turns her head around. "But don't count on him saying yes. If he says no, then that's the end of it." She starts the car and drives us home.

Dad sits on the deck bouncing his son on his knee. "You were gone a long time," he says.

"Takes a long time to shop for five girls." Mom unloads the packages from the trunk. "Found everything we needed and a little bit more." She turns to face Dad. "Delores gives you her well-wishes, said she hopes you're not too distraught by Marj's death. How did everything go here?" She takes her son from Dad's arms.

"Went for coffee then came home. Didn't open the store. Too hard to work while looking after a baby."

"That it is," Mom says. "Do you think we could go out for supper?"

"No," Dad says. "Have to go to the store since I wasn't there this afternoon."

"Come on, Jim," Mom says, forgetting her own instructions about not arguing if Dad said no. "I'm tired. We haven't been to Gas-n-Go in ages. Whatever you have to do at the shop can wait until tomorrow."

"Alright," Dad says. "But this is the last time for a while. Takes a lot of money to raise six kids."

* * *

By the time we're done supper the sun is low on the horizon. Dad fills the tank with gas, then pulls the car out of the parking lot. When he gets to the end of the old road at edge of town, instead of going home, he turns back up the highway towards the city.

"Where are you going, Jim?" Mom asks. "I need to get Cole and the girls home. It's been a long day for all of us. I'm exhausted."

"Going to check on the house," Dad says as he pulls into the Tremblay's driveway. "Thought I saw someone go into the backyard."

"I didn't see anyone," Rose says. "And I was looking that direction the whole time."

"Well then, you didn't see what I saw," Dad says. "Someone went into the backyard while I was filling the tank."

"Who?" Mom asks.

"A stranger, Pat. If I knew who it was, I would have said."

The house looks desolate in the evening light and it's easy for me to imagine a killer hiding around the corner. Dad, untroubled by the sinister atmosphere, opens his door.

Mom reaches across the seat and touches his arm. "I don't think this is a good idea, Jim. We should go to the police."

He shakes her off. "It'll be fine. Stay put and I'll be right back." He steps out of the car and his footsteps crunch on the gravel driveway as he walks towards the porch. He disappears around the side of the house.

Mom leans against the seat and presses Cole to her chest. I think if she hadn't had her son in her arms, she'd have gotten out of the car herself and insisted Dad not leave us alone.

The interior car light blinks on as Rose opens her door.

"Where do you think you're going?" Mom asks.

"With Dad, of course. He needs someone to back him up."

"Close that door right now, young lady."

"Mom, have you never read a murder mystery in your life? Dad can't go out there by himself, for gosh sakes. That's when the murderer comes out of the abandoned cabin or the basement and knocks off the person who ventured out alone, then one by one the others go to see where he's gone and pretty soon there's no one left. I have to go now, before Dad's back there all alone and we don't know what happened."

Rose continues to open the door, putting one foot on the ground. The night air is cool as it spills into the car, drying the sweat on my forehead. We all look expectantly at Mom, sure she'll tell Rose to get back in the car. She surprises us.

"Fine, go and see if he's alright, but run right back here if you don't find him. Do not, and I repeat, do not go any further than the back corner of the house. Do you hear me, Rose?"

Rose nods her assent.

"And when we get home," Mom says, "I'm going to have a talk with you about the books you're buying at Woolworths."

Rose steps into the night, gently closing the door behind her. "Everyone, lock your doors," Mom says.

In the waning light of sunset, Rose's orange overalls glow as she runs down the side of the house and out of sight. Our car becomes quiet, with not one girl talking. Even Cole isn't making a sound. We sit like this for a couple more minutes before Mom speaks.

"Liz, go and find your sister," she says and my heart sinks.

"Aw, Mom," I say, "do I...."

The sound of Rose's footsteps crunch across the yard, saving me from sounding like a scaredy-cat. She pounds on the glass.

Fran pulls the lock up and Rose wrenches the door open. Her voice is breathless. "It's ok, everything's ok."

Mom lets out a sigh, as do I.

"Where's your father?" Mom asks.

"Out back talking to Mr. Pendergrass." Rose climbs into the car. "Mr. Pendergrass said he was out for his evening constitutional and stopped to check on the house like he's gotten into the habit of doing. That's all I know."

Dad and Mr. Pendergrass stroll around the corner of the house. Dad is gripping Mr. Pendergrass's shoulder, but as they near, the gesture becomes a friendly slap. "Squeeze in back, Carl. We'll give you a lift home."

Robin sits on my lap and Fran and Rose slide as close to me as they can. Mr. Pendergrass takes the window seat. He smells like the cool night air and cigarette smoke. He slips a toothpick between his teeth then glances at Dad in the rear-view mirror. I sense tension between the two.

"Patricia," Mr. Pendergrass doffs his cap at Mom. "Sorry for the trouble."

"No trouble," Mom says. "What are you doing out here?"

Dad interjects before Mr. Pendergrass can answer.

"He was out for his evening walk and thought it might be worthwhile to look around for clues and collect the reward the RCMP are offering. Isn't that what you told me, Carl?"

"That's right, Jim," Mr. Pendergrass says. "That's what I told you." He presses his fingers against his knees turning the appendages from tobacco yellow, to white. His cheekbones move as he clenches and unclenches his jaw.

"Carl," Mom says. "You shouldn't be out here. Your life's worth more than a few hundred dollars."

Mr. Pendergrass shifts his eyes to the back of Mom's head. "Why, thank you, Patricia. That's very kind of you to say. I suppose anyone's life is worth more than any amount of money."

"There's nothing left to find, anyhow," Rose says. "Cops took everything away."

Mom whips her head around. "What did you say?"

"That's what I heard," Rose says quickly. "You know, from people who've gone out to look."

Mom slowly turns her head back but not before giving Rose one of her, *you'd better not have been out here alone, young lady,* glares.

"Didn't come out here to intentionally look for things, Miss," Mr. Pendergrass says. "Out for my evening walk and thought I'd poke around."

Dad drops the man off at his house. Mr. Pendergrass touches the brim of his cap and exits the car. We wait while he unlocks his front door and switches on the interior light. He steps inside and closes the door without looking back.

* * *

"Dad was lying," Rose says quietly as we're getting into bed. "When he said he saw a stranger on the Tremblay's property." She punches her pillow then flops down and looks at me.

"He wasn't lying, Mr. Pendergrass was there."

"But he told us he didn't know who it was. When he was walking down the side of the house towards the backyard, I heard him shout *Pendergrass,* before he got to the corner. Unless Dad can see through wood and insulation and whatever else is inside a wall, he wouldn't have known it was Mr. Pendergrass until he stepped into their backyard."

"Why would Dad lie to us about that?"

"Got me," Rose says. "But that's what happened. Maybe he was worried Mr. Pendergrass was going to find a clue and collect the reward before he did."

* * *

He's an odd duck," Dad says.

"Who?" Mom says.

"Pendergrass."

I've been on the floor of my treehouse for an hour, worrying about high school and all that entails, when the outside light blinks on and Mom and Dad, perhaps assuming I'm already in bed, step out to sit on the deck. It's near the end of August, but we're having a hot spell and the house is still too stifling to stay indoors even at ten in the evening.

This afternoon, Mom said she was too tired to make a meal, the third time she's said that since the shopping trip, so Rose and I made sandwiches and lemonade then the whole family ate supper on the deck. For a little while we all relaxed and forgot about the murders and school drawing near. Even Dad was in a good mood, complementing Rose on her overalls and eating three sandwiches. Alex proclaimed that it was the funnest day she's had all summer.

Coffee glugs as Mom fills Dad's cup.

"Went to talk to him today about going to the Tremblay's the other night," Dad says. "Told him I thought it wasn't a good idea until the killer is found."

"What did he say?"

"Said he carried a gun."

"Does he know how to use one?"

"His dad taught him how, just like my dad taught me. Made him practice by shooting the gophers. He became a crack shot; didn't want them to suffer, he said. Told me once he'd rather kill a person than a helpless animal. Marj used to tease him about that."

"Delores said something odd when I had the girls in her shop the other day," Mom says.

"What's that?" Dad asks.

"She said you and Marj were serious in school."

Dad's quiet for a moment. "Surely you know better than to listen to that woman."

"She is a gossip," Mom says. "I knew you and Marjorie dated, but

I didn't know you were serious about one other."

"That's because we weren't," Dad says. "The silly woman should learn to keep her mouth closed. In school she always whispered behind her hand, telling tales, making enemies. Marj suggested taking her into our group, but Stan and I said no."

"Oh?"

"It was enough that she allowed Carl to chum around with us; we didn't need someone we couldn't trust."

"It was good of Marj to take Carl under her wing. High school's tough enough without facing it alone."

"He had no friends until Marj befriended him."

"Marj had a good heart."

"Yup," Dad says. "Everyone loved Marj."

"You've never told me how Carl lost his dad," Mom says.

"Farming accident," Dad says. "Carjack failed. Truck crushed his chest."

"My goodness!" Mom says.

I gasp and press my hand across my mouth.

"We found him," Dad says. "Carl, Stan, Marj, and me."

"That must have been terrible!" Mom says, "finding him dead like that."

Dad takes a drink of his coffee. "The three of us tried to pull him out, but the truck was pressing him to the ground. Marjorie was of no help; wouldn't even look at the man, let alone touch him. Had to leave him there. Besides, Stan and I could see he was already dead."

"Poor Carl," Mom says.

"The carjack company investigated and couldn't prove whether it was an accident, or a defective jack. Paid off Mrs. Pendergrass before she had a chance to sue."

"Is that when his mom sold the farm?"

"Right after the funeral she sold those acres and bought the house Carl still lives in as well as the one next door. There they lived, side by side until the day she died."

"I've always wondered why they wouldn't live together. Carl must have been only seventeen or eighteen. Seems strange they'd live in separate houses. Did she not love her son?"

"I've no idea," Dad says. "But that's what she did and everyone accepted it."

"That's what I found peculiar about his explanation regarding the reward money," Mom says. "There's no way that man is hard up. He's still working and has never married so not had the expense of a family. He would have inherited a large amount from the sale of the farm plus he's never had mortgage payments. And now you tell me his mom had enough money from the jack settlement to buy two houses? Why would he need a few hundred dollars reward money?"

"Like I said, he's odd."

They're quiet for a few minutes and I'm just about to roll over and pick up my binoculars when Dad starts to talk.

"Just to be clear, Pat. Marj and I were never serious. We went out, that's all. Even Carl took her out a few times. Surely you remember high school; everyone dated everyone else. It was puppy-love. Nothing to be jealous of."

"I'm not jealous, Jim. I was simply surprised Delores said you were serious."

"We weren't. After graduation Stan married Abigale, Carl got a job with the township, Marj moved to the city, and I met you and talked you into moving here."

I look through the floorboards; Mom pats Dad's hand. "You were a sly fox, Jim Murphy."

"I was, wasn't I?" Dad says.

CHAPTER FOURTEEN

Like steppingstones, Mom has lined the five of us up against the side of the house. She's handed Cole to me and now stands on the flagstone path that connects the front yard with the back as she puts Rose's camera to her eyes. We're each wearing a new outfit for the first day of school and our hands, scrubbed clean in the bathtub last night, reach up to tug at collars still stiff from lack of wear. Rose is impatient.

"Come on, Mom. All the good desks will be taken if I don't go soon. Just press the button, wouldja?"

Mom lowers the camera and scowls at her daughter. "Robin, move closer to Fran, Alex isn't in the picture." She walks towards us and guides Alex closer to Robin then Robin closer to Fran. When she turns, I notice a red spot on the back of her dress.

"Mom," I say and point.

She peeks over her shoulder. "Oh, thank you, dear." She brushes at the red mark. "I'll change after you're gone to school." She steps to the path and lifts the camera to her eyes.

"Mom," Rose wails.

The moment Mom takes the picture, Rose leaps from the lineup and tries to take the camera from Mom's hands.

Mom lifts the device high in the air. "You know you're not allowed this at school."

"Alright, alright. Thought you might forget with the whole post-baby thing you seem to be going through."

"You'd better watch your mouth, young lady, or I'll make you leave those pants at home." I heard Rose at six this morning, negotiating a deal with Mom to be allowed to wear her orange overalls to school under her dress, in exchange for a month of keeping our room tidy. "And don't forget to go into the washroom and remove them before you sit in your desk. I don't want to get a note sent home from one of the nuns on the first day."

Rose runs to the front sidewalk and hops from foot to foot.

"Wait for your sisters, Rose," Mom commands. "Liz, you show Fran where she's supposed to go, please. I'm busy making a batch of relish and I'm already tired." She pushes the hair off her forehead and I notice dark circles under her eyes.

"Yes, Mom. You told me," I say.

"Can I go?" Rose asks.

"You can go," Mom says.

Fran and I bring up the rear as the three of us run down the street, book bags and ponytails flying out behind us. In the distance, all I can see is Rose's orange pants as she gallops towards grade eight.

* * *

The schoolyard is crowded with kids, some in groups while others stand alone. The ones in groups are horsing around, laughing and talking loudly, brave with the knowledge they have someone to start a new year with. The ones standing alone are doing their best to hide their fear, worried about beginning a new grade without a friend. Jen is waiting for me on the sidewalk in front of The Park. She looks annoyed.

"There you are," she says.

"I have to take Fran in first," I say. "Get her settled in a desk before we leave."

"Then why are you so late? You should have been here twenty minutes ago!"

"Mom had to take our picture. First day of school kind of thing." I look across the playground. Rose is talking to some of the kids that were in her grade seven class, so we leave her to fend for herself and I grab Fran's hand and tug her towards her school. Jen drags her feet as she follows behind, mad she has to wait for me.

Inside, we squeeze between nuns escorting parents who are

pushing reluctant six-year-olds in front of them and pulling curious toddlers behind. I lead Fran towards her room. We stop outside
the door and look in. Older siblings stand by desks, anxious to get
to their own rooms, while parents kneel, quelling tears and patting
hands, impatient to get back to their homes which now have one
less child for a few hours.

I push Fran through the doorway and we find a desk near the
back of the room. Then, I too, kneel down. "It's ok, Fran. You'll be
fine."

She shakes her head.

"If Rose and I can do this, so can you."

Again, she shakes her head. "I want Mom."

"Fran, you're six now. You can't have Mom look after you all the
time. It's either me or no one helping you this morning." I feel bad,
but Jen's pacing outside the classroom and I don't want her to leave
without me. "It's only for three hours." I point at the clock above the
blackboard. "See, I taught you to tell time this summer. What time
does it say?"

Her lips move as she squints at the large white circle. "Five to
nine?"

"That's right. And when both hands are at the top, it will be
lunch time. I'll meet you outside the backdoor by the hopscotch
squares. You can tell me all about what you did this morning when
we walk home. Mom said she'd make your favourite meal, tomato
soup and toasted cheese sandwiches." I thumb away a tear dripping
down her cheek. "Ok?" I say.

She nods without looking at me. I glance back as I walk away;
she's wiping her cheeks with the sleeve of her sailor dress.

"You all done here now?" Jen asks.

"I'm done," I say. "I feel bad. She's shy." I take a step back into the
room, but Jen grabs me by the arm and pulls. "She'll be fine. Come
on. We still have to find our home room. Everyone else will already
be there."

Together, we sprint across The Park towards the high school.
The final bell has rung so with no one outside to slow us down, we

propel ourselves through the double doors. Our footsteps echo as we race down the empty halls.

"What classroom are we in?" I ask.

"Seventeen. Mrs. Cooper is our homeroom teacher."

We pause outside the closed door. I can hear a woman's voice inside instructing kids where to sit. Jen turns the knob.

"Nice of you to join us," the woman I assume to be Mrs. Cooper, says.

We skulk inside amid sniggers and shaking heads.

"There's two desks left at the front. Don't dawdle. You're holding everyone else up."

We spend the next half-hour being told by Mrs. Cooper that she's our homeroom teacher and her subject is English. After today, if we're late, she looks directly at Jen and me, we must go to the principal's office and pick up a late slip or we will not, under any circumstances, be allowed into her classroom. This is the classroom we will gather in every morning, even if our first subject isn't English, and she is the teacher we go to if we have any problems. She hands out a list of books we're supposed to read this year and I discover I've read many of them. I put up my hand.

"Yes, Miss Murphy?" Mrs. Cooper says.

"What if we've already ready some of these?" I ask.

Jen shakes her head and grins along with some kids at the back of the room. I recognize a couple as the girls we saw at the pool in July.

"Then consider yourself lucky as you will be one step ahead of everyone else."

She tells us there will be a class discussion on all the books, and we are to pick three on the list to write book reports for. We are also to write a short story by the end of the semester of no less than ten thousand words on anything that interests us of which we have knowledge.

The bell rings. We have ten minutes to get to our next class, and Jen doesn't have the same class as me.

"I'll meet you at the front doors at noon," I say around people

jostling their way to their own classes. "We can walk home together."

"Sure, Liz, sure," she says. "See you later."

I look back once to see my friend swallowed by the crowd.

* * *

Three periods later the lunch bell rings and the halls become
clogged with students. I squeeze through, eventually pushing my
way outside. Jen isn't here so I step to the grass as I scour the faces spilling out the double doors. Some of the kids who live in the
country break off into groups and sit on the lawn. They open lunch
boxes and paper bags, removing sandwiches wrapped in wax paper
and thermoses filled with soup and milk. Town kids hurry across
the schoolground toward their houses, anxious to fit as much freedom as they can into one hour.

Five minutes later, and knowing Fran and Rose are waiting on
me, I leave, hoping Jen doesn't get mad at me for abandoning her.

Across the schoolyard, I see Fran jumping in the painted hopscotch squares by the back doors of her school. She stops in a shaft
of sunlight to bend forward and pick up her marker and the silver
ribbons Mom tied around her pigtails, sparkle.

Rose is pacing up and down beside her, looking towards the
high school. When she sees me, she raises her palms. I quicken my
pace. "Where the heck have you been?" she says as I draw near.
"Fran and I have been cooling our heels for ten minutes."

"I was waiting for Jen. She said she was going to meet me outside
the school doors as soon as the last bell rang. She never showed up."

Rose points. "Isn't that her?"

I look across the playground. The crowd has thinned and I'm
able to see my friend walking the other direction with another girl.
They have their heads bent close together and Jen is talking with her
hands. She laughs loudly at something this new friend says.

Rose puts her arm around my shoulders. "It's ok, Liz. You still
have me. I promise I'll never desert you for someone else. It's been
my experience that friends just get in the way of your freedom, al-

ways waiting on them to call or cancelling at the last minute, when you could be doing whatever you wanted to do, hours sooner."

I step out of Rose's reach. "Fran, lets go. We don't have all day." When she continues to jump from square to square, I yell, "You have to be back here in less than an hour and if you don't get your ass in gear, you'll be walking home alone!"

Fran runs to me and sticks her hand in mine, ignoring the fact I just swore at her. "Want to know what we did, Liz?" She offers the information without waiting to hear my answer. "The teacher asked who could write out the alphabet. I was the only one who knew how! I wrote it all out on the chalkboard. The teacher, her name is Miss Jacobson, said I was very smart."

"Well, don't let that get around. All you'll get is grief."

"Did you have a good morning, Liz?" she says, not understanding my sarcasm.

"I did not," I say loudly. "I did not have a good morning. I had a crappy, crappy morning and if I never have to go back to that stupid school again, it'll be too soon!" I pull my hand out of Fran's and run home, leaving Rose to help our sister cross the road. I open the front door, run by Mom lying on the couch and the girls watching Mr. Dressup, sprint through the kitchen past counters cluttered with cucumbers that have yet to be peeled, and sealer jars piled in the sink, and don't stop running until I've bounded up the stairs and thrown myself across the bed. I roll to my back and crook my elbow across my face, wiping away my tears.

Fran's and Rose's excited voices echo up the stairs as Mom greets them at the backdoor. She tells them to sit at their places, then, the wood creaking under her feet, she climbs the stairs to my room. I turn over. She knocks.

"Liz, can I come in?"

"I'll be right down." My voice is muffled by the pillow I have my face buried in.

"Did something happen at school?"

"I'm sure Rose told you already. Washout Liz loses her best friend on the first day of school."

"You haven't lost your best friend." She opens the door a crack. "Jen's expanding, reaching out, making new friends," she says without stepping into the room. "We all do it you know, change is inevitable."

"I told her, I told her all summer that I needed her this year. Now she's got another best friend. I can't do this without her."

"Of course, you can, Liz. Talk to some of the other kids. Don't let Jen making friends with someone else stop you from moving forward."

"If you hadn't made me take Fran to her class this morning, none of this would have happened. Jen and I were late, and everyone laughed at us. That's why she left me; she was embarrassed to be seen with me!"

"Jennifer hasn't left you and I'm absolutely positive she's not embarrassed to be seen with you. She's simply exploring her new world." Mom steps into my room. "Come, have a bowl of soup. Franny really wants to tell you about her day. She looks up to you, you know." She strokes my head and I want to stay here, safe under my mother's touch.

* * *

After lunch, Rose, Fran and I stand on the corner to wait for Jen. Rose loses patience and joins a group of kids spinning each other on the merry-go-round. As I'm about to leave, I see Jen part ways with another girl and cross the schoolyard towards Fran and me.

"Where were you at lunch?" I ask, trying to sound like I don't already know or care. "I waited for you. You said we'd meet outside when the bell rang."

"Oh, uh, sorry. Walked home with Holly. Hope that's ok?" She looks expectantly at me.

"Sure," I say. "No skin off my nose. Walk home with whoever you want. I have to take Fran to her class." I grab my sister by the hand and leave Jen staring after us as we run towards Fran's school. When I look back, Jen is already gone. I enter Saint Mary's then start towards the grade one classroom.

"No, Liz," Fran says. "I know the way. My friend is waiting for me."

Olive Drummond is standing by the grade one door peering shyly from under her bangs. Fran skips down the hall then the two of them hold hands as they enter their room. I pause, worried Fran might change her mind and need me, but she doesn't look back. I guess everyone has a friend waiting for them this year but me.

CHAPTER FIFTEEN

"I'm not going," I say to Mom.

"Jen's waiting downstairs. She'll be disappointed."

"She's only asked me to go with her so she won't have to walk into the gym alone."

"You'll be fine. Maybe you'll meet someone new."

I pull my pillow over my head. "No. I won't be fine. I'll be embarrassed and everyone will see what a dud I am."

"If you don't want to go, I'm not going to make you. I only hope you don't regret it."

"I'll never regret not going to a dance where I'll be the only one standing alone. Never in a gazillion years!"

"Fine," Mom says. "I'll tell Dad you're not going and he can drive Jennifer there without you."

I'm quiet.

Mom stands and I hear her take a sharp breath. I look up; her face is pale. She steps towards the bedroom door, her hands on the small of her back.

I sit up. "Wait." I sigh. "Don't talk to Dad. I'll go."

Dad pulls his truck up to the front doors of the school and Jen jumps out. "C'mon, Liz. Everyone is already here."

I follow at a slower pace as she hurries down the sidewalk. She waits for me by the front doors, then runs inside when I catch up.

"Get your ass in gear!" she says. "What's the matter with you?"

"You're only going to leave me to go talk to your new friends. I don't know why I even bothered coming here tonight."

"For God's sake. Move it or I will leave you here by yourself."

She grabs me by the hand and we enter the gymnasium together.

* * *

Two hours later, tired of standing alone after Jen abandoned me within the first ten minutes, I leave the gymnasium. To be fair, she did ask me to join her and her new friends, but when they started whispering and laughing as I walked up, I told Jen I saw someone I knew and left, hoping she'd join me. She didn't.

In the main hall, I attempt to leave the school by the front doors. A chaperone approaches, "No leaving unless your ride is here, Miss," he says.

I back away and walk to the washroom. Girls, a couple of grades ahead of me, are crowded in front of a mirror putting on lipstick and fussing with their hair. I enter a stall while they talk.

"This dance sucks," one of them says. "They're treating us like children just because the murderer hasn't been caught. We could be having a better party in my basement."

"It's like being in prison," another girl says.

"Did you know that in the kitchen off the gym there's a door behind that old fridge? Tommy Burridge showed me the other day. The teachers don't even know it's there. Takes you to the far corner of The Park. It's where everyone goes to make out."

"Come on," one of them says. "Time to get out of here."

Rather than hanging around for another hour waiting on Dad, I decide to take advantage of my newfound knowledge and leave the bathroom to follow the group to the kitchen. I wait as the three of them giggle their way outside, then I enter the kitchen and let myself out. "Close that thing for God's sake," a boy says when I hold the door open too long.

Keeping my eyes averted, I scurry past couples necking in the bushes. The section of The Park between the school and the street-lights lining the sidewalk is dark, and that, combined with trying to come up with an excuse about how I managed to leave the dance alone, causes me to not hear Jen pounding across the playground until she's practically on top of me.

"I see you found the door behind the fridge, too," she says when she catches up. I turn to look at her.

"You'd better wipe off your mouth before your mom sees," I say as I point to her smeared lipstick. Her blouse is untucked and the velvet bow that was pinning her bangs back, has come loose and hangs at the nape of her neck; she pulls it out and stuffs it in her pocket.

"Thanks," she says, a sheepish grin on her face. "Talk about good timing. If you hadn't walked past, I don't know what I'd have done. Told him my friend needed me so I had to leave." She tucks in her blouse.

"So glad I could be of service to you," I say.

"What's eating you?"

"You sure you want to be seen with me? I guess walking in the pitch black is as safe as you can be from being seen with the loser in the class."

"Huh?"

"Those friends of yours are nothing but snobs. Can't you see that? I left and you forgot all about me. I stood alone for an hour!"

"I thought you said you saw some kids you wanted to talk to. What happened to them?"

"They all came with each other; I was like a fifth wheel."

Jen puts her hand on my shoulder, I shake her off.

"Come on, Liz. Don't be mad. I thought we were friends."

"I've heard rumours about those girls you're trying to buddy up to," I say.

She shrugs. "Holly says the rumours are sour grapes started by jealous people. You should have stayed with us. I didn't realize you were alone."

"Whatever," I say.

"Holly says she can introduce me to some of the boys she knows."

"Holly says, Holly says. Is that all you can say?"

"Just trying to make some new friends. It's high school! That's what you're supposed to do, isn't it? We still have each other but maybe some new friends too? Ok?"

I lift my hands in the air. "Be friends with whoever you want."

A shadow appears in front of us and we both jump. Mr. Pendergrass steps under a streetlight.

"Oh," I breathe. "It's you, Mr. Pendergrass. You scared me."

"You two shouldn't be out here alone after dark."

"We're heading home," I say.

"I'll follow you to make sure you're safe," he says.

"It's ok, Mr. Pendergrass," Jen says. "We're just about at the Murphy's." She points to my house.

He nods then stops walking to watch us walk home.

"Sheesh," Jen says, as we run down my street. "That man's scarier than Ichabod Crane. All he needs is a head under his arm."

We cross the street in front of the Henderson's, walk down the front sidewalk of our house, then turn down the flagstone path. The house lights are on, but Dad's truck isn't parked outside the garage.

"You'd better come in," I say. "I hope Dad hasn't already left." We enter the house. "Mom," I call. "Dad doesn't have to pick us up. We walked home." I add, "With Mr. Pendergrass," so she won't get angry.

Mr. and Mrs. Olyphant step out of the living room. They've been watching the evening news. "Your parents aren't here, Liz. Your dad took Pat to the hospital."

"He's taken Mom to the hospital? What's the matter with her? Is she sick?"

"Let's wait and see, shall we? Marvin will drive Jennifer home and you can go to bed. I'll stay here until your dad gets home."

"I want to know what's wrong with her," I shout. "Tell me."

"She was bleeding a bit, that's all. It happens to some women after they've had a baby."

"So, she'll be alright then?"

"Like I said, Liz, let's wait and see. You go to bed now. Rose is waiting for you."

Jen gives me a hug. "Go upstairs and talk to your sisters. They need you more than I do."

I tiptoe past my sisters' bedrooms, but I needn't have bothered.

When I open the door to my room, Rose, Fran, Robin and Alex are huddled in the middle of my bed. Rose looks up; her cheeks are wet with tears.

"Oh, Liz. Mom was bleeding, I saw it on her dress. And her face was white. She didn't want to frighten us, but she looked so scared."

I sit on the edge of the bed. Alex crawls into my lap then wraps her arms around my neck and tightens her grip. I peek around my youngest sister's head. "What did Mom say was wrong?"

"Dad told us to go to our rooms, he wouldn't let us talk to her. He yelled up the stairs for us to stay here, then he phoned Mrs. Olyphant. He left before she even arrived. What's wrong with Mom? Why did Dad have to take her to the hospital?"

"I don't know exactly what's wrong, but I think it's something that happens to women when they have a baby. She'll be alright."

I tap Alex and Robin on the nose. "Time for bed, you two."

"I don't want to go to my bed," Robin says. "I want to sleep here."

"We can't all sleep in the same bed," I say. "There's no room."

Alex sticks out her lip then throws herself across my pillow.

"Alright." I pull the covers up to their chins, then without changing my clothes, I lie down on the foot of the bed and begin to sing. "To-Ra-loo-ra-loo-ral, to-ra-loo-ra-li. To-ra-loo-ra-loo-ral, hush now, don't you cry. To-ra-loo-ra-loo-ral, to-ra-loo-ra-li. To-ra-loo-ra-loo-ral, that's an Irish lullaby."

CHAPTER SIXTEEN

Morning arrives and the memory of why I'm sleeping on the end of my bed still in the clothes I wore to the dance, jolts my eyes open. How I managed to sleep through my sisters clambering out of my bed, I'll never know, but the room is empty save for me. Someone has pulled a blanket over my shoulders and I scrunch it tight under my chin. I stay like this for quite some time, dropping in and out of sleep until I hear the sound of the phone ringing through the open bedroom door.

"Hello," Mr. Olyphant says.

It's quiet while he listens.

"Yes, I understand. We'll see you in a bit."

"Is Mom ok?"

Even from our bedroom, I can hear the panic in Rose's voice.

"Your dad is on his way home. Why don't we let him talk to you?" Mr. Olyphant says and my stomach clenches.

"Why can't you tell us?" Rose screams. The next thing I hear is the pounding of her bare feet as she runs up the stairs. She bursts into the bedroom. "Something's wrong with Mom, I know it," she yells. "They won't tell us because we're kids." She throws herself across the bed, pummelling her fists into the covers. "I'm tired of being treated like a baby!"

I reach over and stroke her hair. "Don't worry. Mom will be ok. She'll be home to look after us just like she always has." I try to sound strong but I know Rose can hear the doubt in my voice.

Rose sobs as she gasps for air between words, "I can look after myself."

"Well then, maybe it's a good thing you're so independent. When

Mom gets home, she might be too tired to look after anyone except Cole. You and I might be looking after Fran, Robin and Alex, as well as ourselves for a while."

Rose and I climb under the covers and hold onto each other as we sleep. We don't wake up until we hear muted voices a few hours later.

"She just fell asleep, went unconscious in the truck and never woke up." Dad sobs. "There was so much blood."

"I'm sorry, Jim," Mrs. Olyphant says. "Be thankful she didn't suffer."

I sit up. Rose opens her eyes and looks at me. Immediately the two of us know what's happened.

"How am I going to raise six kids by myself? I can't do this alone. Why the hell didn't she go to the doctor? All the time being a martyr, that woman! I told her she needed to see a specialist, but she said she was worried about leaving the kids again so soon after the murders. Well, now she's left them for good!" His voice breaks.

"We'll help, Jim. You have us."

A sound, so foreign as it reverberates up the stairs, I'm sure there must be someone else in the kitchen. Our dad doesn't cry, doesn't need others to console him, doesn't need anyone else to keep him strong. I want to run to him but I know he wouldn't want my sympathy.

Rose and I wait for someone to climb the stairs to our room. Normally it would be Mom coming to console us, to tell us the news that someone is sick or someone has passed on. Like when Mrs. Olyphant ended up in the hospital with a stomach ailment. She was there for a week and had surgery and now can't have fried foods anymore. Or the time Mrs. Davidson from across the street died while making her morning coffee. She was like a grandmother to us, knitting sweaters, bringing us into her house to warm up, and always on the lookout if we needed help with something. Mom was taking her some fresh baked cinnamon buns and found her dead on her kitchen floor from a heart attack. Mom came upstairs and told us that time. Said everyone had an hour to be called to God and it was Mrs. Davidson's time. But today, I lie in bed and wonder who it will be. Who will make the trek up the stairs to tell us our mother is dead?

After a long wait, the stairs creak with Dad's heavy step. He walks past the younger girls' doors and knocks on ours.

"Yes," I say.

He clears his throat. "Can I come in?" His voice is thick.

"Yes," I say again.

He opens the door but does not step across the threshold. Nor do Rose or I run to him for comfort. "I've something to tell you," he says. He rubs his hands across his unshaven face. His eyes are red, and his hair is disheveled. He's still in the same clothes he had on last night when he dropped me off at the dance. There's blood on his cuff turning it from green to red. "Your mother has passed on." His voice catches. "Can you please help Mrs. Olyphant with your sisters?"

He closes the door and Rose and I don't move until Mrs. Olyphant comes up the stairs late in the afternoon to tell us supper is on the table.

* * *

"Will this be ok?" Fran asks Mrs. Henderson as I walk past her bedroom. She's holding a yellow dress in her hands.

"Perhaps it's a bit too bright," Elva says. She pulls another dress out of the closet. "Here, this will do." She hands Fran the sailor dress that she wore the first day of school.

Alex and Robin are already dressed and playing dolls in the living room as they wait with Mr. Henderson for the rest of us to join them. I walk past their empty bedroom and enter mine.

Rose is supposed to be getting dressed; Mrs. Henderson has a navy dress laid out on our bed waiting for her, but instead, she's sitting in my treehouse wearing her orange overalls. It's chilly out today and her red hair blows wild in the wind. I join her.

"I don't think Mrs. Henderson will let you wear that," I say. "You're supposed to wear something dark to a funeral. You know, to show everyone how sad you are? I think it's a show of respect."

"If people don't know I respected my own mother, then the hell with them." Her voice is quiet as if speaking to herself. "This is what I'm wearing and Mrs. Henderson is going to have to tear it from my own dead body if she wants me to wear something else. Mom loved these overalls; she told me so the day she bought them for me."

I acquiesce. "You're right, Rose. As far as I'm concerned, Mom would love the way you look. I think it's the perfect outfit to wear today."

From the treehouse we see Dad pull Mom's station wagon out of the garage. He drives down the alley and disappears around the corner to park on the front street. He honks the horn.

"It's time to go," I say.

"Why do you think she didn't say she was sick?" Rose asks. "Why did she wait so long to go for help? I heard Mrs. Olyphant say to Mrs. Henderson that if Mom had gone to the doctor sooner, she'd be here today."

"I don't know, Rose. Perhaps she thought she'd get better on her own."

"I'm mad at her but I don't want to be."

"I think we all are," I say.

* * *

A long line extends out the door of the church as the congregation waits their turn to jot their name in the book that has been placed in the vestibule. As we pass the queue, the men remove their hats while the women reach to stroke the little ones' faces. Alex shrinks from their touch and I pick her up. The group of us, led by Dad who's carrying Cole, walk down the aisle to the front pews.

Mom's coffin has been placed by the altar and a picture of her set in a gold frame is standing on the lid. I picked the picture from Rose's collection, and Rose had it enlarged. It was that hot day a few weeks ago when we ate supper outside and Alex declared it was the funnest day of the summer. Rose took candid shots of every-one and caught Mom with her face rosy and glowing in the heat as she poured the lemonade. Alex was right; it was the funnest day all summer. The organ music stops and Alex climbs onto my lap. Father Mackinnon begins to speak.

"We're here today to mourn the loss of one of our own. Patricia Murphy was a woman who lived in this community for many years, a woman who blessed our town with six children. A woman everyone knew and loved."

I want to stand up and shout, *Quit speaking about her as if you can't love her just because she's dead.*

"She will always be in our hearts." Father Mackinnon's eyes fall on us. "In your hearts."

Alex whispers in my ear. "Is there something wrong with Mommy's heart, Liz?"

I shake my head and say *shush*. The little girl slumps against my shoulder.

"We ask you to help this family in their time of need. To give your love, and your time. They'll need our support for many months to come."

Cole starts to fuss and Dad passes him down the row. I sit Alex on the pew beside me and take my brother in my arms. I pat his bottom and he settles down.

When Mass comes to a close and before the coffin is wheeled to the back and the lid raised for viewing by those who wish to partake, I stand and hand Cole to Mrs. Henderson. Then as per instructions from Dad, I take my sisters home. Though I feel like a child leaving my own mother's funeral, I hadn't argued with Dad about not being able to see Mom one more time. I want to remember what she looked like the last time I saw her, not made up by some stranger who imagined what she looked like when she was alive.

Alex and Robin, who've been sitting for two hours as quietly as a two-year-old and three-year-old are able, chase each other up the sidewalk. I'm sure their giggles can be heard through the open windows of the church.

* * *

"I'm hungry," Rose says as she stares into the fridge. All the way home she complained how she wished she could have stayed, but a sandwich and cookie wasn't worth enduring the neighbours' rubbing her head or kissing her on the cheek.

"Make yourself a sandwich. You know where everything is," I say.

"I'm hungry too," Robin says. "I want Mom to make me a sandwich."

"You know that can't happen," I say. "You know Mom isn't coming back."

"Why isn't she coming back?"

"Because she's in heaven. We've already talked about this."

"But why is she in heaven? Does everyone go to heaven?"

"No, not everyone."

"Who doesn't go to heaven," Fran asks. "Bad people?"

"Yes, bad people," I say.

"Like the man who killed the Tremblays," she says.

"That's right."

"Why?" Robin asks.

"Why what?"

"Why won't he go to heaven because he made someone dead?"

Two days ago, Robin overheard Dad talking to Mr. Krieger about the Tremblays and she came to me asking if Mom was dead because she was murdered. I explained to her in as little detail as possible that the Tremblays were dead because a bad person killed them but Mom died because she was sick.

"Because it's a sin to kill someone, silly," Rose says. "Don'tcha know that?"

"The doctor made Mom dead," Robin says.

"The doctor didn't kill Mom," I say.

"But she died," Robin says. "Didn't he try hard enough to make her better?"

"I think he tried as hard as he could," I say. "Mom was too sick."

"Didn't Mom want to be with us anymore?" Fran asks.

"That's the question of a lifetime," Rose says.

"Of course, Mom wanted to be with us," I say. "She thought she'd get better. I know she wouldn't want to leave us."

"Who's going to look after us now?" Fran asks.

"You'd better learn how to make your own sandwiches, that's all I can say." Rose tosses the cold meat and mustard onto the counter then slams the fridge.

"Rose," I say. "Be quiet. We have the Hendersons and the Olyphants," I say to Fran. "And Dad. They'll look after us."

"And you," Robin says. "We have you, Liz. You're just about grown-up. You can help look after us too."

CHAPTER SEVENTEEN

"A fairy, a fairy," Alex says as she jumps up and down.

"Ok," I say. "Robin, which one do you want?"

"I wanted to be the fairy," she says. "Alex always gets to pick first."

"What about a princess? A princess wears a pretty dress like a fairy, only princesses are real. Fairies are make-believe. And this dress is purple, your favourite colour."

"I want to be the princess," Alex says. "I want to be someone real, not make-believe."

"You've already decided on the fairy costume. You can't change your mind."

She sticks out her lip.

"Well," Rose says, "I'm going to be a cowgirl." She plucks a white hat and cowgirl shirt from the costume rack. "I can wear the holster Aunt Frieda gave Cole for a baby present and ride the hobby horse that's been kicking around the house for years."

"Fran," I say. "What about you? Have you decided yet?"

The little girl shrugs her shoulders. "Maybe a clown? Mom sewed a clown costume last Halloween that no one wanted to wear."

I put my arm around my sister's shoulders. It's been six weeks since Mom died and already the littlest ones are getting used to the idea of not having her around, but Fran still suffers.

Fran squints up at me. "What are you going to be?" she asks.

"I can't go trick-or-treating this year. I have to take you guys out then stay home and hand out candy."

"Quit being a martyr," Rose says. "You're acting like Mom. Dad said he and Mrs. Olyphant would look after Cole and hand out candy so you could go out trick-or-treating and you refused."

"Don't call Mom a martyr!" I yell. The clerk glances at us then goes back to restocking the cigarette packages. "Ok. I'll dress up when I take you guys out. Jen said she'd help."

"I thought she had new friends," Rose says.

I scowl at my sister. "She cornered me in the washroom last week and said her mom told her this would be the last year she's allowed to go, so she asked if she could go with us. I told her I wasn't going to dress up and collect candy, but she could help me take you guys out and collect some candy of her own if she wanted to."

"Sorry. Last I heard you and she weren't talking. Glad to hear it's all worked out."

"I didn't say it worked out. She asked to go out with us, that's all."

"So, because her new friends are too sophisticated for Halloween, she's using you to go trick-or-treating with your sisters."

"So, she's using me. So what? Maybe she'll see she still wants to be friends with me. Maybe I'm being the grown up by letting her go out with us!"

"Ok, no need to get huffy. Anyhow, it's good you'll have Jen to help because I'm going out alone. Cover more ground that way."

"No, you're not," I say. "The police said kids either have to have a parent with them, or be in a group with someone older."

"That's so stupid," Rose says. "It's been over three months; the killer is long gone. You and Jen walked home from the dance and you weren't murdered."

"Stupid or not, it's the way it is. Anyhow, you're the one who said it's when people are alone that they get knocked off."

* * *

Robin twirls in her purple princess dress. "I look so pretty," she says as she stares at herself in the full-length mirror that's hanging on the back of Mom and Dad's bedroom door.

I pull Alex's wings on over her fairy costume which in turn is pulled on over her winter coat, then tug a toque down over her mop of strawberry blonde curls. I'm glad it hasn't snowed yet so the girls don't have to trip over their costumes while wearing winter boots.

The day before Rose's first Halloween, there was a blizzard that left the sidewalks plugged with snow. Rose wore my ghost costume which, even though Mom had pinned it up, kept falling down with the weight of the snow in the hem. Rose, in her hand-me-down boots which were too big, must have tripped a dozen times before the evening was done. Mom said that Halloween was proof Rose was going to be stubborn because the little girl kept going, determined to keep up to me. When we got home her ghost costume was ripped and muddy but Rose had a smile on her face as big as the Jack-o-lantern we'd carved.

"You know you're not a real princess," Rose says to Robin.

"Mom called me her princess," Robin argues.

"That's because it was her pet name for you. It doesn't mean you're actually a princess. The only way you can become a real princess is to marry a prince. Unless you're born into royalty, which you weren't." She waves her hand at the little girl who's looking confused. "Never mind." She turns to the bedroom window. "Finally, it's dark outside. I thought we'd have to go out in the daylight with these little kids."

"I don't wanna go out in the dark," Fran wails. "I'm scared."

"You can't go hallowe'ening in the daylight, for gosh sakes," Rose says. "What's the fun in that?"

"It isn't real, Fran," I say. "Its make-believe. We pretend we're scared because it's fun."

"Yeah, it isn't real," Rose says as she picks up the abalone shell comb from Mom's dresser and pulls her hair into pigtails. "You know there's no such thing as scary monsters that hide under your bed, or ghouls who live in your closet."

Fran's face turns white.

"Rose," I say. "Be quiet."

"Ok, ok." She looks at her sister. "I'm just trying to reassure you, Fran." She tosses her winter coat onto the bed where our mitts, toques, and coats are piled. "I'm not wearing a coat. It throws the line of my cowgirl shirt out."

"Rose, it's thirty degrees outside. If you don't wear a coat you'll freeze. And mitts too, and a toque."

"Cowgirls don't wear toques! We wear cowgirl hats."

"Either you put a toque on under that hat or you're not going anywhere," I say.

"You're not the boss of me," she says.

From the living room, Dad says, "Wear a toque, Rose."

Rose makes a face and mouths, *wear a toque*, knowing Dad's only telling her what to do because Mrs. Olyphant is here. She pulls a toque over her thick hair, dons her parka then tugs the sleeves of her shirt over the bulky coat, pulling the material across her chest to do up the buttons; the shirt gapes under the strain of being stretched so tight. "Hurry up. I want to get out before all the good candy is gone," she says as she presses her cowgirl hat on over her toque.

I pick up two ghost costumes that I made from an old sheet Mom didn't get cut up into rags before she died, then usher the group into the front porch. Mrs. Olyphant joins us. Rose's camera is in her hands.

"You get in the picture too, Liz," she says. "Put on your costume."

I drape one of the sheets over my head and the five of us stand in a row under the bare light bulb hanging from the porch ceiling: me as a ghost, Rose as a cowgirl, Fran as a clown, Robin as a princess, and Alex as a fairy.

* * *

"That house is haunted." Jen points to the deserted bungalow next to Mr. Pendergrass's whose house is in darkness.

My sisters and I stopped at every house on the way to Jen's, and the little girls have quite a haul of candy at the bottom of their pillowcases.

I've stuffed my costume into my pillowcase and am carrying Alex's bag as she's having trouble not dragging the thing on the ground. A group of kids runs past us, a roll of toilet paper trailing in their wake.

"No, it's not," I say. "Don't tell them things like that. You don't have to get up with them in the middle of the night crying because they've had a nightmare. It's only a house that no one lives in anymore."

"You're wrong," Jen says. "There's a ghost who lives there."

"Jen," I say, "there's no such thing as ghosts and you know it."

"Uh-uh. I've seen him. He's tall and skinny and his cigarette glows in the window. He watches me when I walk past. Anyhow, I thought Catholics believed in ghosts. You know, the Father, Son and the Holy Ghost?"

"That's entirely different," I say. "And ghosts don't smoke."

"How would you know? Have you ever seen one?"

"I just know. They're dead. They can't hold onto anything, they're ghosts."

"So, you do concede there are ghosts."

"No, I do not."

"But you said...."

"Stop it, Jen. I do not believe in ghosts and I don't want you telling my sisters that there are such things."

"Ok, already. Jeez, you'd think you were their mother or something."

"May as well be," I say under my breath.

Fran, Alex and Robin don't hear what I said, but Rose does. "I don't need someone who isn't my mother but tries to act like she is, to tell me there's no such thing as a stinking ghost," she says and runs ahead. "I'm going to see if there's someone home." She rides her hobby horse up the path of the deserted house.

"Rose, no," I say, but then think better of it. No one lives here, she can knock until next Halloween for all I care.

Rose hops onto the step and turns to wave at us—the back end of the hobby horse hits the front door. Suddenly, she jumps off the step losing her hat in the bushes, and runs down the dilapidated path. "Someone said something to me," she says as she races past the five of us. Fran, who's already spooked out here in the dark, follows her sister down the sidewalk, trying not to trip over her clown shoes and losing her red nose on the way.

"Now see what you've done?" I say to Jennifer. "I'll be up with them all night having nightmares." I shout at Rose who's already reached the end of the block. "No one's there, Rose. No one said anything to you. It's your over-active imagination because Jennifer told you the house is haunted."

"Is not! I saw a figure, a tall figure and he said, *keep your eyes open tonight.*" She repeats, "Keep your eyes open," in a monotone voice. "And I do not have an over-active imagination. I'm the most practical member of what's left of this so-called family!"

"Fine, you saw a ghost and he told you to keep your eyes open."

"Did I say it was a ghost? It was a person and he spoke to me. Scared me, is all." She picks up Fran's nose and brushes off the dirt then presses the red ball back on the little girl's face. She pats the top of her toque as she and Fran rejoin us in front of the house. "I have to get my hat. It fell off in the bushes."

I grab the tail of her horse and pull. "Leave it," I say.

"But I don't look like a cowgirl without it, just some doofus on a kid's toy horse."

"I'll get it," I say. "I don't want you scaring Fran again."

The path is crumbling and old, but it's been swept clear of snow. The white hat lies deep in a bush under the front window and I set down my pillowcase and climb into the middle to retrieve it. I put my nose to the glass. The room is empty, no person, no ghost, no furniture, no nothing. Not even a speck of dust like one would expect in an abandoned house. I step out, hat in hand. "You know," I say, "I think Mr. Pendergrass owns this house and he might be your smoking ghost. The living room is cleaner than ours and you know what a fuss-pot that man is. Isn't this the house that belonged to his mom before she died?" I ask Jen.

She shrugs. "Got me. There's been no one living there since I was born. Maybe it's his mom who's haunting the place," she says.

"His mom is not haunting the place. No more talk about ghosts." I point across the street. "That's our last house then it's time to take the girls home."

"I don't want to go home," Robin complains. "I want some more candy."

"You can barely carry what you have. It's time to go home to bed. Mrs. Olyphant said to have you back by eight."

"Then you and me can go out," Jen says. "Do some serious trick-or-treating."

I don't say anything, not sure if I want to be alone with her. Except for the occasional walk home when Holly isn't available, tonight is the first time I've spent any length of time with her since the night Mom died.

By the time we drag the girls and their pillowcases home, I'm carrying Alex, Jen is carrying Alex's bag and Rose is carrying Robin's bag. I set Alex down in the front porch then open the door. The girls run inside eager to show Dad and Mrs. Olyphant their loot. I stick my head in. "Dad, we're back. Jen and I are going out now. We shouldn't be too long."

"I want to go with them," Rose says. "I hardly got any candy. No one wants to give the good stuff to an eleven-year-old cowgirl when there's a three-year-old purple princess and a two-year-old pink fairy standing in front of them. All I got was the stupid squished caramels and boxes of dried out Raisinets. They got all the chocolate bars."

Glad Rose can be an unsuspecting buffer between Jen and me, I say, "Sure. You can come with us. As long as it's ok with Dad." Jen scowls while Rose raises her eyebrows at me, probably suspecting my motive.

"Liz, take your sister with you," Dad says before he realizes I've already agreed. "Oh." He stands up and switches channels on the television. "And stay in the neighbourhood."

True to her nature, Rose argues. "But we can't, Dad. We've already gone to every place between the Olsen's and here. We have to go to some new houses or no one will give us anything."

"Fine," Dad says. "Stay off the highway."

Mrs. Olyphant frowns but doesn't say anything.

As we're leaving, I hear the theme music to Bonanza start.

* * *

"There's a house we didn't go to." Rose points at the Johnston's across the street from Mrs. Seamer's at the end of the block.

Jen, unhappy an eleven-year-old is tagging along says, "Forget about candy. I've got a better idea. Although now that your baby sister is here, maybe it's not such a good plan."

"Don't call me a baby!" Rose shouts. "I'm eleven years old, soon to be twelve. And I'm more mature than you are."

"Well," Jen says. "I'm closer to fifteen than fourteen and I'm far more mature than you."

"Are not," Rose says.

"Am too," Jen says.

"Are no...."

"For heaven's sake," I say. "You're both acting like children. We need to get a bit of candy in our bags or your mom," I say to Jen, "and Mrs. Olyphant," I say to Rose, "will wonder what we've been doing out here tonight."

"You got that right," Rose says. "Dad wouldn't notice if different children walked through the front door, let alone his own kids without any candy."

"Ok, already, Rose. I've heard enough of your complaining about Dad! He's doing his best."

"Actually, Liz, I'm not complaining, just stating facts. I like the independence his inexperience with this parenting gig has given me."

I pull my ghost costume out of my pillowcase and drape it over my head then toss Jen hers. I stomp down the front sidewalk of Mrs. Johnston's house and shout, "Trick-or-treat." Jen and Rose fall in line behind me and hold out their bags.

After collecting enough candy so Mrs. Olyphant and Jen's mom won't be suspicious, Jen, getting more and more impatient, says, "That's enough of this kid stuff. I want some excitement."

"I need more candy," Rose says. "I hardly got anything this year."

"Baby," Jen says.

"Atheist," Rose says.

"Quit it!" I say loudly. "If not more trick-or-treating, what's your big plan, Miss Better Idea?" I ask Jen.

"I want to go to the Tremblay's."

"No," I say quickly, suspecting what she was going to say. "I am not going to the Tremblays. If something happens, I'll be the one who gets into trouble." I slump to the curb. My ghost costume shines under the streetlight.

Rose sits on the curb beside me and puts her arm around my shoulder. "I know it's a big responsibility being the oldest, and now with Mom gone you feel that weight even more. But really, I'm fine by myself. As far as I'm concerned, you are relieved of any responsibility of looking after me."

"Are you two going to sit there and flap your jaws?" Jen says. "'Cause I'm going down that road whether you come with me or not."

"Jen," I say. "I really don't think this is a good idea. Dad said we're to stay in town."

"No, he didn't. He said we couldn't go on the highway. We can walk down the old road then when we get to their house, we can cut through the ditch. We'll be on the highway for less than a minute."

"It's still something Dad wouldn't want us to do."

"He's not my dad so I don't have to listen to him," Jen says.

"You don't have a dad to tell you what to do. Maybe you'd stay out of trouble if you listened to mine."

"And just because you're the mom now," she snaps at me, "doesn't mean you're my mom. I can get myself out of trouble just fine without you coming to my rescue!"

Both of us stop before we say more.

"What are you guys talking about?" Rose says.

"Nothing," I say.

"Never mind," Jen says.

"Ok," Rose draws out the word. "Remind me not to be as weird as you two when I turn thirteen."

I rub my hands down my face. "I'm not going out there, Jen."

"Then I'll go by myself." She starts walking towards the old road.

"Jen, stay with Rose and me, please," I say to her back. "Come hallowe'ening with us. Get some more candy. This is our last year."

Jen turns. "All the more reason to see what this house looks like on the scariest night of the year. Next Halloween all I'll be able to do is stay home and hand out candy, and you'll be stuck taking your sisters out for at least another five years, probably more like ten. My mom is certainly not going to allow me to be one of those teenagers who goes out to push over outhouses or hang toilet paper in trees. It's now or never."

"Jen," I plead, but she's skipping backwards and motioning for Rose and me to follow.

Rose takes a step in Jen's direction.

"No, Rose. I forbid you."

"Don't say that, Liz. You know that makes me want to do it even more. Come on. We have to make sure she stays safe, atheist or not."

I sigh and stand up from the curb. Then, still wearing my ghost costume and dragging my mostly empty pillowcase behind me, I follow my sister and my friend towards the road that runs past the house where seven people were slaughtered just over three months ago.

CHAPTER EIGHTEEN

"I should be leading the way before we trip over each other and roll into the ditch," Rose says as she steps on the hem of Jen's costume for the third time. She's leaned her hobby horse against Mrs. Seamer's elm tree, tucked her hat into her pillowcase, and now the two of us are following my friend down the road. We've already passed The Gas-n-Go Café and without light from the sign, the old road is dark, the crescent moon not yet clearing the willow trees that separate the old highway from the new.

In the distance, headlights appear and Jen quickly pulls off her ghost costume and stuffs it into her pillowcase. A car, full of screaming kids being driven from farm to farm to collect candy, races past, and I drop to the shoulder of the old road.

"We shouldn't be here," I say as I pull my costume off as well. "We should have stayed in town. This was not a good idea."

"Oh, come on. There's no murderer out here. Nothing's happened since July. Whoever killed the Tremblay's has flown the coop ages ago." Jen begins down the road again.

"You heard what Mrs. Witherspoon said," I say from behind Rose who's in the middle of our parade. "That he walks among us."

"And the cops said there's no evidence to support the fact that he's still in town." Jen says over her shoulder. "Who are you going to believe? Some crazy old lady or the police?"

"I don't know why everyone thinks it's a man," Rose says. "It could be a woman."

"I doubt a woman would kill kids," I say.

"I don't know about that," Rose says. "I'm sure there's a woman somewhere who has it in her. Maybe her mom died and she had to raise her siblings alone. Or maybe it was a jealousy thing. Mr. Tremblay was an old flame and the killer felt jilted because he married Mrs. Tremblay instead of her. Or maybe Mrs. Tremblay threatened to tell a secret about an old friend and that got them all killed."

"There it is," Jen announces when she stops to look across the road.

Rose and I stop behind Jen and look through the tangle of tree limbs at the two-storey house on the other side of the highway. Because the place is vacant, the yard-light isn't on and all we can see from this distance is the outline of the walls and roof. An owl, hidden against the star-studded sky, hoots.

"Do you know that owls hunt away from their daytime roost?" Rose says. "It's supposed to allow them to sneak up on their prey easier."

"Are we going to stand here and talk about owls?" Jen says.

"I'm close enough," I say.

"I'm going to look in the window," Jen says.

I extend my arm in front of me, inviting her to cross the ditch. She doesn't move.

"Don't think I won't," Jen says. "If you think I'd walk all the way out here listening to you complain about how we shouldn't be doing this, to simply turn around and go home, then you don't know me very well."

"Go ahead," I say. "I'm not stopping you."

When she realizes I mean what I say, she faces the house, tromps down one side of the ditch, pushes her way through the willow trees, up the other side, then crosses the highway. She stops at the end of the Tremblay's driveway and looks back at Rose and me.

"She wants you to go with her," Rose says.

"I know," I say.

"Well, aren't you going to? She is your best friend, is she not?"

I don't answer.

Rose studies my face. "If something happens to her, you'll never forgive yourself."

Jen looks small against the backdrop of empty fields as she slowly walks towards the vacant house. She glances back; I pretend to look at the stars.

"Well," Rose says. "I'm not going to let your best friend do something stupid all by herself. Are you?" She doesn't wait for an answer and descends into the ditch.

Deciding I would rather stay in a group than be left alone in the dark, I follow Rose through the willow trees, cross the highway, then stop beside the two of them standing at the bottom of the Tremblay's driveway. Together, the three of us walk towards the house, then climb the steps and peer into the living room window. Unrecognizable shapes lurk in dark corners of the room.

"That's the furniture," Rose says. "When the Tremblays first died and the For-Sale sign went up, the couch and chairs were displayed around the room. They even kept the pictures on the walls. Like it was when the family lived here. They thought showing what the room looked like furnished would help sell the house. Guess no one wants to buy a murder house so they've covered it up."

"I'm going around back," Jen says then jumps off the porch. Rose follows.

"No," I say, "we shouldn't," but they've both disappeared around the corner before I can finish my sentence. "God Almighty," I mutter as I too jump off the porch.

The shadow of the house is causing the backyard to be as black as our basement when the lights are turned out and I stop by the back corner. "Where are you guys?" My voice is crisp in the cold air and all I can see is my breath.

"Over here," Rose whispers, "by the hedge."

I cross the backyard, not knowing I've reached the hedge until I feel its stiff branches poke through my mittens. Standing this close, I can make out Jen's and Rose's shapes, but I can't see their faces.

"I heard something," Jen says from the gloom. "I think there's someone here. Someone other than us."

"We should go. I don't like this," I say.

"It's only a skunk," Rose says. "They're nocturnal. Or it could be a fox, maybe even a snake. They forage for food during the day, but they sometimes move at night. Although in the cold weather they don't move around as much. It's called brumation, not hiber...."

"Shush," Jen says. "I'm not kidding. There's someone out there, in the field."

"You tried to scare me once tonight, I'm not falling for that again," Rose says. Her elbow pokes me in the ribs as she starts undoing the buttons on her cowgirl shirt. "May as well take this off; no candy all the way out here where you've dragged us."

Jen and I turn our attention to the field beyond the hedge, the field where Mr. Tremblay and his son were murdered. To the right is a berm that separates his acreage from the road, to the left, miles and miles of flat land that was planted to wheat last spring. Seeds Mr. Tremblay would have been optimistic for as he sowed the golden kernels under the warm earth, not knowing he wouldn't be around to harvest the crop. The land was eventually harvested by his neighbours, the profits given to the estate.

A figure is standing in the middle of this empty field, and a cigarette glows as if suspended in mid-air. Rose, who's been struggling to rip the cowgirl shirt off from overtop of her coat, begins to curse. I place my hands on the sides of her head and turn her eyes towards the land. Whoever is there takes another puff and the red ember burns through the darkness.

"Probably some high school creeps trying to scare us," Rose says.

"Maybe it's the smoking ghost and he's followed us out here," Jen says.

"I thought we'd already established that there are no such things as ghosts," Rose says.

"Are too," Jen says.

"Are not," Rose says.

"Hush," I say.

The cigarette glows one more time, then its red end drops to the ground.

"He's stubbed it out," I say. "He heard us talking."

In the silence, footsteps begin pressing the stubble flat. It's a sound we all know well, being raised in the country as we have been. A crunching kind of sound, like the breaking of bones.

"We have to go." No one moves. "Now!" I say in a whisper so forced it makes my throat hurt.

Dropping our pillowcases to the ground, Jen, Rose and I turn and run. Behind us, branches crackle as someone breaks through the hedge.

We streak around the side of the house, past the front porch then down the gravel driveway. Jen is in the lead and I can see her outline on the highway as she bolts towards town. Rose is behind her, and I'm the last in this race. When my feet hit the asphalt, I peek over my shoulder to determine if I'm about to be tackled to the ground but stop running when I see Stevie Drummond standing by the corner of the house. He's laughing so hard, he has his hands pressed to his belly.

"What the hell?" I turn to call to Jen and Rose. "Come back. It's only Stevie." Rose turns around, but Jen is too far away to hear me. "What do you think you're doing?" I yell at Stevie.

"Just scaring the pants off a couple of girls," he says. "Look at that scaredy-cat sister of yours; running so hard you'd think she was going to be murdered. Maybe you need your mommy to hold your hand," he shouts at Rose.

Rose is a blur as she speeds past me; Stevie turns to try and get away, but Rose, anger spurring her on, has no trouble catching up and tackles him, pushing the boy to the ground. She jumps on top and starts punching him in the face and pummelling his chest. "I do not need my mommy," she says with each swing of her fist, "to look after me. I'm old enough to look after myself."

I pull at her arm. "Rose, stop. You're hurting him."

She looks at me and when I see the fury on her face, I take a step back before I, too, get punched.

"Rose," I say softly, "you've taught him a lesson. You can get off him now."

Stevie's nose is bleeding and his lip is split. His eyes are wide between outstretched fingers. Rose stands and walks to the other side of the driveway.

"I'm telling," Stevie says as he climbs to his feet. "I'm telling everyone what you did. You're crazy!" He dabs his bloody nose with his sleeve.

"Go ahead, Stevie," I say. "Tell everyone that a girl beat you up."

"I will," he says. "I'll tell and you'll be in...." He looks confused. "Give me your candy. I won't tell if you give me your candy."

Rose, her back to us says, "Are you blind as well as ignorant? Do you see any candy? It's in the pillow cases we dropped when you crashed through the hedge." Pointing behind her to the backyard of the Tremblay's, she says, "If you want it, go ahead and take it, for all I care."

Stevie looks at Rose, then takes a step towards the backyard but changes his mind. "Nah, I don't need Halloween candy. That's for babies." He makes a wide girth around Rose, stopping at the bottom of the driveway. "You think you're so smart," he says. "I was behind you all the way from town, you didn't even see me. I followed you up the driveway, then waited by the front porch for you to come out. I wasn't anywhere near the hedge." With those words, he takes off down the highway faster than Jen was running.

I touch Rose on the arm.

"Sorry," she says without turning around. "Guess I lost my temper," she raises her palms, "again."

"It's ok," I say. "It's been a tough couple of months."

She lifts her head; in the light of the crescent moon, her face is streaked with tears. "I miss her, Liz. I miss her so much I don't know what to do."

"I know. I miss her too." I put my arm around her shoulders. She grabs onto me and we stand locked together for a few minutes while Rose sobs into my shoulder. When we separate, she turns to cross the Tremblay's driveway.

"Where are you going," I ask.

"To get my candy." She wipes her eyes with the back of her orange mittens.

"I'm not going back there," I say as the distance between us gets wider. "I don't need candy that badly. Too many people out here tonight, and being scared once is enough for me."

Rose stops next to the house and squints into the blackness. "Yeah, maybe you're right. I'll come back when it's daylight. We'd better go and find that friend of yours. She's going to think we were murdered."

* * *

Rose and I find Jen sitting by the hedge that lines the sidewalk in front of the Krieger's house. She has her head in her hands and jumps to her feet when she sees us. "Where were you?" she whispers. "I thought I was going to have to tell your dad you were murdered!"

I peek around the hedge to our house. Through the living room window, I can see Mrs. Olyphant in the glow of the floor lamp as she watches television. Dad's chair is empty.

"C'mon," I say to Jen. "We'd better walk you home before your mom sends out a search party. We're already half an hour late."

"What happened?" Jen asks.

"Stevie Drummond was the one who was chasing us. Rose beat him up," I say. "It wasn't a ghost or the murderer, only Stevie."

"Yeah," Rose says. "Thanks for suggesting we go out there tonight. I had such a good time. All I ended up with is no candy and a bump on the nose. Remind me to invite you again next year."

We drop Jen off at her house then, unhindered by our candy bags, we sprint up the street, enter the porch and open the front door. Dad is by the back door, hanging his coat up in the mud room.

Mrs. Olyphant stands and greets us. "Where's your pillowcases?" She asks when she sees our empty hands.

"Left them at Jennifer's," Rose says. They were getting too heavy to carry. We'll pick them up tomorrow. You were out, Dad?" she asks, peering around Lois.

Dad sits in his chair. "Went to the hardware store. Last Halloween there was some damage done and I wanted to make sure no windows were broken this year."

"Was there? Damage this year, I mean," Rose asks.

"No, actually, there wasn't," he says after a pause. "Not that it concerns you."

I check on the girls. Robin is snuggled up with her bag of candy and Alex still has her pink fairy costume on. Fran is reading by the light of a flashlight. "Turn that off, Fran, and go to sleep. It's after nine-thirty."

I climb into bed beside Rose. "I don't remember Dad saying there'd been damage to the store last Halloween," she says. "But like he said, it's none of my business."

* * *

The next afternoon, as we're walking home from school, Rose says, "I need to talk to you." Fran is running ahead, anxious to get home and show her sisters her new candy. After lunch, she took some Tootsie Pops and Rockets to school when I told her the nuns will let her trade with her friends during afternoon recess. They used to allow us to trade at the morning recess as well as afternoon, but when kids started bouncing off the walls, they changed it to afternoon only so the kids wouldn't be high from sugar rushes until they got home for the day.

"What about?" I say.

"I went to get our candy."

"You went to the Tremblay's? When did you go there?"

"At recess."

"Rose!" I say. "You're not supposed to do that. The nuns will give you detention if they find out you left the grounds during school hours."

"They didn't see me. They were settling a fight over a candy trade. I saw my chance and took it. All the kids were sharing and swapping and I had nothing."

"So, where's our candy?" I ask.

"The bags were gone."

"There were probably all kinds of kids out there scaring each other after we left. Someone took it. Maybe Stevie even went back. We told him exactly where we'd dropped it."

"Why do you think he stopped chasing us?"

"Because he thought it was such a big joke. All he wanted was to scare us."

"While Jen was high-tailing it down the highway ahead of me, I looked back. Wanted to make sure you weren't being murdered."

"Thanks," I say.

"I saw the person who crashed through the hedge and I don't think it was Stevie," Rose says.

"It had to have been Stevie; there was no one else out there."

"He said he wasn't by the hedge. He said he never left the drive-way. Know what I think?" Rose says. "I think there were six people at the Tremblay's last night." She counts her fingers hiding inside her mitten. "You, me, and Jen, Stevie hiding beside the porch, Jen's ghost in the field who crashed through the hedge," she raises the other hand and pokes her thumb up under the wool, "and someone we never saw. I think whoever crashed through the hedge wasn't chasing us, he was chasing the person we never saw."

CHAPTER NINETEEN

"The teacher says I need glasses," Fran says as we walk home after school. It snowed last night for the first time and Rose is hurrying home to get her camera, grumbling about all the great photographic material that's being wasted.

Before bed last night, Rose and I checked the basement and found all of our boots, as well as extra toques, mitts, and scarves. I'm glad Mom was good at organization and every box was labelled with what was inside and what age group the clothing belonged to.

"Tell Dad when he gets home from work," I say to Fran.

"He won't hear me," she says.

Unfortunately, Fran is right. Immediately after Mom's funeral, neighbourhood women descended on our house cooking and cleaning and babysitting. Dad seemed fine with it, at least for a while. After two weeks of having women underfoot telling him where to sit and what to eat, searching for his clean shirts that were hung up differently than the way Mom hung them, and having to wait in the porch while the floors dried, he'd had enough. He told the neighbours that once Rose and I were home from school, they could leave. I'm not surprised; Dad's never been one to take much from anyone. Mom told me that his dad lived by the creed that a man had to look after his own.

The first few weeks after relieving the neighbours of their duties, Dad would come home for lunch and would never be late for supper. He'd tuck his youngest daughters into bed and rock Cole to sleep. He appeared to be stepping up to the plate, and I was grateful. Now, most days he eats lunch at the hotel restaurant, and doesn't get home for supper until after I've already fed the kids and put the littlest ones to bed. On the rare days when he does manage to make it in the door before bedtime, he eats in silence, holds Cole for a few minutes then goes to bed with barely an acknowledgment of his daughters.

For Rose's twelfth birthday last week, I made a cake and we sang happy birthday without Dad. I gave her a new roll of film and a photo album from Woolworths. Assuming he wouldn't remember, I put all our names including Dad's on the card, though I doubt I fooled Rose. She said thank you to all of us but has never said anything to Dad.

Monday, Wednesday, and Friday, Mrs. Olyphant drives into town to stay with the girls while Fran, Rose, and I are at school. Tuesdays and Thursdays, Mrs. Henderson crosses the street and does the same thing. Both women have argued with Dad that his daughters could use a bit of help, but so far, Dad has refused. They've often started supper, and when I get home, I finish making the meal while Rose looks after Cole, and Fran sets the table. When we're done eating, Rose and I do the dishes while Cole kicks and coos at the mobile in his playpen and Alex and Robin watch television or play with their dolls. After dishes, Rose and Fran sit in the office to do their homework, I read the little ones their bedtime stories, tuck them into bed, give Cole a bottle and put him to bed, then do my own homework. Most nights, I'm in bed by ten. I don't think Dad notices how I've fallen into Mom's job, or cares.

"I'll call and see if they'll let me book you an appointment," I say to Fran as we walk in the back door. "I'm home, Mrs. Olyphant," I shout. We take off our winter gear and hang it in the mud room, then enter the kitchen.

"He's got a runny nose," Lois says as she passes my brother to me. Cole, who's now four months old, lifts his head and smiles his baby smile. I'm sure he's going to grow up thinking I'm his mother.

"Did Dad come home for lunch today?"

"No," she says. "He called and said he was having a bite at the hotel. Said he'd be home around seven and you're to keep a plate warm for him." She rubs my back. "Give him time, Liz. He'll come around," but the look on her face tells me she believes otherwise.

She leaves me standing with Cole on my hip, and Alex, who's not talking as much as she used to, holding onto my leg while she sucks her thumb. I make a decision to talk to Dad tonight. This cannot be our lives for the next ten years.

"I want a snack," Rose says.

"Grab yourself an apple."

"Dad hasn't been for groceries for two weeks. The apples are all gone."

"Have a banana then."

"They're covered in black spots."

"Find something, Rose. For God's sake, I have to make supper."

"If Mom were here, she'd get mad at you for swearing."

"If Mom were here, I wouldn't have to swear."

I put Cole in his playpen and take the ground beef from the fridge. Mrs. Olyphant has put the frying pan, as well as a pot of water which she's already brought to a boil and turned off, on the stove; steam is rising to the ceiling. The noodles are measured out in a four-cup container on the counter and the can of mushroom soup is opened and sitting beside the noodles.

"Not ground beef casserole," Rose complains. "I'm so sick of that I'll puke if I see it on the table again. And that's something you don't want to see."

I drop the package of meat on the counter. "You make something then."

"Me! I don't know how to cook."

"Well, it's time you learnt. You're not much younger than me. By the time I was your age Mom had already taught me how to make macaroni and cheese and chocolate chip cookies. I'm retiring."

"And if Mom hadn't died, she'd have taught me too. But I guess that ship has sailed. So, since you're the only one of us who can cook, we'll starve if you quit."

"Then quit complaining." I tear open the package of hamburger and begin to stir fry the meat, then turn on the burner to bring the water back to a boil.

"I wonder what Christmas will be like this year," Rose says. "Pretty dismal, I imagine."

I look into the living room remembering the Christmas trees that have stood in the corner, twinkling in the dark.

"It will be fine," I lie as I try to reassure Robin and Fran. "Dad will give me some money and I'll buy a tree and gifts. We'll write the Santa letter in the office just like Mom always did. Santa won't forget about us just because Mom isn't here."

"Want to bet?" Rose says.

"Rose, be quiet." My voice is harsh. Rose hasn't believed in Santa for five years, but this is not the year to spoil it for the others. "Santa will bring us all gifts, just like always."

"I want Mom," Fran says. "I want Mom to make us Christmas cookies, and buy us presents and put up the tree." She wipes her wet cheeks with the heel of her hand.

I have no more time to comfort her, no more time to lie and tell her that everything will be fine. I am not the parent. I'm a thirteen-year-old girl who barely has a friend and who's had the job of raising a family shoved onto her. I pour the noodles into the pot and dump the soup into the ground beef. When the noodles are soft, I pour everything into a casserole dish and slide it into the oven. When it's cooked, I scoop Dad a plateful and pop it in the oven with tinfoil on top. The kids and I clean up the remainder of the casserole as if we hadn't eaten the same meal three days ago. Cole sits in his highchair propped up by pillows and I feed him an entire porridge bowl of rice cereal and banana while eating my supper.

When the meal is done, the little girls play while Fran mops the floor and Rose and I do the dishes. Then I put Alex and Robin to bed and get Fran and Rose sitting together in the office doing their homework. Fran has some cursive letters to practice as she already knows how to print, and she sticks out her tongue as she swirls her pencil over the shapes. Rose complains about having to learn history. She says the world is cursed to repeat itself no matter how much we learn from our past, so learning history is moot. I tell her she's right and learning anything is a waste of time so why doesn't she simply quit school right now. She gives me a patronizing smile and retreats into the office to finish her homework.

It's eight at night and I've finished giving Cole his last bottle. I'm tucking him into bed when the back door opens and Dad shuffles inside. He hasn't worn the winter coat I hung for him in the mud room last night and the shoulders of his thin shirt are caked with snow. I pull his plate out of the oven and set it on the table then tear off the tinfoil. He takes his chair. He's shivering.

"You need to wear your coat, Dad. You're going to get sick dressing like that in this kind of weather."

He picks up his fork and pokes at the casserole, now overheated and dry. His face is gaunt and I wonder if he even goes to the hotel for lunch or simply doesn't eat all day.

"The teacher told Fran that she needs glasses. You have to book her an appointment."

He doesn't answer.

"I tried calling the optometrist this afternoon, you know, the one you and Mom go to? But the receptionist said they needed to talk to an adult. They said they couldn't make the appointment without talking to you."

"They'll have to wait a couple of days. I'm busy all day tomorrow and the next."

"The teacher said Fran can barely see the blackboard."

"Then she'll just have to move her desk closer to the front, won't she?"

"She's already done that, Dad."

He swipes his arm across the table, pushing his supper to the floor. The plate shatters and noodles and ground beef slide across the linoleum. "I told you they'll have to wait."

Cole starts to cry. "See to your brother, Liz." He places his head in his hands.

Startled by the commotion, Rose and Fran have come to the doorway of the office. Fran looks scared. Rose looks pissed off.

"I said, see to your brother, Liz," Dad repeats as Cole's cry becomes frantic.

"No, Dad. You see to your son."

"What did you say?" he shouts.

I speak again, making my voice louder than his. "I said, he's your son, you woke him up, you look after him."

Dad spreads his hands on the table and stands—his cufflink glints green in the ceiling light. Fran retreats into the office. Rose stays where she is, her arms crossed stubbornly over her budding chest.

My voice shakes. "I've been doing everything around here." I say. "I could use a little help. I mean, a thirteen-year-old shouldn't have to pick out underwear for her mother to wear in her coffin or decide if she wants an inexpensive casket for burial and a display casket for the viewing. A thirteen-year-old shouldn't be rushing home to change her brother's diaper or make supper for her sisters. I should be spending time with friends, not arguing with a receptionist at the eye doctor to please make an appointment for my six-year-old sister because my dad is too busy and my mother is dead."

Without hesitation, Dad says, "Well, that's life, kiddo. We all have crap we have to do. Get used to it." He leaves us and closes his bedroom door behind him. He must have picked up Cole as the crying stops.

* * *

"Why can't we put the tree on the sled and make Alex walk?" Rose whines as we struggle up the sidewalk. "It won't hurt her, she's got legs. It's only a few blocks."

"Because we'd get home about midnight?" I say imitating Rose's irritating tone. "You know how slow she's walking these days. I can't carry her that far; she's getting too big."

Alex has reverted to being a baby. She's crawling whenever she has a chance and talking baby talk instead of using words.

"We're not going to get home much before midnight doing it this way," Rose says. "As a matter of fact, I think we won't get home until after midnight. And you can bet your bottom dollar we'll freeze to death out here before Dad misses us. He barely notices anything we do anymore."

Each year for as long as I can remember, on the last day of school before Christmas, me, Mom, and whatever sisters I had at the time, would pick out a Christmas tree from the lot behind Fogg's Grocery Store. We'd put it up and decorate it that afternoon, then when Dad came home from work, he'd put the star on top. We'd eat our evening meal in the living room with only the tree lights to light the room. It's a tradition that I imagine won't be repeated.

This year, after leaving Cole with Mrs. Henderson, the five of us have gone to the tree-lot alone. I brought up the subject with Dad a few weeks ago about buying a tree, but his response was to not bother him about such mundane matters. Not wanting to elicit another outburst, I told the girls we'd get the tree on our own. Conditions at home have deteriorated to the point I barely talk to Dad for fear his temper will flare again.

Alex is on the toboggan and Fran and Robin are tugging her along while Rose and I attempt to carry the tree. Mrs. Henderson offered to take care of Alex as well as Cole, but when the little girl's sobs reached a crescendo pitch, I didn't have the heart to leave her there; both for Alex's throat, and Mrs. Henderson's ears.

Not knowing how much Christmas trees cost, I'd brought six dollars with me but the price list stapled to the fence surrounding the lot said twelve dollars for a tree this size. Mr. Fogg, a short balding man of about forty with an easy-going demeanour, saw me trying to explain to my sisters that I didn't have enough money for a six-foot tree and we'd have to settle for a three-footer this year. The man quick-stepped over to us on his stubby legs and explained that every year he has a prize of a half-price tree, any size, for the hundredth tree sold. This year, he said, our group happened to be his hundredth sale. Fran and Robin jumped up and down and yelled, "We won, we won," while Rose rolled her eyes, recognizing a lie when she heard one.

"Don't drag your end," I say to Rose. "You're tearing branches off."

"Am not. It's you who's not lifting your end high enough."

"If you'd left your camera at home, this would have been easier."

"Quit telling me what to do, you're not my mother." She takes one hand off and opens and closes her fingers. "My hands are getting stiff holding onto this GD frozen trunk. Probably have frost bite when I get home. And my mittens are sticking together from the sap. How am I going to get that off? I'll be sticking to my camera. We should have brought two toboggans."

I drop my end to the ground. "You know, Rose. I've had enough of your grumbling. We'd already be home if you'd put the same energy into carrying this thing as you're doing into complaining." I stop when I realize Rose is right and I do sound like a parent.

Rose opens her mouth, presumably to lip off to me when Mr. Pendergrass strides up.

"Need some help, ladies?"

"No," I say. "We're fine."

"Yes," Rose says. "We could use a hand."

Mr. Pendergrass smiles and takes Rose's end. Then hoisting the entire tree onto his shoulder, he grabs the toboggan with his other hand and begins to lope in the direction of our house. Rose, Fran, Robin, and I run to keep up. Ten minutes later he has the tree, the toboggan, and Alex, deposited in the front porch.

"There you go, girls. Merry Christmas." He doffs his ever-present cap.

Rose stands on the sidewalk and watches as he walks away.

"What are you staring at?" I ask.

"I don't know. There's something familiar about him, that's all."

"Well, duh. Of course, he's familiar. It's Mr. Pendergrass. You've seen him a gazillion times in your life."

"No. That's not what I mean. Something else about him is familiar but I can't put my finger on it." She lifts her camera and snaps a shot.

* * *

We haven't been to church since Mom died. Without her here to push us, we've let the Sunday ritual slide. And knowing Rose would put up a fuss, I haven't had the energy to force everyone to attend. Dad, who used to make sure he had the house to himself Sunday mornings, now doesn't appear to care about our lapse in practicing our faith as he usually gets up before the rest of us and goes to the shop to do God knows what. Because of his indifference about what we do, it's been easy to stay home and play games in our pyjamas, instead of having everyone dressed and out the door by nine in the morning. As Saturdays are filled with errands—grocery shopping which Dad helped with for a few weeks, but now, while Rose watches the kids, I make the trek to Fogg's pulling as much home as I can fit on the toboggan. Laundry which Mrs. Henderson does some of during the week but Rose and I do the rest on Saturday then sort and fold the pile after the kids have gone to bed. Catching up on dishes which Fran has begun doing without me asking, bathing the girls, vacuuming, cleaning the bathroom—I enjoy my one day of semi-rest. But it seems my lack of enthusiasm for taking the kids to church has come to an end.

Every Christmas Mr. Tremblay, whose hobby was wood carving, erected a nativity scene outside the church. Its life-sized occupants he'd carved out of the willow-tree wood near his house, worshiped the baby infant from the first Sunday in December until mid-January. The display has been the highlight of midnight Mass for as long as I've been born and before, and people crowd around to take pictures right up until Father announces the service is about to begin. Much of the excitement has to do with it being Christmas Eve as children and adults alike feel the magic in the air. The rest of the fervour is because on Christmas Eve, the wooden figures come to life when they are replaced with a real sheep, a real donkey, and a real cow, which are tethered inside the stable. There is also a real woman playing Mary, a man playing Joseph, as well as three wise men, various shepherds and angels, and the highlight, a real baby representing baby Jesus. If you're chosen to play one of these roles, it's considered an honour. Refusing is rarely done. You have to be on your death-bed to have a legitimate excuse.

This year, because of the murders, there was a church meeting to decide what should be done about the display. A few of the town's residents suggested the tradition not be observed out of respect for the Tremblay family, but others argued they knew of no better way of honouring them than to keep the tradition alive. It was decided the custom remain, and Mr. and Mrs. Olyphant offered to take over the responsibility of storing and erecting the wooden cut-outs as well as casting town members when the cut-outs were replaced on Christmas Eve.

When Lois asked me if Cole could be Jesus, I said yes, even though my first reaction was to decline. I'd much rather stay home, get the kids to bed with the pretence that if they didn't get to sleep as soon as their heads hit their pillows, Santa wouldn't come. When they were asleep, I was going to put the meagre assortment of gifts Rose and I managed to buy with the money Dad gave me, under the tree that Dad did not help decorate, and go to bed. I doubt Rose or I will dream of sugarplums this year.

I don't know how Mom did it for as long as she did. She seemed to revel in being a mother, never complaining about having too much to do, never overwhelmed by the noise and commotion five girls can cause. There were times she'd even join us in our mayhem, dancing around the kitchen and singing at the top of her lungs. Though when Dad would come home from work, we'd have to settle down. Sometimes we'd still be giggling and he'd get angry, not understanding we weren't laughing at him, but laughing at what we'd been doing moments before he opened the back door. I used to think if he'd let loose once in a while, he might not be so serious about having to work to support a family. Now, with all I have to do, I'm beginning to understand how he feels.

This year, by the time the tree was decorated—which amounted to as much tinsel on the floor and in the girls' hair as on the tree—I was exhausted. I stood on a chair and lifted Alex in the air to put the star on top, then barely got supper on the table. I certainly didn't serve it under the tree like Mom used to do. The star is tilted but no one has bothered to straighten it.

When I think back to the last few weeks of Mom's life, I see how tired she was and I feel terrible I didn't say something. I should have asked her what was wrong, told her to get some rest and I'd look after the kids. At the very least I should have suggested she go to the doctor. I remember her not participating in our water balloon fights or games of hide and seek. She had the best places to hide, like in the pumpkin patch with Rose's orange sweater over her shoulders.

At the time, I put her non-participation down to having had a baby. It never dawned on me she wasn't feeling well. Perhaps she did complain, but being so involved in my own life, I didn't hear. Or perhaps, because it's been three months since her passing, time has fogged my memory. Or perhaps, and this one occurs to me often, she played the martyr and just did not say a word about how she felt when she should have been yelling from the rooftops that she was sick. But one shouldn't speak ill of the dead.

There are two Masses on Christmas Eve, one at 8 o'clock and one at midnight, and Father has said that if you attend either of these, your obligation for Christmas morning is taken care of. At the 8 o'clock Mass, Jesus is replaced by a real baby. Because Cole is Jesus, at supper last night I announced that we would be going to Mass on Christmas Eve this year.

The little girls became excited about staying up late with the hopes they might see Santa as he made his way to our house, while Rose groaned at my pronouncement and said there was no way she was going. She said God had disappointed her this year and she, like Jen, had become an atheist. Science was her God and if she didn't already have friends at the Catholic school, she'd switch to the public-school system. Luckily Dad was still at work or he would have thwacked her on the ear. Even though he won't attend church, I know he isn't an atheist. I've heard him in his room at night asking God why He's forsaken him.

I told Rose that if she didn't attend Mass, then Santa wouldn't bring presents to our house because he would know she was being bad. And while Rose simply snorted at this, Alex, Fran, and Robin got so upset, Rose had no choice but to agree to attend or be the one responsible for ruining Christmas. But that didn't mean she wasn't going to complain.

* * *

"Do I have to wear a hat? I don't want to."

"Just wear a toque, Rose. We have to walk anyhow. You don't have to wear your usual Sunday hat, I don't care."

It's Christmas Eve and Dad has stayed late at work again. I don't know what he could be doing there tonight, but I won't ask. He told me, when last week I got the courage to question him on his whereabouts, that it's not my place to ask why he doesn't come home at meal time. He went on to say that *Since Mom's been gone, I have to look after the sales, the ordering, as well as the books and it takes every waking hour to keep up to everything and if you want to continue to have food on your plate and a roof over your head, this is how it's going to be.* I wanted to say, *tell me about it,* but I kept my mouth closed.

Rose said Mom's death hasn't altered Dad's behaviour one iota and he's exactly the same as when she was alive; still opting out of his parental obligation because it doesn't interest him. I'm inclined to think that because Mom did the majority of the parenting, he simply never learned how, and Dad, being Dad, is afraid of trying and failing. The little girls no longer ask where their father is like they used to when Mom first died.

Rose tugs her toque on. "I think it's dumb that females have to wear hats to church. Men don't. What's wrong with Jesus seeing the top of my head? I should be able to go to church in my birthday suit if I want to. I'm his creation."

"I thought you'd become an atheist?" I say.

"Yeah, well, it seems tonight I have no choice but to pretend to believe. Either that or not get any presents. Not that there's much to be excited about this year." She pulls at the straps of her overalls. "And I'm wearing these." The orange pants are short on her. I suppose the next thing I'll have to do is talk Dad into giving me money to go to Hampton's.

"Wear whatever you want," I say.

"Will Santa be there?" Robin asks.

"No, Santa won't be there," Rose says. "What do you think? He's no...."

"Rose," I say. "Be quiet. It's Christmas Eve, for gosh sakes."

"I was only going to say he's busy flying with his reindeer delivering presents, he doesn't have the time to be involved in this part of Christmas." She zips up her coat then, after tugging on her socks, shoves her feet into her boots. "Look at it this way, Robin. There's two parts to this holiday, the church stuff and the presents stuff. Baby Jesus is the church stuff. We're celebrating His birthday. That's why we're going to church on a Friday night."

"So why do we get presents if we're celebrating His birthday?"

"That's a very good question, Robin. We give gifts because the three wise men gave gifts to the baby Jesus. Frankincense, gold and myrrh. Therefore, in the giving of gifts to each other, we're honouring Jesus."

"So, Santa should be part of the church stuff. He's like the three wise men giving gifts." Robin says. "I'll bet he's there tonight."

"In my experience in attending midnight Mass," Rose continues, "Santa has yet to make an appearance. All that happens is we stand outside in the cold and look at the people in the manger while the donkey and the sheep poop in the hay. Then Father gives a sermon loud enough to be heard over the noise of kids whispering about what Santa is going to bring them, and crying babies wishing they were home in their beds. Mostly I think everyone has forgotten the part about the wise men giving gifts. People only give gifts because they want to get some in return."

I change Cole's diaper because he has to lie in the manger for at least an hour and I don't want him to have a wet bottom outside in the cold. He certainly doesn't look like a newborn anymore, but there's been no other babies born in the town since his birth. Which is odd. Usually the women around here, much like the land, are very fertile. At five months of age Cole can sit by himself for a few moments at a time and can roll over from his back to his tummy and push himself up to his hands and knees. He has not yet figured out how to crawl, thank goodness.

When everyone has their coats and boots on, we troop to the backyard and I sit Alex on the toboggan with Cole—who's dressed in Alex's pink snowsuit, which used to be Robin's which used to be Fran's—balanced on her lap.

It snowed last night, so pulling the sled isn't hard, except for the places people have been eager beavers and already shovelled. Rose and I have always been the ones delegated to shovel in our family, but this winter, with so many other things to do, neither of us have had the time, and the shovel is far too large for Fran to wield around. As a consequence, the sidewalk in front of our house is packed hard with six inches of the white stuff.

Mr. Krieger has shovelled our snow on occasion, but since he's getting older, he sometimes only manages to get his cleared. The man is outside adjusting his Christmas lights, something else I didn't get done, and the sled drops off the edge of snow as we begin to pass their house. "Evening ladies," he says. "Off to Mass, are you?"

"Yes, Mr. Krieger," I say. "Cole's baby Jesus this year."

"Oh my. Maybe I'll take a stroll down and see him in action." He nods at the pink snowsuit. "Kind of looks like a female version of Baby Jesus in that getup, doesn't he?"

I sigh. He does and I hope Mrs. Olyphant has a blue blanket to swaddle him in. Mom was going to buy a blue snowsuit but didn't get around to it before she died. And it never occurred to me that most of the clothes Cole has been wearing these past five months, except for the ones given as baby gifts, have been pink.

Rose says, "There is no documented proof that Jesus is a man. Did you know that, Mr. Krieger?"

Our neighbour looks surprised.

"The Bible may talk of Jesus being a man, but that was written by men, so who's to say they didn't twist the facts? In my opinion, women would be far better at being God, or Prime Minister, or any leader, for that matter."

* * *

A crowd has gathered in front of the manger when we arrive. I lift Cole off Alex's lap and he grins at me. In the past week he's sprouted one tooth on the bottom but I don't recall him being crabby about it. When Alex teethed, the whole town knew. I think Cole, being passed from person to person part of the time, and left in his play-pen or crib the rest of the time, is going to grow up rolling with the punches.

"Liz," Mrs. Olyphant says as she pushes her way through the crowd. "I should have picked you up. I thought your dad would be driving you. I forgot the blue blanket." She sees the pink snowsuit and beings to laugh. "If there were ever a year for a pink Baby Jesus, this is it. Your mom would have been proud." She gives me a hug.

She leads me and my brother through the throng and I lay Cole in the hay. Giggling ensues as flashbulbs pop. I look at Rose.

"You forgot your camera," I say.

"Didn't forget," she says. "Didn't want to take any pictures of my brother playing Jesus. Though now, in his pink snowsuit, I wish I had."

Alex, Robin, and Fran, becoming disinterested in seeing their brother do what he does everyday—kick, grin, and be the centre of attention—have left the crowd and are standing behind us looking up. Fran starts to shout.

"I see him, it's Santa. I see him!" She raises her yellow mittened hand to the sky. "Up there, it's Santa, I know it is."

The crowd, including Mary, and Joseph, the angels, shepherds, and wise men, wander out of the stable. Fifty heads look to where my sister is pointing. A few parishioners begin to murmur things like, *"What the hell,"* and *"In God's blazes, what's that,"* when I too spot Santa and his reindeer, flying higher than Mrs. Witherspoon's fence. He has his hand in the air as if waving to the crowd below, and is calling *ho, ho, ho* as he sails upward. Some of the children wave in return while Santa and his reindeer remain aloft, then just as quickly pull their hands back as the red suited man plummets to the earth. A puff of smoke rises above the top of the fence before we hear the sizzling sound of water putting out the flames and Mrs.

Witherspoon's disembodied voice cursing loudly. The children in the crowd start to scream that Santa is dead. Suddenly I realize what this is.

"It's Mrs. Witherspoon's Christmas decoration," I shout. "I saw her making it last summer. She built a roller coaster for Santa to ride on. He was supposed to jump from one track to another. Looks like he must have crashed."

Most of the people laugh about eccentric Mrs. Witherspoon, but a few complain that her yard is a disgrace and she should be made to clean it up. I turn back to the manger. Cole is not lying in the hay.

"Cole," I shout. "Has anyone seen my brother?" I run into the display. "Cole, where are you?"

Mr. Pendergrass calls to me over the heads of people from the other side of the manger. He has Cole in his arms and is stroking his cheeks while Cole smiles like the Baby Jesus into the man's face. I rush up to them.

"Found him trying to crawl over to the donkey," he says. "Probably would have made it too, if not for this snow suit. Thought I'd better rescue him before he was stepped on. He had a Guardian Angel watching over him tonight, that's for sure." He hands my brother to me.

"Thanks, Mr. Pendergrass."

"My gift to you," he says. "Merry Christmas to you and your sisters."

Rose stands by my side and watches him walk away. "Remind you of anyone?" she asks.

"Who, Mr. Pendergrass?"

"Couldn't think of it when he carried our Christmas tree home, but tonight, it hit me. He looks like Jen's ghost."

CHAPTER TWENTY

Instead of Mrs. Olyphant greeting us after school, a strange woman stands in front of our stove stirring something in one of Mom's pots. Steam rises from the pot as she lifts the spoon to her lips then adds a couple shakes of salt from the shaker on the back of the stove. Alex and Robin sit at the kitchen table colouring while this woman holds Cole, who plays with the apron string tied around her neck. The apron, printed with pictures of raspberries, was Mom's favourite because it reminded her of us; her raspberry patch.

The moment Alex sees me, she jumps down from her chair and runs to my legs. I pick her up. She wraps her arms around my neck and squeezes hard. "Izzy, Izzy," she says.

"You know how to say my name, Alex. Don't talk baby talk."

"You must be Liz," the woman says as she wipes her hands on the apron. "I'm Patricia Gillespie. You can call me Pat if you like, or Mrs. Gillespie. Whatever you're comfortable with. I thought your dad would be here to introduce me, but he seems to have stepped outside." She looks towards the living room. "He's hired me to cook the meals, do housework and babysit you and your sisters. And, of course, Cole, here." She pinches my brother on his chubby cheek and when Cole smiles at this stranger, I feel a pang of jealousy.

Rose has kicked off her boots and is padding her way across the kitchen floor in her bare feet. Her mouth drops. "We have a babysitter?" she asks.

Dad opens the front door and a waft of cold air enters along with him. He has the mail in his hands. "Girls," he says. "You're home. This is Mrs. Gillespie, your babysitter."

The woman nods. "I'll arrive at seven in the morning and stay until Cole is in bed at night."

Rose shouts, "What the hell, Dad?"

"Quit swearing, Rose," he says. "I can't be in two places at once. I have to work. It costs money to raise six kids."

"And you'd rather pay someone to look after your own children, than pay someone to work more hours at the store?" On her way up the stairs she screams, "I hate you!"

Dad yells after Rose to put on her slippers before she gets chilblains, as she pounds down the hall, slamming the bedroom door behind her. "Sorry about that, Patricia," he says and I wonder if he even realizes the babysitter has the same name as Mom. "Rose is a bit high-strung."

The words come out of my mouth before I can stop myself. "Rose is not high-strung," I say. "Being her father, you think you'd realize she's the most level-headed person in this family. She might be outspoken, and react to situations too quickly, but the last thing she is, is high-strung!" By the time I'm done talking, I'm shouting.

"That's enough, Liz."

"No, Dad, it isn't. You think because you lost your wife, you can do whatever you want. Show up for a meal, don't show up for a meal. Help around the house, don't help out. Discipline the girls or let me look after it. You've missed three birthdays so far; Rose's, Alex's and Robin's. And now this? You should have talked to us about what you had in mind, asked us what we thought." Alex buries her face in the collar of my sweater. "Rose and I are more than capable of looking after ourselves. We don't need a babysitter. We need a parent."

Dad steps forward and I'm afraid he's going to slap me. Instead, he pries Alex from around my neck. Then, pushing Fran and Robin ahead of him, he takes the girls upstairs.

I stare at the woman. "Dad didn't need to hire you. We're fine on our own."

"He told me you said you could use a bit of help. That you've been doing everything alone."

"I meant I wanted him to help." I hold my hands out to Cole. He comes to me easily.

In the quiet we hear Dad telling Alex to stay in bed until she calms down. I imagine her gulping for air as she tries to control her sobs and I want to run to her and hug her to my chest.

He descends the stairs and joins us in the kitchen.

"Listen, Mr. Murphy," Mrs. Gillespie says. "I didn't mean to step on anyone's toes. Perhaps this wasn't such a good idea."

"You didn't step on anyone's toes," Dad says. "I've hired you to look after my children, make the meals and do housework, and that's what you're going to do whether they object or not." He speaks to me. "Before Christmas you said you wanted some help, so I got you some help. Both Lois and Elva have been hounding me that you're doing too much. Now, here I am trying to do the right thing, and all you can do is embarrass me and embarrass Mrs. Gillespie. I have to get back to work. I want you and your sisters to take down the Christmas tree before you go to bed tonight. It's two weeks past Christmas already!" He enters the mud room and puts on his boots and winter coat. "Mind your manners and do what Mrs. Gillespie tells you," he says before he slams the door behind him.

Mrs. Gillespie's face is red. "You know, I'm going to have enough to do with a baby and three young girls to look after. If you and your sister, the one who ran upstairs...."

"Rose," I say.

"If you and Rose promise to be responsible young ladies, you don't have to come to me about every little thing. If it's important, I'll be glad to help. If you need me, ask. But if you're alright on your own, as I imagine you are, that's fine by me. We just won't tell your dad."

In bed after supper, which was roast beef, potatoes and gravy, and cauliflower with cheese sauce, the best meal we've had since Christmas at the Olyphant's, I tell Rose what Mrs. Gillespie said. "Looks like you finally got the independence you've been wanting."

"Huh. I don't know how I feel about that. It's kind of weird not being wanted."

"Don't say that, Rose. Dad wants us. He's overwhelmed. Raising a family is not an easy job."

"You got that right," Rose says. "I don't know why I'm surprised that he's hired someone to do it for him."

"Quit talking like that. Dad loves his kids."

"Hey, don't you think it's kind of weird the babysitter has the same name as Mom?"

"I'm hoping it's a coincidence."

CHAPTER TWENTY-ONE

"Where are you going?" Rose asks.

"Out with Jen." I turn my head away from the bathroom mirror.

Rose peers around me. "What's that on your face? Lipstick?"

"What if it is? I'm old enough to wear makeup. Everyone does."

"Not everyone. Only the girls who want to be noticed by boys."

"No," I say, my voice rising. "I'm wearing it because it looks nice. It's what all the popular girls wear."

"And you know why they're popular, right?"

"Because they're smart and funny."

"Give me a break," Rose says. "They're popular because they do what boys ask them to do. I believe the term is *putting out.*"

I can't believe the words my sister has learned. Without Mom to monitor her reading material, she's buying whatever she wants at Woolworths.

"They do not!" I say. "They're popular because they're pretty and outgoing. What do you know about that anyway?"

Rose throws her hands in the air. "Have it your way. And I know more than you think. Mom explained everything to me last year. She must have had a premonition."

"All I know is, Jen invited me to go out with her and her friends, and I accepted. I've been stuck here for too long. It's time to expand my horizons, grow up a little. Aren't I supposed to rebel and get into trouble?" I brush my hair into a ponytail. "You wouldn't understand. You don't have raging hormones yet."

"I thought you said they were snobs? I thought you didn't like them because they were stuck-up and rude?"

"Well, maybe I was wrong. Maybe they're simply more mature

than me."

"There's been talk on the playground," Rose says.

"And what are you kiddies talking about? How to swing the highest, or run the fastest? How to make the best snow-angel?"

"That's so funny I forgot to laugh." Her eyes meet mine in the mirror. "I've heard Jen's name mentioned when I pass groups of kids."

"Jen?" I pinch my cheeks then put my brush in the vanity drawer. Mom's makeup is at the back of this drawer, but I've not touched it since she died. "Why would kids from your school be talking about Jen? She didn't even go to Saint Mary's."

"Same playground, same gossip; you know that. I heard talk about a gang led by Holly Black, and they're trying to get your friend to join them."

"Jen isn't in a gang," I say. "Unless you call a group of girls who are friends, a gang."

"Not that I care what Jen does," Rose says, "because I don't. I only hope, since you seem all fired up to stay friends with her, that I don't pass the merry-go-round some recess and hear them talking about you."

"I don't need my sister, who only recently turned twelve, to look out for me, someone who turns fourteen next week." I pull my eyes from hers in the mirror. "Jeepers creepers, Rose. You're making a big deal out of nothing. I'm reaching out, making new friends. Mom told me I needed to move forward and that's what I'm doing. What am I supposed to do, hang out with you for the rest of my life?"

"What these girls want you to do to be accepted into their group is not *moving forward*. And I don't mean this as a criticism of your friend, but don't you think it's weird they're allowing Jennifer Olsen into their group? She has no money, no nice clothes, no popular friends. Her mom doesn't own her own business. Jen hasn't anything those girls are interested in other than friendship and that's not what they're after. And if you meet them today, they're going to want something from you too."

"You don't know anything. I'm meeting them at two. Gotta go."

In the hall, Alex approaches me sucking her thumb. "Up, Izzy, up," she says.

"I'm busy," I say. "And take your thumb out of your mouth. You're not a baby like Cole. You're three years old now."

Tears drip down my youngest sister's cheeks and Rose bends to pick her up. "I know I'm only twelve years old," Rose says, "but even I can see that you and I are more mature than any of these, so called, popular girls, will ever be."

* * *

Jen and her friends are waiting for me at the end of the block in front of Mrs. Seamer's. They're whispering behind their mittens as I approach. Holly steps forward.

"You're late," she says. "What were you doing, reading a book?" She laughs at her own joke.

"I had to talk to my sister. She's been...." I stop when I see them start to snicker. "Our Mom died a few months ago and she misses her." They stop snickering.

"Let's get out of here," Holly says, "before we all start to cry."

There are five of us in this procession and I fall in at the end of the line. The snow-plough was down the highway last week, one of the few times it's ploughed during the winter months, but the old road is reliant on local traffic, and people walking to Gas-n-Go to keep it passable. As a consequence, the shoulder we're on is packed with snow and the path, only one person wide, forcing us to walk in a single line. Jen slows her gait and whispers over her shoulder.

"What are you doing? Trying to make a fool of me? Quit talking about your dead mother, for God's sake!"

We turn in at the driveway, enter Gas-n-Go, and follow Holly to a booth. Each of the girls slide across the seat filling up both sides, and being the last in line, I have no place to sit.

I attempt to grab a chair. "It's taken," the boy sitting at the table, says.

"No, it's not," I say.

He lifts his legs and places his feet on the chair. "Now it is," he says and laughs.

An employee approaches. "You can't take up two seats." He pulls the chair out from under the boy's feet and places it at the end of the booth crowded with my companions.

Holly speaks. "Now that we're all finally sitting, we need to fill the newcomer in on what she has to do to join our group."

"My name is Liz," I say.

Holly continues as if I've not spoken. "There's an initiation before you can be seen with us around the school. See if you're someone we want to associate with."

"What do you do? Blindfold me while I eat grapes you tell me are eyeballs, or spaghetti you tell me are worms?"

She shakes her head. "No, our initiation is a little more sophisticated than that."

I laugh, thinking she's joking, but the look on her face is so serious, I wonder if what Rose said about them was right.

The waitress arrives to take our orders. She's a matronly woman who's worked here for decades. Her voice is gravelly as she repeats our orders of Cokes while scrawling on her order form.

When she's gone, Holly says, "We want you to take something. From a store. Something that doesn't belong to you."

"You want me to shoplift?" I say too loudly for Holly's liking.

"Keep your voice down," she scolds. She turns to Jennifer. "Is your friend stupid or something?" She turns back to me. "It's not that difficult, at least not for you."

"What do you mean, not for me?"

"Well," she looks around the table trying to stifle her laughter. "You can walk in and not be suspected of anything."

"Why wouldn't I be suspected if I'm stealing?"

She can't hold it in any longer and begins to laugh. Each high-pitched squeal is followed by a snort that sounds so ridiculous coming from such a pretty face, I almost laugh along with her. Her friends look the other way. "Because, silly," Holly is finally able to say, "we want you to steal something from your dad's store. He's not going to be suspicious of you like he is of us. The moment we walk in, he watches us like we're a gang of thieves. I ask you; do we look like thieves?" She bats her eyes and places her hand against her cheek. "Anything will do. A hammer, a paint brush, a handful of nails, it doesn't matter. As long as you come out of the store with something you didn't pay for or your dad didn't give to you. And," she adds, "that he doesn't know you have. All you have to do is go to say hi then slip something into your pocket. Easy-peasy."

"I want to go home," I say.

"I want to go home," Holly mimics. She reaches towards my face. "Look at you with the pink lipstick smeared all over your baby mouth. Baby Face Murphy. That's what I'm going to call you. Some-one needs to teach you how to put makeup on properly."

I push her hand away and stand up. "I'm not stealing anything from Dad's store. I'm not that desperate for a friend."

Holly's face has turned red. "If you say anything to your dad about this, you'll have no friends left to your name. I'll bad-mouth you to every student from the most popular to the lowest of the low. No one will want to be seen with you, I can promise you that. And when I say bad-mouth, you won't believe the stuff I can come up with."

I leave, Jen follows. "Nice friends you have," I say as we stand outside Gas-n-Go.

Jen looks at her boots. "Sorry, I didn't know what she was going to ask you to do."

"Give me a break! Even Rose warned me. I told you last summer I didn't trust them. I don't know why I came here today."

"It's a handful of nails. That's not so bad," Jen says. "Your dad won't miss them."

"That's not the point! It's still stealing. I don't want any part of this. I don't understand why you want them to be your friends."

"You're right, you don't understand. You with the money for anything you want. You with sisters who will always be there for you. You with the good grades and the green eyes. Me, I'm just a skinny kid with no money, passable looks, and hand-me-down clothes from my mother." She waves her hand at me. "Of course, you wouldn't understand."

"Money for anything I want!" I say. "Obviously you haven't been to our house lately. Don't do this. Please, Jen. Come home with me. We can talk about boys like we used to. We can even go to The Park and you can have a cigarette if you want. I still have them in my drawer."

Jen says nothing. I turn to leave.

She grabs my arm. "Wait, Liz. Don't go."

"I'll stay if you leave those losers. If you're going to be friends with them, count me out."

She hesitates.

"Goodbye," I say and walk away. I turn around once and see her re-entering the restaurant.

* * *

I plod along the shoulder of the old road, not even stopping to watch the rabbits as they chase each other across the field. When I reach my street, I run the rest of the way home. Mrs. Gillespie is in the kitchen.

"Where's Rose," I ask.

"She left right after you with that camera of hers. Don't know what she could find to take pictures of today."

"Do you know where she was going?" I ask.

"No idea. She said she had something to do and she'd be home in a few hours. That's all I know."

Without taking off my boots and coat, I leave the house to look for Rose. At The Park, I scan the kids faces as they slide down the toboggan hill. Rose is not among them. I pass between the schools, then peer down the road towards the Drummond's to see if she's hiding in the ditch taking pictures, but don't see her. I walk past the businesses on Main Street and look through the window of Woolworths where she buys her photo albums and film, but she's not there. Finally, I make my way to Jen's street, and see her standing in front of Mr. Pendergrass's house.

"Hey, Rose," I say. "Whatcha doing?"

She turns. "You wouldn't do their little initiation?"

"How did you know?" I ask.

She snaps the shutter then points the camera at a different part of the house. "I told you, I hear things," she says.

"Guess I should have listened to you."

Rose takes out her notebook. "Here, let me jot down that hell has just frozen over."

"Haha, very funny."

Rose puts her arm around my shoulders. "You can follow me around if you want. We're sisters; I'm not allowed to desert you."

"Thanks," I say, looking at the toes of my boots.

She lifts her instamatic and snaps a few shots of Mr. Pendergrass's house.

"Why are you taking pictures of Mr. Pendergrass's house?"

"While you've been busy trying to find yourself, I've developed a theory."

"About what?"

"Tell you later."

Across the street, Sister Veronica has been chatting the ear off a neighbour of Jen's and she now begins to cross the road towards us. Even though she has her habit pulled up to her knees, there's bits of mud splashed on the hem and I wonder, not for the first time, if nuns have a multitude of the black dresses lining the rods in their closets. She arrives in front of Rose and me then drops the edge of her habit to the ground and brushes out the wrinkles.

"Hi, girls." She points a gloved hand at Rose's camera. "Gorgeous day for picture taking."

"Yes, Sister, it is," Rose says.

Sister Veronica stands tall with dark eyes, clear skin, and a face that's beautiful without makeup. I wipe my mitten across my mouth leaving a pink streak on the navy wool.

"Look at that blue sky and frost on the branches of the trees. Great photographic subject matter. The world is a wonderous place, is it not?" She sighs with delight as she looks around her. "What are you taking pictures of today, young lady?" she asks Rose.

"Plants that have rotted off with the cold, muddy tire tracks. Close ups of the decaying leaves frozen to the ground. You know, artsy stuff." She snaps a few shots of the road.

Sister Veronica taught Rose in grade four so knows her well. "Everything is God's creation, I suppose," she says without missing a beat. She faces Mr. Pendergrass's house. "Mr. Pendergrass certainly does have the tidiest yard in town. Even in the winter it looks neat and trim with not a thing out of place." She looks at Rose. "If you like the disorderly style of pictures, you're not going to find it pointing your camera in that direction."

"I was thinking of doing a comparative study. Disorderly as opposed to neat and tidy."

"Very interesting," Sister says. "You should probably ask permission first. Perhaps Mr. Pendergrass doesn't want his house to be photographed."

"Yes, Sister," Rose says.

"I'm off to the grocery store," she says as she once again pulls the hem of her habit high exposing the black stockings underneath. "Sister Rebecca needs her skim milk. She insists it helps her lose weight, but if you ask me, it hasn't made a lick of difference. God's plan for that woman was simply to be on the plump side." She giggles then puts her finger across her lips. "Don't tell her I said that, now."

"No, Sister," we say in unison.

When the woman has toddled out of sight, Rose turns her attention back to Mr. Pendergrass's house. She snaps a few more pictures. "Let's go," she says. "I've something to tell you."

Rose and I hike to our side of town and pass our house where I see Mrs. Gillespie standing on a chair as she dusts the ceiling light in the living room. The girls are standing beside the chair their heads craned back, watching her. We stop in front of Mrs. Seamer's.

"I think Mr. Pendergrass knows more than he's telling," Rose says.

"What do you mean?"

"I think he thinks the murderer is someone we know. Either that or he is the murderer."

"Mr. Pendergrass thinks we know who the murderer is?" I say.

Rose stomps on my toe.

"Ow," I shout. "Why'd you do that?"

"Because that's not what I said. I said, he thinks the murderer is someone we know."

"Ok," I draw out the word. "What makes you think that he thinks the murderer is someone we know?"

"He's been hanging around us since last summer. He rescued Fran from the tree, although that might have been luck that he was there at the right time. But he did save Cole at Christmas and he was there when you and Jen walked home from the school dance when he told you to go home. He carried our Christmas tree home like he'd been watching us, and I believe it was him at the window last Halloween. The one who told me to keep my eyes open."

"That could have been your imagination," I say. "Jen had been talking about ghosts and Fran was scared out of her mind."

"I'm not that easily swayed by others," Rose says.

I pick up a handful of snow and squeeze it into an icy ball. "He has shown up at times when we needed help, that's for sure. What makes you think he's the murderer?"

"He's trying to throw me off his trail."

"Huh?" I say.

"Think about it. What better way to hide in plain sight than to pretend to be looking out for our safety? He told you last summer that I needed to be careful about who I talk to. Maybe he's worried I'm going to figure something out. And," she says, "what about Mrs. Witherspoon's prophecy? She told Mr. Pendergrass he'd become famous after he died. There's nothing like giving a deathbed confession in order to become famous."

"Just because some old lady said Mr. Pendergrass would become famous after he died that makes him the murderer?" I turn towards Mrs. Seamer's house and see her in her living room window. She waves at us and we wave back then move further down the road.

"I'll concede that you were right about Holly Black wanting more than friendship from me, and you may be right about Mr. Pendergrass looking out for us, but you're not right about him being the murderer. I think when he told me that you should be careful about who you talk to, he was genuinely worried."

"Remember when the Tremblays were alive and their yard was always a mess with toys, gardening tools, dog poop, oil cans, cardboard boxes; nothing was ever picked up, thrown out, or put away?" She points in the direction of the yard that has since been cleaned up. "It could have drove Mr. Pendergrass crazy. Went berserk and killed them all."

"You think the mess drove him crazy?" I say. "No one commits murder because someone's yard is messy. Mrs. Witherspoon would have been knocked off years ago if that was the case. You can do practically whatever you want to your yard in a small town and no one says a thing. You're simply considered quirky."

"Ok, ok. So that's not a probable scenario. I just know he's on my list of possible assailants. He still goes to the Tremblay's every day. I've hidden in the ditch and seen him staring at their house. He watches for a while, then he turns around and comes back to town."

"So, he's different. I heard Dad tell Mom last summer that he thinks Mr. Pendergrass is an odd duck. You need to quit spying on people, Rose. One day someone will find out you are snooping on them and get mad."

"Never happen. I'm too good at what I do."

"You know you're a twelve-year-old kid, right?"

"Who's going to be a forensic photographer when she grows up. I've been reading all about them. They go to crime scenes and take pictures and deduce theories. Do you know there's something called a body farm? That's a place where unidentified dead people are left under specific conditions for scientific study later. Frost, rain, heat, bugs. Then the bodies are monitored daily. You can tell how long someone has been dead by studying how fast they decompose. I've already begun my own studies. When Mom would trim a roast before she cooked it, I'd steal the leftover blood and scraps of meat.

I've even taken some of the ground beef you're so fond of cooking to determine how long it takes the blood to congeal and the meat to rot and maggots appear. I keep the samples in a one-quart sealer in a cupboard in the basement."

"That's really gross, Rose."

She looks into the distance. "There's something else," she says.

"What?"

"I made a discovery while I was in the basement. I was checking on my meat then stopped to look at our measurements, you know, where Mom marked our heights from year to year on the side of that old cabinet? When I looked up to see if I'm taller than last year, I saw something hanging over the edge. It was Dad's grade twelve yearbook. There's pictures of Mr. Pendergrass and Mrs. Tremblay together, of the four of them, actually."

Rose has grown recently; last summer she wouldn't have been able to look me in the eye and I realize how much time has passed since Mom died and how much of our lives she's missed. "The four of them?"

"Mr. Pendergrass, Mr. Drummond, Marjorie Hampton who became Mrs. Tremblay," she says, "and Dad. They were all friends with Mrs. Tremblay in high school." She's quiet for a moment. "Have you ever wondered why Dad didn't stay friends with any of them after high school? He never went to visit the Tremblays when they were alive. He never goes to the Drummond's. And last summer when Dad had the neighbourhood men over to have a drink after Cole was born, that's the very first time I remember Mr. Pendergrass ever being at our house. I'm thinking there was some sort of competition between the three boys to have Marjorie as their girlfriend. I think they all had a crush on her and that's what broke them apart. And don't forget, both Dad's family and Marjorie Hampton's family were wealthy. And love, jealousy, or money, sometimes all three, are always the reasons murder is committed in books."

CHAPTER TWENTY-TWO

The cold wind blows causing our scarves to sail behind us like flags. The walk home from school is hurried as the temperature is well below freezing. We don't even stop to make snow angels in The Park like we sometimes do. Everything, as far as the eye can see, is frozen six feet into the ground. February on the prairies.

Rose gets to the door first and we hustle inside. "Mrs. Gillespie," she shouts. "We're home. Alex, Robin, where are you?" No one answers. "What are you guys doing, playing hide-and-go-seek?"

The kitchen lights are on, the furnace is running, and the television is tuned to *The Littlest Hobo*. "This is weird," I say. "Dad would never allow Mrs. Gillespie to go out and leave everything on. You know how frugal he is."

A tea towel covers a bowl of bread dough that has risen too high and now sags onto the counter. Vegetables that were being chopped into salad are strewn on the kitchen table, the task left unfinished. I walk over to the mess.

"She left in a hurry," I say. "What's this? Raspberry dressing?"

Rose leans close and sniffs. She picks up a spoon and dabs a splatter. "This is blood. My guess, it's been here a couple of hours. Kind of sticky but not real wet."

"Blood?" I frantically look around and notice a trail of red drops leading to the front door. My eyes lift to the living room window—my heart is pounding—and see Mrs. Henderson hurrying out her front door. She's carrying Cole in her arms and holding Alex's hand while Robin crosses the street unaided. None of them have on winter coats. "There's the kids," I say. Rose flings open the front door.

"What happened, Mrs. Henderson?" I grab Alex and spin her

to me. "Are you hurt?" I reach for Robin. "Did you get cut, sweet-heart?"

"No, no, child," Mrs. Henderson says. "Your sisters are alright. Mrs. Gillespie cut herself. Your dad took her to the doctor for stitches."

I sag to my knees and hug Alex and Robin close.

"Mrs. Gillespie was crying," Robin says. "She chopped off her finger."

"She chopped off her finger?"

"Just the tip," Mrs. Henderson says. "Not the entire thing. Your dad came home from work in the middle of the day, which he never does and scared her to death. He'd apparently been cleaning out the basement at the hardware store and his clothes and face were covered with dirt. Well, you know how particular your dad is about his looks. Pat was cutting up carrots when he came barrelling in the house to clean up. She looked up just as the knife went down. Cut off the top of her index finger on her left hand. Could have been worse. At least she didn't cut off her entire finger. Would have scared me too if I'd been Patricia."

I take Cole from her arms. "When do you think they'll get back?"

"I don't know. I only know your dad said to bring the kids back when you got home from school, so here they are." She looks me in the eyes. "I'm sure they'll be home soon, don't worry. Everyone's alright. Kids were a bit frightened at first, what with all the blood, but I played eye-spy with them and they calmed down."

"Thanks, Mrs. Henderson."

I lay Cole in his playpen and hand him his milk. He's learned how to hold onto his own bottle at a younger age than Alex did and I have to think this is only because he has no choice—either hold his own bottle or go thirsty. I'm mopping the blood off the floor when the back door opens and I glance up. Dad is standing in the doorway of the mud room. His face is streaked with dirt, and his coat, covered in dust. Not wanting to cause a fight, I don't say anything. But Rose, who is coming around the corner, doesn't hold back.

"What happened to you? You look like a pig who's rolled in the mud."

"Took a load of garbage from the store to the dump," Dad says. "Mrs. Gillespie will be off work for a few days, back next week. Elva is coming over tomorrow to look after the girls and Cole. She'll leave when you get home from school." He looks at his watch. "Need to shower and get back to the store. Don't expect me home before you go to bed."

After he's gone Rose says, "I've never known Dad to do that job in the winter. He's always complained that the backhoes this town uses aren't big enough to dig holes when the ground is frozen six feet down. He always waits to clean the basement until spring."

CHAPTER TWENTY-THREE

It's Saturday, bath day for the three youngest and Mrs. Gillespie sent Rose and me to the drugstore to buy shampoo. It's been three weeks since she cut off the top of her finger, and last Tuesday the bandage came off and the stitches came out. When she arrived at our house, we all gathered around to marvel at the jagged scar where the end is missing. She says it doesn't hurt but sometimes I see her massaging the shortened appendage or wrapping it in a wet facecloth she's heated in the oven.

With money for shampoo in hand, Rose and I left the house in the early afternoon, but after we made our purchase, we stopped at the school rink so Rose could snap a few shots of the kids learning to skate before the daylight began to fade. Consequently, by the time we arrive home, it's already four. Dad, whom we haven't seen much of since Mrs. Gillespie's accident, is next door talking to Mr. Krieger. The sun is low in the sky and the two of them are standing in the last of its winter warmth on his perfectly shovelled sidewalk.

"The police finally issued an arrest warrant for Drummond," Dad says. "Found some evidence in his backyard. It's about time, is all I can say."

I pick up the broom and sweep the snow from the front step while Rose brushes off the windowsill and handrails with her mittens, both of us stalling our entry into the house.

"What did they find?" Mr. Krieger asks.

"The gun used in the killings."

"My God," Mr. Krieger says.

"What did he say?" I whisper.

Rose shushes me.

"How do they know it's the same gun?"

"They compared the bullets they took out of the Tremblays bodies to ones they fired from the gun they found. I guess they matched."

"Where was he stashing it?" Mr. Krieger says.

"In the rafters of a shed next to their house," Dad answers. "Wrapped in a quilt."

"You'd think they would have already searched his property."

"Couldn't. There was never any evidence giving them cause."

"What made them look in the shed now, after all these months?"

"I reported some inventory missing. And because he's broken into the store before, that was enough for the police to get a warrant to search his house and property," Dad says. "Found the gun, along with the stolen merchandise hidden all over the shed. Guess living in the bush can do things to your mind, make you lose the ability to think clearly."

"They found the gun?" I ask Rose.

"He's being set up," she says. "Someone under suspicion of murder would never hide the murder weapon on his property. He'd take it out to the middle of a lake and drop it to the bottom, or toss it in the landfill where it would never be found. The last thing he'd do would be to hide it in a place that would implicate him. I don't care how mixed up he is."

Dad looks at Rose and I, then puts his hand on our neighbour's shoulder and together they walk up the sidewalk, closer to the Krieger's front door. They're not in the sunlight anymore and the distance and gloom, muffles their voices.

"You read too many murder mysteries," I say to Rose. "There's a lot of stupid criminals in the world. The police wouldn't have charged Mr. Drummond unless they were sure."

"But you heard Dad. They only searched the shed because he told them there'd been merchandise stolen from the store."

"What are you saying?"

"Not saying anything," Rose says. "Could be Mr. Drummond is guilty and he really did kill the Tremblays and steal from Dad, then was crazy enough to stash the items in his own shed. Or," she says, "it could be someone else stole the items and hid them at the Drummond's. They knew he'd be suspected because he's stolen from Dad before and the cops would have cause to search his place. Who knows?"

Rose and I finish clearing the snow before entering the house.

Mrs. Gillespie balances Cole on one hip and a jar of beets that Mom canned two summers ago, on the other. I rush forward and take my brother from her before she drops one, the other, or both.

"Can you bathe the girls for me?" she asks me. "They can eat supper in their pyjamas."

"I guess," I say. She sets down the sealer and I pass Cole back to her. "Come on, Rose. Give me a hand."

"She didn't ask me," Rose says.

"Haven't you missed them? We haven't been around them much lately." I point at Alex and Robin playing on the living room floor. Fran is curled up on the couch, her nose deep in a book. "Come on," I prod. "It'll be fun."

With Rose lagging behind, the five of us troop upstairs to the bathroom. Fran lies on her bed to continue reading while I fill the tub. Rose takes off the little girls' clothes.

"Alex," Rose exclaims. "Where's your diaper?"

"Patricia says I'm a big girl now." I hadn't noticed till then that she's not talking baby talk like she was a month ago. "I go to the bathroom on the toilet like my sisters," Alex says. "I don't need to wear a diaper. They're for babies like Cole."

"And I can count to twenty," Robin says. "Mrs. Gillespie taught me how." She demonstrates her skill, missing numbers seven and thirteen. "And I have all my baby teeth." She pulls at her lips, making a face to show us her white smile.

Rose and I look at each other wondering if we'd have missed this much if Mom hadn't died. I think Mom would have ensured we were involved. Family was everything to her.

I help Robin into the tub while Rose lifts Alex and sits her in the water. The two of them giggle and splash in the bubbles for fifteen minutes, then with more water on the floor than what is left in the tub, we take them out and dry them off. They run to their bedroom to get their pyjamas on and I call Fran for her turn.

"I can do it myself," she says to me. "I don't want you watching. And I prefer showers to baths now. Mrs. Gillespie says I do a really good job of washing my own hair."

"Ok," I say. "Call if you need help."

She doesn't call and ten minutes later is scrubbed clean and in her own pyjamas.

* * *

In the living room as we wait for supper, while Fran, Alex, and Robin play dolls in front of the television, Rose bombards Dad with questions. It will be the first time he's eaten a meal with his children in over a month.

"What were you and Mr. Krieger talking about, Dad?" Rose asks.

"Not your concern."

"Do they think Mr. Drummond is the murderer?"

"Like I said, it's not your concern."

Rose doesn't give up. "They found stolen items from your store in his shed?"

"They did."

"And the gun used in the murder?"

"Yes, Rose."

"I think they've charged the wrong man," Rose says. "I think Mr. Drummond is being set up. I've been developing my own theory these last few weeks."

Dad, who's been attempting to read the newspaper, lowers the pages and peers overtop. I'm sure he'd like to ask his daughter what her theory is, but either he doesn't want to encourage her to keep asking questions or he's afraid of what her theory will be. He says nothing.

"You and Mr. Drummond were friends in high school, right?" Rose asks.

"I was, Rose. I was also friends with Mrs. Tremblay, Mr. Pendergrass, Mr. and Mrs. Henderson, Mr. Fogg and Mr. Krieger. Like I told the police, it's a small town, I know just about everyone. I was born and raised here."

Rose is quiet. I can practically hear her brain whipping up a plan. "It's a nice night, not as cold as it has been. I think I'll get my skates up from the basement after supper," she says.

I frown at her. Rose has never liked ice skating. Biking on the country roads where she can leave a dust trail behind her for miles, she loves. Skateboarding up and down every sidewalk in town, she adores. Even sitting on the toboggan then screaming with joy all the way down the hill at the north end of The Park, she's crazy about. But bundling up in her winter coat and ski pants then slapping some blades on her feet just to travel in an endless oval, she hates.

"I'll go with you," I say. "I haven't skated yet this winter."

"I'll be fine on my own," she says.

"I insist. I'm coming with you. It's more fun to skate with someone else, than to skate alone." I put my arm around her shoulder. "We'll have some sisterly time together. Besides," I say, "I love *The Skaters' Waltz*."

Rose sticks her finger in her mouth and pretends to gag.

"Supper's ready," Mrs. Gillespie calls from the doorway.

* * *

"So, what's up with the skating lie?" I ask. The sound of the snow under our boots, crunches in the cold night.

The long laces of our skates are tied together to form a loop that hangs around our necks and the skate guards clack together on our chests as we walk. Two years ago, Rose's skates belonged to me, as is the case with much of Rose's clothes, coats and shoes, which she's never hesitated to complain about as her taste in just about everything is far different than mine. But the skates, she never said boo about because she knew she wouldn't be using them very much.

"Not a lie," she says. "I said I was getting my skates up from the basement, and I did. Never said anything about using them."

"I take it we're not going skating?" I say.

"Since when have you known me to go skating voluntarily? I only went when Mom made me help Fran. Dad couldn't care less if I skate. Or swim or bike or go to school for that matter."

"I think he'd be upset if he found out you were playing hooky." I stop walking, Rose does not. I say to her retreating back. "You haven't been playing hooky, have you?"

"No, I haven't been playing hooky," she says as she continues to walk away from me. "Don't you know me better than that? I need to finish school so I can become a forensic crime scene photographer. And the only reason Dad would be upset if he found out I was skipping school is because it's against the law. Not because he'd be worried about me not getting an education."

She's right about that. Our dad is very keen on obeying the rules. No spitting on the sidewalks, no jaywalking. No going on the pond in the winter when the red flag is flying, no cutting across peoples' lawns, no stealing. No playing chicken with trains, and no skipping school.

Rose pauses by the rink, I run to catch up. "So, where are we going?" I ask.

"To the Drummond's," she says.

"No, Rose. We're not going to the Drummond's. Dad would be mad."

"You can go home if you want, I didn't ask you to come with me, you insisted. I came out here to go to the Drummond's and that's exactly what I plan on doing." She leaves me standing by the rink boards.

"Why do you want to go there?" I call.

"To see what I can see."

She tries to run ahead but the skates bouncing on her chest get in the way. She swings the laces over her head, walks towards the nearest bush and drops them to the ground.

"Are you going to leave your skates there?" I ask.

"Maybe I'll luck out and someone will steal them."

She kicks them behind the low-lying scrub, passes between the schools, walks quickly down the next two blocks, leaves the sidewalk and begins the trek along the avenue that leads past the Drummond's. Not wanting someone to steal my skates because I really do enjoy the winter activity, I leave them around my neck and try to catch up.

It's cloudy out tonight, causing the street to be pitch black. The only flickers of light to help me keep my bearings are coming from the houses buried deep in the bush beside the avenue and farmhouses far across the field on the other side, and neither offer enough light to help me see my feet. Without the weight of her skates slowing her down, Rose moves faster than me, and because her winter coat is navy blue, a hand-me-down from me, I soon lose sight of her in the darkness. Every so often, when the ambient light from the houses catches her at the right angle, her orange mittens and toque, not hand-me-downs, shine like a disembodied head and hands in the distance. If Rose had her druthers, she'd pick orange for everything she wears.

"Rose, slow down. I can't see you."

"It's not my fault you wouldn't leave your skates behind."

"What's the rush? Their house isn't going anywhere."

"I don't want the crime scene to be compromised."

"Crime scene to be compromised? What do you know about crime scenes?"

"I know more than you think," she says. "I've read about footprints, and fingerprints, and evidence left behind that can incriminate someone."

"There you go again using words most twelve-year-old's have never even heard, let alone know the meaning of. And there's been no crime committed on the Drummond's property; the crime was committed at the Tremblay's."

"According to Dad, evidence from the murder was hidden in Mr. Drummond's shed. If that's not a crime scene, I don't know what is. Besides, everyone knows that the police never release all the information. Maybe there were other body parts taken besides a tongue."

"Well, I for one, do not want to find someone's ear buried in the dirt!"

I bump into her in the dark. She's standing with her legs spread and her arms crossed over her chest and doesn't budge an inch when we hit.

"Then go home, Liz. No one's forcing you to tag along."

Our freckled noses are practically touching and I breathe in the fresh scent of my sister. When Mom was alive, Rose insisted she buy her Ivory Soap, unlike the rest of us who use Dove, so predictably Rose smells like ginger root. Either she's buying it herself with the leftovers from her allowance Dad sometimes remembers to give us, or she has a supply of it stashed somewhere in the house. I take a step back.

"Someone has to keep you safe," I say.

Rose turns and plods off in the dark. This time I stay close behind.

After a couple of wrong turns, we find the right driveway and push through snow that's so deep, no car could have driven down it all winter. I haven't been back since I was here with Father Mackinnon the last week of July, and surprisingly, the place looks better in the dark. No cracks in the windows or siding can been seen. The rickety steps are hidden by the shadows, and the broken and discarded toys are buried somewhere in the snow. The little bit of smoke trailing out of the chimney is inviting against the black sky and I hear the occasional sound of children's laughter coming from within. Rose and I crouch by a bush a few feet away from the step. She works her hand in her pocket then tugs out a flashlight. With her mitten over the bulb, she turns the device on. The light glows orange through the wool.

"You had a flashlight all this time! Why the heck didn't you use it on the road?"

"Lower your voice," she spits at me. "Because I didn't want any of the neighbours to see, of course. I wanted the cover of darkness to hide us." She points the light towards the shed that sits beside the house. "I'm looking in there first."

"I'm not going inside that dirty old shed."

"Suit yourself."

She turns off the light and crouch walks towards the building. When she reaches the structure, she stands and shines the light on the hasp then slowly opens the door just wide enough for her to squeeze inside. I watch the light, as if it's alive, swirl between the cracks of the weather-worn siding. Five minutes later, as I'm panicking about whether or not Mr. Drummond is hiding in the shed and murdered her, she emerges and crouch walks back to me.

"Well," I say when Rose doesn't offer any information. "What did you find?"

"Nothing," she says. She takes off her toque and shakes out the cobwebs then brushes the dirt off her coat. "Just dust and mouse droppings. There's a moth-eaten blanket in the middle of the floor that must have fallen from the rafters. Probably where the cops found the gun. But that's all."

"Thank God," I say. "Let's go home."

She begins to crouch walk away from me again.

"Where are you going this time?"

"To get closer to the house. Those walls look pretty thin, maybe I can hear something."

"Rose," I say. "You've searched the shed, that's enough. It's time to go home. You're not going to find anything snooping into their private lives. And I'm pretty sure peeking in someone's window is against the law."

"Are we going to have that conversation again? I already said, it was your idea to come here with me, not mine. If you want to go home, then go home. I'm fine on my own."

I stay where I am.

"Alright then," she says.

Again, she leaves me alone beside the bush. A moment later I see the beam of the flashlight glowing orange next to the house. The light makes its way around the edge of the building, coming to a stop at the far corner.

"Psst," Rose says from the darkness. I don't answer. "Get the heck over here, Liz," she whispers.

Reluctantly, I leave the safety of the bush and crouch walk in her direction. With my skates hindering my mobility, twice, I fall forward. By the time I get to her, my knees are wet and my nose is red from falling face first into the snow. "I thought you said I could go home?" I say. "That coming with you was my idea and I could leave if I wanted to?"

"I need a lookout to tell me if someone is coming down the driveway. There's a window on that side of the house," she points. "I'm going to investigate."

"No, Rose. I want to go home. I've followed you down the dark road in the middle of the night. I waited by myself wondering if Mr. Drummond was going to come out of the bushes and murder me while you searched the shed. Now I've fallen on my face walking like a duck over here. I've had enough."

Suddenly Rose switches off the flashlight. It becomes so dark I feel as if I've gone blind. She pushes me out of sight around the corner and falls to the ground beside me. In the silence, the sound of boots crunching down the snow plugged driveway, bounces between the trees. From a position close to the ground, we peek around the corner of the house and peer into the abyss. My eyes have become accustomed to the blackness and I'm able to make out the shape of a person. The form is big enough to be a large man and the outline and swagger of the body is familiar. I grab Rose by the shoulder and pull her back. We flatten our bodies to the ground, and from this awkward position, the only thing in our line of sight is the rotting wood of the back doorstep. With our faces inches from being seen, a pair of boots step up to the house. He knocks.

The door opens and light spills onto the step.

"Hello Gail," Dad says. "Can I come in?" The light blinks out as the door closes behind him.

CHAPTER TWENTY-FOUR

Rose and I lie in the snow without moving.

"Well," Rose says quietly. "That wasn't entirely unexpected."

"Rose, that was our dad! And he's in the house of someone the police have accused of murder! What if he gets killed?"

"That's not the question we need to be asking ourselves. What we should be asking is, what possible reason could Dad have to be in the house of a suspected murderer?"

"I don't care why he's in there. I'm leaving. I've had enough excitement for one day. Hell, I've had enough excitement for one lifetime and I'm only fourteen years old!"

I attempt to crouch walk away but Rose grabs the hood of my coat and pulls. I fall backwards into her lap.

"No," she whispers as she looks down at me. "We can't leave now. We have to see what's going on."

"Are you crazy?" I hiss. "What do you propose we do? Knock on the door? Say, *Hi Dad. Saw you go inside and just wondering what you're doing here?*"

She closes one eye and looks at me. "I said I was going to look in that window," She points over her shoulder at the only window in the house which is not boarded up, "and that's what I'm going to do. And you have to come with me. We're sisters."

I rub my frozen mitt over my face. "I don't want to know if Mr. Drummond stole from Dad or killed the Tremblays, and I don't want to know what Dad's doing in the house. As far as I'm concerned, he's here to tell Gail how sorry he is for her troubles and offer her some money."

"You're wrong. Our dad didn't even hug his own children when their mother died; why would he care about this family? There's some other reason he's here and I'm not going home until I see inside."

Rose crawls away, and before I'm able to right myself, she's under the window. I linger in the snow for a moment longer, looking into the sky dotted with stars, imagining myself home in my warm bed. After a few more moments of delaying, knowing I have no choice but to stay, I sigh, lift my skates off my neck, then dragging them behind me, follow Rose to the house.

Rose is standing on a pile of bricks. The hood of her navy coat is pulled up to cover her orange toque, and only her eyes are higher than the windowsill. She lowers her head and motions for me to come closer.

I shake my head.

"They're not facing the window. Dad has one hand on Gail's shoulder and the other in the pocket he keeps his wallet in."

"He's offering her condolences and cash," I say. "Like I said." I set my skates on the ground, then climb onto the pile of bricks, poking my head beside Rose's. Gail and Dad are on the other side of the room facing each other. Their voices are reedy through the thin glass.

"I'm sorry for your troubles, Gail," Dad says as he pulls his wallet out. "You need to tell your dad to turn himself in. It will go much better for him if he does." He hands her some money.

"I don't know where he is," Gail mumbles. "Said he knew who the killer was and it wasn't safe for him here."

Rose and I lower our eyes. "That's what I said months ago," she whispers.

We raise our heads.

"He's innocent," Gail says. "He swore on Grandma's bible. I have to believe him. He's my dad!" She wipes tears off her cheeks.

"If he makes contact with you, tell him to come and talk to me," Dad says as he again reaches into his wallet. "Tell him," he passes her some more bills. "Tell him I'm his friend, always have been, no matter what's happened in the past. Can you tell him that?"

Gail hesitates, then shoves the money into her pocket. "I know he isn't the best of fathers," she mutters, "but he's not a murderer."

"I have to go," Dad says. "Send your dad to me, tell him we need to talk."

"Mr. Murphy?" Gail says.

Dad turns.

"Mom told me everything that happened in high school."

"I don't know what she could have possibly known about me," Dad says. "She and I ran in different circles."

"If all this hatred," she spits out the word, "is about some silly high school fling, then bygones should be bygones."

Rose's foot slips, and she tumbles to the ground taking me with her. I grab her hand and pull her up, then, clutching my skate laces, we take off into the field as someone opens the door.

* * *

Rose dropped the flashlight when she fell and it's a long trek home across the summer fallow in the dark. Once, we see Dad's outline walking up the road and we crouch in the field to wait while he passes.

"Dad was trying to bribe her," Rose says. "He thought if he gave her money, she'd give up her dad."

"You think so?" I say.

"What else could it have been? When was the last time you saw our dad voluntarily giving anyone money for nothing. He always expects something in return."

With my skates hampering my progress, I trip over mounds of snow that have accumulated in the chaff poking out of the uneven ground. By the time we arrive in our backyard, I'm so cold my teeth are chattering and I have straw sticking out of my mitts and stuck inside my toque.

"You should have left your skates behind the bush like I did," Rose says.

"What would Dad say when there's nothing to hand down to you next winter?"

Rose closes one eye at me. "Like Dad would notice, and like I'd care," she says.

"We'll have to go back and get yours tomorrow."

"Uh-huh," she says. "I'll make sure to rush out first thing in the morning. Where was that bush again? I can't quite remember."

Mrs. Gillespie is in the mud room getting her boots and coat on. "Cole's in bed," she says. She looks me up and down. "What happened to you?"

"Fell. Not a very good skater," I say quickly and Rose smiles.

"You should use a chair, like the little kids." She says to Rose, "Where are your skates?"

My mouth opens to come up with a lie, but Rose is quicker than me.

"There's a place this year, at the rink I mean, where you can store your skates so you don't have to keep taking them back and forth. In case you forget to bring them."

"Really?" Mrs. Gillespie says. "I suppose that's a good idea. Though I don't know what kid would walk all the way to the skating rink and forget to bring their skates."

"You'd be surprised," Rose says.

When she's gone, Rose says, "We make a good team."

"I've been hanging around you too much," I say. "Getting too easy to lie." I grab her arm and stop her from going inside. "Did you see the person on the other side of the field we crossed? He was smoking. Like at Halloween."

"What am I, blind? Of course I saw him."

"What are we going to say to Dad about seeing him tonight?" I ask.

"I don't know about you," Rose says, "but I plan on saying nothing. Ask no questions, tell no lies, I always say."

We enter the house. Dad's sitting in his chair with the TV on, his head back and his mouth open. From this angle he looks like any other dad, snoring in front of the television after a hard day's work. Until I remember that his friend and her family were murdered just a few short months ago, and his wife of fifteen years is dead and he has to raise six kids by himself. At the moment, his life is not like any other dads and I feel sorry for him. He stirs in his chair and looks over his shoulder.

"Dad?" Rose says.

"Yes?"

"Did you go out tonight?"

I poke her in the back, she swats at my hand.

"I walked to the rink," Dad says.

"Thought we saw you. By the time we skated over to say hi, you were already gone."

"You were having such a good time I didn't want to bother you. Watched for a minute and went home. Going to bed. You two should do the same."

We climb the stairs. Light shines under Fran's door but I walk past. She's probably reading, wishing her mother were here to tuck her in. The little ones' lights are out as they sleep, lost in their innocent dreams.

"You said you weren't going to say anything," I say to Rose, toothpaste bubbling out of the corners of my mouth. I spit into the sink. "What happened to that plan?"

"It kind of came to me and I thought, I wonder if he'll lie or tell the truth. If he lies, he's covering something up." She too spits then puts her mouth to the tap, swishes and spits again. "If he tells the truth, then he doesn't have anything to hide and was truly at the Drummond's to help."

"I don't think he's hiding anything," I say. We rinse our brushes and put them in the medicine chest. "He's embarrassed about helping that family, that's why he said he was at the rink instead of where he really was." We walk down the hall, kick off our slippers and get into bed. "Dad doesn't like people to see that he has a soft side." I'm still shivering and we pull the comforter up to our chins.

"Aren't you going to tell me I was right?" Rose says.

"About what?" I say.

"About the boys. Dad, Mr. Pendergrass and Mr. Drummond. Gail said her dad and our dad hated each other because of a high school fling." She yawns. "I said that a long time ago. I need to talk to Spooky."

"I thought you didn't believe in what she does."

Rose plumps her pillow. "Never said I did. But she's lived here a long time, remembers things about this town, things others have forgotten. Maybe she remembers something about their friendship, about what tore them apart." She breathes deeply as sleep overtakes her.

CHAPTER TWENTY-FIVE

As quite often happens on the prairies when spring is on the horizon, overnight the weather takes a turn for the worse. From my bedroom, I can hear Fran in the kitchen, begging to please be allowed to go to The Park to meet her friend. Mrs. Gillespie tells her no, it's too cold; the same reason Rose and I decided not to go to Mrs. Witherspoon's today.

"But I have to go," Fran says. "She's waiting for me. I have something to give her."

"There's nothing important enough one six-year-old has to give another six-year-old that warrants her going out in twenty below temperatures."

"Is too," Fran says. "Just because I'm six doesn't mean I don't have something 'portant to do."

"The only way you're going anywhere, young lady, is if one of your older sisters takes you and I'm quite sure they'll be smart enough to stay home. If you got frostbite your father would hang me from the rafters by my apron strings. And I'm willing to bet your friend's mother isn't allowing her to go to the playground today either."

Fran, who in the past wouldn't argue about anything, shouts that her friend doesn't have a mother and her sister lets her do whatever she wants. She stomps up the stairs and slams her bedroom door. She's changed since beginning school, becoming argumentative and obstinate, no longer the quiet little girl we're used to dealing with and I wonder if it's Mom's death that's affected her.

I leave my bedroom and stop in the hall to watch Robin and Alex as they play in their bedroom. A Raggedy Anne doll has been placed on her back with her cloth hands crossed over her chest. Various dolls sit around that doll, and Ken, Barbie's boyfriend, is standing at the front. His arms are extended as he addresses the crowd of assorted dolls.

"What are you playing?" I ask them.

"Funeral," Robin says. She points at the Raggedy Anne doll. "This is their mommy. She died." She points at Ken. "This is the priest. He's saying the prayers for their mommy's soul to go to heaven. He's telling the people at the funeral," she points at the congregation of dolls in attendance, "that their mommy will always be in their hearts. He's asking them to help the family because they don't have a mommy anymore." There's an empty shoe box at the back of the circle of dolls. "We're putting Raggedy Anne in the box and keeping her in the porch until the spring when we can dig a hole in the garden to bury her."

Shocked that she remembers what Father said at Mom's funeral, I say, "You're going to bury Raggedy Anne in the garden? You'll never be able to play with her again."

"That's what happens when someone dies, Liz. You never see them again until you go to heaven too."

I leave them to go and find Rose.

Since I've become friendless, I've been turning to my sister more and more for company. I find her in the front porch, snuggled under a blanket on the couch. Her notebook leans against her bent knees. "Whatcha doing?" I ask.

"Nothing."

Names, joined together by lines, are written in various spots on her paper.

"Doesn't look like nothing to me," I say. "Looks like you're trying to figure something out."

"Maybe," she says.

"Well?"

"Well what?"

"What are you trying to figure out?"

"Can we go to your treehouse?" Rose asks.

"I'm not supposed to go out there when the roof is slippery. You know that."

"You've done it before, you just never told Mom."

"I've never been out there when it's twenty below. What's wrong with right here?"

"I need some privacy to talk and Mrs. Gillespie is always popping up."

Mrs. Gillespie opens the porch door and begins to vacuum the floor around our feet. "It's too cold out here, girls," she says. "You should move to the living room."

"It's ok," I say. "We're hot because we were doing jumping jacks. You know, trying to get some exercise because we can't go outside today."

"Well, I need to finish vacuuming while the pie dough is resting in the fridge. It gets too sticky to roll out when the furnace is cranked so high." She rubs the end of her missing finger. "You shouldn't stay out here much longer; you'll catch your death."

I lift my feet so she can vacuum underneath. "Only a few more minutes, Mrs. Gillespie. Then we'll be cooled off." I've never been able to call her by her given name being as how it's the same name as our mother's. I have, however, heard Dad call her Patricia on more than one occasion. When she's gone, I say, "There's a bag of sand in the mud room. I suppose we could spread that across the cat-walk; make it less slippery. We need to sneak it upstairs, though."

Rose stands abruptly; the blanket falls to the floor. "I'll distract Patricia, while you get the sand."

Inside, Mrs. Gillespie rolls out the dough on the kitchen table. She glances over her shoulder. "All cooled down?" she asks as I head towards the mud room.

"We are," Rose says.

"I left a note in my coat pocket about what chapters I'm supposed to do for math class," I say to Mrs. Gillespie. "Need to get it so I can finish my homework." She turns her back to me to continue rolling the dough and I enter the mud room.

Rose engages the woman in a conversation about making pie.

"That looks challenging," she says.

"What, this?"

"I could never do that without it crumbling to bits."

"You mean, your mom didn't teach you how to make a pie?"

"Said some things got done faster if she did them herself. Eventually she would have taught me but, you know, she kind of died."

"I suppose she was a busy woman. But a girl needs to learn how to make a pie. How are you going to make pies for your husband when you get married?"

"I'll buy them from the grocery store. Or maybe my husband will be the one who stays home and makes the meals while I work to support us."

I've been using their voices as a cover to hide the sound of my feet, weighted with the sand as I lug the bag towards the stairs, but come to a halt when Mrs. Gillespie stops talking.

"Let your husband stay home!" she says. "While you go to work! Of all the ideas." She unrolls the crust off the rolling pin and drops it onto the apples that have already been cut and sugared in the pie plate. "Next time I make a pie I'm going to have you help. This is something every young lady needs to learn how to do. I suppose Liz doesn't know how either?"

"She doesn't. But I'm sure, being the oldest, she'd love to learn."

I begin to thud the bag up the stairs. Rose turns on the radio.

"I don't like music while I work," Mrs. Gillespie says.

"No?" Rose says loudly. "Our mother always had the radio on. We would dance around the kitchen to entertain her while she worked. She thought it was great fun."

"Well, I'm not your mother." Mrs. Gillespie clicks the music off.

I have one more step left and the bag thumps on the wooden floor.

"What was that?" Mrs. Gillespie says.

"Excuse me," Rose says. "Probably the eggs I had for breakfast. Sometimes they give me gas. Well, nice talking to you," she says then bounds up the stairs behind me and my bag of sand. She joins me in our bedroom.

"Why did you tell her I want to learn how to make a pie?" I say. "Now she's going to try and teach me and I already know how, it's you who doesn't."

"Asked and answered in the same sentence," Rose says. "Where's the sand?"

I'm pointing at the bag when our bedroom door bangs open; Fran stands on the other side. Her hands are in fists, and her face is contorted in such anger, she looks like a poster I saw outside the Twin-Plex Theatre a couple of years ago advertising an up and coming horror movie. It was taken down when parents complained. "I want to go outside," she says. "I need to meet my friend." Her lips barely move as she talks.

"Mrs. Gillespie said it's too cold." I open my window and pull out the screen.

"You can't go out there," Fran says. "Mom said the roof is too slippery in the winter."

"Mind your own business," I say.

"I'm telling Mrs. Gillespie." She runs half-way down the hall.

"Wait," I call. "I'll take you to meet your friend. But you can't tell anyone I'm going to the treehouse."

She turns. "When?"

"When what?"

"When will you take me to meet my friend?"

I look at the clock on the bedside table. "It's two o'clock now. I'll take you at three."

"Two-thirty," Fran says.

"Three or not at all," I say.

"Ok," Fran says. "But Olive is supposed to be there by two-thirty and she won't wait long."

"Go and call her. Tell her you're going to be late. Do you know her phone number?"

"They don't have a phone," Fran says.

"Well, it's three or nothing," I say. "Get your snow pants on and wait in the mud room. Tell Mrs. Gillespie I'm taking you. But you can't tell anyone what we're doing."

Fran looks at the clock. "I can tell time you know. And I'm leaving at three if you're not ready."

"Have you noticed that kid is getting too big for her britches?" Rose asks after Fran has left.

"I think it's not having Mom around anymore. And don't complain, you've been big for your britches since you were two years old." I look at the slippery roof. "Maybe we should stay inside to talk. It looks pretty slick out there."

We hear giggles coming from Alex and Robin's bedroom. One of them says, "shush."

"There's no way I can talk about this in the bedroom," Rose whispers. "And what if Dad comes home and goes into his bedroom? He can hear every word we say from down there. We have no privacy in this house except out there." She points out the window.

"And you're sure this is that important?"

"I'm sure."

"Help me lift this over the ledge."

Together we lug the sandbag over the window ledge and lean it against the house. I open the closet and take out our warmest sweaters. There are some old gloves on the shelf and I toss Rose a pair.

"Grab the extra blanket off the bed, would you?"

Rose puts on her sweater then drapes the blanket around her shoulders. She sticks her notebook under her shirt. "Wait." She opens her dresser drawer and pulls out a book, sliding it under her shirt along with her notebook. "Dad's yearbook," she says.

I climb out the window ahead of her. The moment I step through, the wind catches my hair and lifts it straight in the air. Without an elastic in my pocket, I tuck the tangled mess into the back of my sweater, then reach into the bag of sand and throw a handful onto the cat-walk. Some of it blows over the edge of the roof, but most of it sticks. I hold the rail with one hand and with the other, scrape the sandbag a few inches forward along the catwalk. I take my first step. My foot slides before finding purchase on a pile of sand. Rose steps out.

"Be careful," I say. "It's windy."

I throw another handful of sand, drag the bag a few more inches and take another step. The wind tears at my sweater, blowing it open and the icy blast freezes me to the bone.

"Are you ok?" I ask Rose but my voice is blown away. I reach back; she touches my gloved hand with hers.

The two of us continue inching forward, with me throwing a handful of sand every few steps until we arrive at the relative safety of the treehouse. I sit on the bench and hug my arms around my body. I can't stop shivering. Rose wraps the blanket around our shoulders. The wind is howling between the wooden slats of the walls, sounding like someone has stepped on a cat's tail. The branches sway and crack into each other and the treehouse sways along with the tree.

"Holy cannoli," Rose says between the clacking of her teeth. "Maybe this wasn't as good an idea as I first thought." I feel the blanket begin to shake. I look at Rose, she's laughing.

"Remind me to never let you talk me into anything again," I say.

"You g-g-gotta admit, it was k-kind of f-fun."

"Fun?" I say.

Still stuttering from the cold, she says, "We did something we didn't think we could do. I don't know about you, but I've always liked challenging myself," she says as she pinches the blanket under her chin.

"I think your sense of adventure is slightly different than mine," I say. "Why have we risked our lives to come out here?"

She pulls the books out from under her shirt and flips the notebook open; the pages blow in the wind; she presses them flat. "I've made a chart," she says as she shows me her notebook.

At the top of the page, is the name Marjorie Hampton. On the right side and slightly lower, she's written Carl Pendergrass. On the other side of the paper is Stan Drummond's name and at the bottom of the page, is Dad's name. There's a line drawn from each of the boys' names to Marjorie Hampton's at the top, and beside each boys' name she's written the word, dated.

"So, what's this mean?" I ask.

"It's their circle of friends," she says.

I tap her chart. "Dad told us he was friends with Mr. Krieger, Mr. Fogg, and Mr. and Mrs. Henderson in school. You should put them on your list too."

"They didn't date Marjorie Hampton, whereas these three," she points at the boy's names, "did. I believe these three," again she points at their names, "were all vying to be Marjorie Hampton's boyfriend. I think that's what connects them to the murders."

"Just because they dated, doesn't mean they're involved in the murders."

"This was a murder of passion. It had to have been committed by someone close to her."

"It could have just as easily been committed by someone who didn't know her as a teenager. Someone she knew as an adult."

"It could have, but I don't think so. Grudges that linger for years are more likely to become blown out of proportion. And because there was violence, this had to have been a grudge that festered for a long time." Rose wags the yearbook at me. "There's lots of pictures in here of the four of them together." She opens the yearbook to point out a few of the pictures. Captions beside them say things like, *the fearsome foursome,* as they walk down a hall arm in arm, or, *the four musketeers,* while they play tennis on the court behind the school. "That corny stuff high school yearbook editors think is witty," Rose says. She shows me a picture of Carl Pendergrass and Marjorie Hampton sitting together on the school bleachers. The photographer has caught Carl gazing at Marjorie with a look on his face of pure adoration. "See how he's looking at her? If that's not love, I don't know what is." She turns to a dog-eared page, pressing the spine flat and taps a picture of a boy and girl dancing. "That's Marjorie Hampton and Dad," she says. "Look closely at the person in the background."

I tighten the blanket around our bodies while Rose holds the book close to my face. Leaning against the gym wall is a young Mr. Pendergrass and he's watching Dad and Mrs. Tremblay as they dance. He does not look happy.

Rose turns the page to the class picture of Mrs. Tremblay and reads the caption written beside the picture. "Jim and Marjorie sitting in a tree, k-i-s-s-i-n-g. I think Mr. Pendergrass was jealous of Dad dating Marjorie Hampton. I think he wanted to marry her. But I don't think she felt the same about him."

"God, Rose. There're all kinds of love triangles in high school. It's like *The Edge of Night* in that building. Mr. Pendergrass being jealous of Dad dating Mrs. Tremblay has nothing to do with the Tremblay family getting murdered. I heard Dad tell Mom last summer that they all dated her. It was puppy-love, he said."

Rose chews on the end of her pencil. "There's something else, something I'm missing that's all tangled up with the jealousy thing. And why aren't they all still friends? They live in the same town, see each other at the store, at church, at, well everywhere. It's just weird. Like something came between them."

We sit and shiver for a moment as the wind howls around us.

"Well," I say. "This isn't as wild as your messy yard theory. But the RCMP said it was a random killing. A crazy stranger. Even you said last summer that he was probably already lying on a beach in Mexico. You said that no one sticks around after doing something like that, not even crazy people."

"I don't think so anymore. I think crazy people stick as close to the crime scene as possible. I think Spooky Witherspoon is right and he walks among us."

CHAPTER TWENTY-SIX

Rose looks up from the yearbook towards Dad's store. "Did you see that?" she says.

I turn my head and look in the same direction as her; the wind takes my breath away. "What?" I say when I see nothing.

"I thought I saw, never mind." She flips the page on the yearbook. "There, it happened again," she says as she glances up. "Smoke, coming from behind Dad's store."

I look over my shoulder. "Someone's burning garbage."

"In the winter? In this weather? I don't think so. I suppose it could be someone trying to keep warm, but..." She stands, placing the yearbook and her notebook on the bench behind her. "It's thicker now. And it's Sunday. You're not supposed to burn on Sunday. I'm going to look."

I pick up the yearbook and Rose's notebook and toss them inside the bench, then take out my binoculars and peer across the rooftops. A column of smoke wafts intermittently from behind Dad's store. "I'm coming with you," I say.

We inch our way along the catwalk and climb inside the house. I look at the bedside clock, it says quarter to three. We clomp down the stairs, into the kitchen, and enter the mud room; Fran's not there.

"Where's Fran?" I call to Mrs. Gillespie who's changing Cole's diaper.

"In the mud room waiting for you. She told me you said you'd take her to The Park to meet her friend, of all the silly things. I told her I doubted you'd said that but she could wait there if she wanted to as long as she had her winter things on."

"She's not there," I say. Rose and I don our own winter gear and rush out the backdoor.

With our zippers flapping, and our toques barely covering our hair, Mrs. Gillespie calls after us asking where we're going, but we don't turn around to answer her.

"I'll go to the store," I say, "you check The Park for Fran."

Rose turns down the flagstone path to the front yard to race towards the schools, and I run down the alley and head to the store. When I arrive, the back door is banging open and closed, causing smoke to billow erratically into the alley. "Dad," I shout. "Are you here, Dad?"

I hear a voice. It's not Dad.

"Is there someone in here," I shout.

A tiny voice cuts through smoke that gets thicker the further I step inside. "I'm here, Liz. Help me, please."

"Fran," I say, "is that you?"

"It's me, Liz. Help me," she says.

Rose runs up to the back door. "Fran isn't at The Park," she says breathlessly. "What are you doing? You shouldn't be inside!"

"Fran's in here," I yell. "Go to the firehall. Tell them Dad's store is on fire!"

Rose doesn't argue and takes off.

"Hello," I call again as I take a tentative step further inside. "Fran, are you in here? Where are you?"

"In Daddy's office. I'm scared, Liz."

I drop to the floor to avoid the smoke. The heat is close and I wipe away the tears streaming down my face as I try to ascertain which direction I'm going. I've been coming to this store since the day I was born, but with my vision so badly obscured, I can barely tell which direction the ceiling is, let alone where Dad's office is.

"Keep calling, Fran. Keep talking. I can't tell which way to go."

"I'm here, Liz, I'm over here."

On my hands and knees, I move towards Franny's voice. Paint cans, the display that sits against the wall next to the office, are visible through the smoke. Their paper wrappers are warping in the heat, but they're not yet on fire. The office door is partially closed. I reach out and push it open. The door is hot to the touch.

"Fran, I call, "Where are you?"

"Under Daddy's desk."

"Is Olive here? Is Dad here?"

"No. Only me," she says.

"It's ok, Franny. Everything will be ok."

I stay in the doorway and look inside the room; the smoke isn't as thick as in the main part of the store. The catalogues from wholesalers across North America have tumbled off the bookshelves to the floor. The curtains Mom made have fallen down, and the filing cabinet is tipped over. Our family picture which sat on top of the cabinet lies broken in two. Filing drawers have spilled paper everywhere and I know I have to hurry because the papers will be quick fuel for the flames. Fran has pushed the chair out from under the desk and is curled underneath.

"I'm here," I say. "Come out, the desk isn't on fire."

"I can't, I'm scared."

"I'm scared too," I scream. "If you don't come out the office will be on fire soon, and then we'll be stuck." I look over my shoulder. The flames are moving quickly from the front of the store to the back and smoke is wafting in through the now open office door.

"I can't, Liz."

"I'm coming to get you."

I hear sirens and pray I can rescue Fran before the fire reaches this far. I crawl through the doorway and into the office. I flatten my body closer to the floor as I try to get air into my lungs. "Fran," I gasp, "I'm here." I reach out my hand. "Grab my hand, just grab my hand."

"I can't see you," she says.

"For heaven's sake, Fran, if you can climb that tree last summer you can grab my hand. God almighty, just do it or we'll both die in here!" My voice has risen to a shriek, yet through the noise of the fire in my ears, I can only feel it vibrate in my throat.

Her little fingers clasp onto mine and my hope for escape increases. I curl my fingers onto hers and drag her out from under the desk then pull her to my chest.

"Let's go," I say.

I look out the office door into the shop. The path I just crawled through is consumed floor to ceiling by flames. One by one the paint cans catch on fire and pop, spilling their contents across the floor. I turn and look around the office for a way out. The light shining through the bare windows shows me our escape.

"This way," I say.

Without letting go of Fran's hand, I move behind the desk and push on the window. The glass is hot but it doesn't budge.

"Throw the chair through," Fran says. "Throw Daddy's chair through the window!"

I pick up the chair. It's heavy in my hands, but when I loft it in the air and out the window, it feels as light as air. The glass shatters and with strength I didn't know I have I push Dad's desk up to the broken window. Fran and I scramble on top and climb through the jagged opening. We run into the alley just as a fireman, who's following Rose, jumps out of his firetruck and runs towards us. Dad's truck screeches to a stop behind the firetruck. He jumps out and picks Fran up in his arms. We cross the alley to stand beside the loading dock of the fabric store behind us, away from the flames licking out the back door.

"Is anyone else inside the building?" the fireman yells.

I shake my head.

"Are you alright?" Dad asks Fran.

"It wasn't me, Daddy. It wasn't me."

Dad pulls her away from his shoulder and looks her in the face. "What do you mean, it wasn't you? Did you start this fire?"

Fran begins to sob.

"What does she mean, Liz? Did she start the fire? Did you?"

"Me? No, Dad. Rose saw the smoke from the treehouse and we came here and found the store on fire."

As if in a dream, the fireman moves us to the front street. Townspeople have assembled on the sidewalk opposite Murphy's Hardware to watch the firemen douse the flames. Dad leaves Fran, Rose and me with Mrs. Henderson while he talks to other shop owners, questioning them about what could have happened. I rub the tears from my cheeks, my fingers turn black with soot. In the short time I was getting Fran out, Dad's store has been reduced to rubble.

The firemen gather around one spot in the back corner of what's left of Dad's store. It's where the office was, close to where Fran was hiding under the desk and I wonder if they've found the source of the fire.

CHAPTER TWENTY-SEVEN

I have Cole snuggled between Rose and me in bed. His little body is warm against mine, and I stroke his soft cheek. The girls, including Fran, have gone to bed, though I doubt Fran is asleep.

As we stood and watched the firemen extinguish the blaze, an ambulance drove up to the scene and a body was removed from the rubble. Dad drove us home in his truck as Rose quizzed him on whose body it was, but he said it was too badly burnt and couldn't be identified yet.

At home, while curled up in a kitchen chair, Fran told Dad, me, Rose and Mrs. Gillespie what had happened.

At school on Friday, her friend Olive had asked her if she'd seen a purple bag filled with marbles. She said she lost them last summer when she returned the wagon to our yard. Fran told Olive she knew where they were.

"How did you know where they were?" I'd asked Fran.

"Robin told me. She was peeking into your bedroom when you put the bag in the bottom drawer."

Olive told Fran that if she met her at The Park on Sunday with the marbles, she'd share them with her. Since it was so cold outside, Fran decided to take the matches so the little girls could have a fire to keep warm.

"Like when we'd go on a winter picnic with Mom," Fran had said. "Remember, Daddy? We'd go to the campground and have a fire to keep warm while we made a snowman?"

Dad stopped Fran there. "What were you doing with matches in your drawer, Liz?"

"I was ...." I begin to say. Rose cuts me off.

"I found them at The Park, Dad. I was going to throw them out but put them in our dresser because, uh, I thought I might like to give smoking a try."

Dad opened his mouth to give Rose heck, but closed it, deciding, I suppose, he'd deal with her later. I'd started to tell Dad the truth but Rose kicked me in the shin.

Fran said when her friend wasn't at The Park, she decided to go to the store. Because she was afraid one of us would see her and tell her to come in from the cold, she went the long way around using the sidewalks instead of going down the alleys so she wouldn't pass her house. The back door of the store was unlocked, and she went inside.

"Why didn't you want to come home?" I'd asked.

"Because I wanted to see my Daddy," she said, trying not to cry. She looked at Dad and rubbed her eyes, red from the smoke. "You weren't there. I called and called, but you didn't answer."

"Did you light the matches?" Dad asked.

"No, Daddy. I didn't burn your store. I threw the matches in the garbage can. You know, the one you have by the front door for people to put their candy wrappers in? They caught on fire by themselves."

"Why didn't you go home when you couldn't find me?" Dad asked.

"I was scared you'd get mad at me when the matches caught on fire, so I hid under the desk." Tears dripped down her cheeks and she'd palmed them away. "Why was all your stuff on to the floor?"

"What stuff?" Dad asked.

"The picture of us. The catalogues you order from. Mom's curtains. They were spilt all over the floor." Fran asked.

"The fire, Fran. The fire made them fall."

It appears it was all an accident, a horrible accident, but the store is gone and Dad is very, very angry. He's angry at Fran for going outside on such a cold day and for stealing the matches. He's angry at Rose for having the matches in the first place and at me for allowing Fran to go outside alone. He did question Rose and me as to what we saw when we were in the treehouse, but he said nothing to us about crossing the catwalk in winter.

* * *

I sleep fitfully, as does Rose, and when we get up in the morning, Dad has already left the house.

I ask Mrs. Gillespie where he is.

"Gone to look at what's left," she says. "From what you told me yesterday, nothing much, I imagine."

"Do they know whose body it was?" I ask.

"They do."

"Who?" I ask.

"Why don't we let your dad tell you," she says.

We finish our porridge, then Rose and I bundle up to walk to the store. The street is filled with people gawking at the ruins. The road, blocked off at each end to prevent vehicle congestion at the scene, is slick with ice from the firefighters' hoses and the windows of the buildings across the street from Dad's store are blackened with soot. Telephone poles tilt in the alley behind the store and icicles cling to the burnt wires that drape to the ground. Each time the lines sway against the wood they send a shower of ice cascading down. Mrs. Henderson is standing beside me and I ask if she knows whose body they found. She tells me it was Stanley Drummond.

"What was he doing in the store?" I ask.

"I don't have any idea, child," she says. "He has broken into your dad's store before. Perhaps that's what he was doing again."

Along with everyone else, Rose and I stare at the remains of Murphy's Hardware. The once handsome structure looks like photographs I've seen in history books of bombed out buildings in Europe after the second world war. Jagged half walls, heavy with ice, line the perimeter of the burned-out lot, while piles of debris fill the centre. The majority of the rubble is cloaked in ice, making the mounds of irregular shapes look like modern art sculptures. But, like a tornado that takes out some buildings while leaving others untouched, some of the wreckage is bare of its frozen sheath, and everything from tape measures, to hammers, to cans of oil and sponges, stick out of the blackened piles at odd angles. The fire department has set up sawhorses around the fire zone to stop individuals from entering, and people crowd as close as they can manage without crossing the barrier. Rose and I squeeze between the bodies and step to the front of the mob. In the far corner of the cordoned off area, where his office would have been, Dad picks through the rubble. He's kicking at this and that and every once in a while, bends forward, rubbing at the ice, as if trying to see what's underneath.

"Dad," I call. He doesn't hear me. "Dad," I call again. He lifts his head and glances at Rose and me, but returns to his task, totally ignoring his two eldest daughters. Then despite people telling me it's unsafe, the building I've considered my second home for the past thirteen years, draws me in. Rose joins me and together we stumble our way around what used to be Murphy's Hardware. I try not to look down for fear of crying, but familiar articles draw my eyes to the ground.

There's the paintings of the Mona Lisa and the Arc de Triomphe, Dad ordered thinking someone would buy them to hang in their house. The frames are half gone; the pictures as black as charcoal. I remember Mom telling Dad they'd never sell; that farmers want pictures of wheat fields and granaries, not pictures of far off places they will most likely never see. But Dad was insistent. The pictures didn't sell and have greeted me as they hung on the wall by the front door for the past twelve years.

I stub my toe on the remnants of a rocking horse Dad got in last fall before Mom died to boost his Christmas sales. He had five of them and sold all but one. He was saving it to give to Cole for Christmas, which I forgot about, as, I presume, did he. Now it's no good to anyone. All that remains are the seat, a few strands of tail, and the charred and blackened head.

The set of copper pots and pans I tried to talk Mom into using, from which she recoiled saying she didn't need any new-fangled cook-wear to make a decent dinner, have spilled out of their box, the shiny orange hue now caked with ash and slick with ice.

I make my way closer to Dad, closer to the spot where I rescued Fran. A piece of glass twinkles through the cinders and I bend forward to look. Mom's face sparkles back at me through a layer of ice. It's the family picture that sat on the filing cabinet. We had it taken after Alex was born but before Cole came along. We were going to get another taken with all eight of us, but Mom had been too tired to arrange a time we could all go. Guilt that I've been carrying around since Mom died, overwhelms me and tears run down my face. I attempt to break the ice with my hand but it's too thick. I kick at a pile of debris nearby that's not been coated in an icy tomb and, finding a hammer, pound at the ice until I'm able to pry the picture loose. I brush off the glass and pick up the five by seven photograph, stuffing it in my pocket.

Dad, a few feet away, starts to kick at something. When he's unable to break through, he pulls his jackknife out of his pocket and stabs at the thick ice over and over. He pries a badly burnt drawer out of the mess, and takes a small box from inside. It appears to be unscathed by the flames and he drops it into his coat pocket.

"Did you find what you're looking for, Dad?" I ask.

His eyes are red, his cheeks, ruddy from the cold. There's a trickle of blood on his lip from biting it out here in the freezing temperatures and he wipes the back of his hand across his mouth leaving a red streak. He has no toque or gloves on and doesn't have his winter coat done up. "Didn't find anything," he says. "Nothing to find. Years of work," he sifts ash through his fingers, "all gone. Glad your mother isn't here to see."

Rose and I leave the area. Jen waits behind the sawhorses.

"I'm sorry, Liz." She touches my hand.

Rose steps in front of me and with her mouth close to my friend's ear, she whispers so softly, all I can see is Jen's hair being wafted by Rose's breath. The blood in Jen's face drains away and she looks like she's going to faint. When Rose is finished, she takes a step back and the only words she says loud enough for me to hear are, "I hope you get cancer and die."

Jen shakes her head. "I didn't...." she starts to say, but Rose grabs my arm and pulls me away.

"Come on, Liz," my sister says. "She's not a friend of ours any-more."

I look over my shoulder as Rose and I run down the street. Jen's watching us, a sad look on her face. She takes one step towards me, then hangs her head and turns towards her own house.

"What did you say to her?" I ask when we stop running.

"Only that Fran stole the matches you were hiding for her and lit one inside the shop and that's what caused the fire. I told her I know what she's been doing with her friends and if it wasn't for the fire, I'd turn her into the police today."

"You shouldn't have said that. Fran said she didn't light a match. She said they started on fire by themselves when she dropped them in the waste basket."

"I don't give a rat's ass! I mean, grow up, for God's sake!"

"Why'd you tell Dad the matches were yours if you hate her so much?"

"You were going to confess and I knew if I blurted out they were Jennifer's, Dad would think I was only trying to save your skin." She shrugs her shoulders. "He already thinks I'm the black sheep, what's one more sin?" she says. "You know, I was thinking in bed last night; how would the fire cause all those things to fall off the shelves in the office, like you and Fran said, if the fire wasn't even there yet?"

"I don't know," I say. "I just know that's what I saw."

With no place else to go, we head home.

* * *

For the next few weeks we go through the motions. Get up, go to school, come home, eat, do homework go to bed. We don't see much of Dad, grief stricken as he is with the death of wife, and now the loss of his store.

The fire department determines that the matches Fran said she didn't light but threw into the waste basket, caught on fire from a smouldering cigarette someone had carelessly dropped inside. Dad, who isn't a smoker, said, because the fire happened on a Sunday and no one had been in the store that day except for Mr. Drummond, he must have been the one to drop the cigarette into the can.

The other bright spot in this never-ending tragedy is, the person the RCMP charged with the Tremblay murders is dead, and the townspeople are finally, after eight months, resting easy.

CHAPTER TWENTY-EIGHT

"What are you doing out there?" I call from our bedroom window.

"What?" Rose says from the treehouse, her hand cupping her ear.

I call louder. "I've been waiting downstairs for ten minutes, what's taking so long?"

"I'm looking for my notebook. I want to take it with us to Mrs. Witherspoon's. I'm sure I dropped it here the day we saw the smoke."

"I put the notebook and yearbook inside the bench."

Rose lifts the lid and pats around the storage space. She closes the bench and stares at the seat then looks at me standing at the bedroom window. "Well, they're not here and I certainly didn't take them with us to the fire," she says. "You must have done something else with them. Or come out here after and picked them up."

"I haven't been out there since the fire. They should still be in the bench."

"Maybe Fran took them. Or Dad. He might have come up here to see what we saw the day of the fire. He did seem interested when we told him we were up here." She places her hands on her hips. "Now what am I going to do? I need that yearbook. It's the closest thing I have to a lead. And my notebook contains all kinds of pertinent information."

"All I know is I put them in the bench. If they aren't there, I don't know where they've gone." I look at my watch. "Our appointment is in twenty minutes. We have to get going."

* * *

When we approach the stone house; the flag which announces Mrs.

Witherspoon is with a client, is flying. Rose leads the way to an anteroom.

"How did you know this was here?" I say. "I've seen this building when I've looked around her backyard at her artwork, but I didn't know it was a waiting room. I thought it held the junk she used to build her stuff."

"About the time Dad hired Mrs. Gillespie, I came here to ask Mrs. Witherspoon to contact Mom. I wanted to tell her Dad wasn't holding up his end of this parenting deal and had handed us off to someone else. I was mad and wanted Mom to know."

"You didn't!"

"I only did it to let off some steam. I figured I couldn't tell Father Mackinnon. He'd tell me all the same clichés everyone else was saying. That *a man needs to grieve* and *to give him time*, or, *he'll come around*. So, I came here. It felt kind of good, like going to confession. After I said my piece to Spooky, a weight lifted and I felt better."

"What happened? Did you talk to Mom?"

"Of course not, Liz. There's no such thing as the living being able to talk to the dead."

"What did Mrs. Witherspoon tell you?"

"That," she makes quotation marks with her fingers, *"the reason for Dad's behaviour will eventually be clear."*

"That's all? Just wait and see?"

"Yup. *As with everything in life, only time will reveal the truth,* she said."

Out the window we see the flag being lowered. We wait the required five minutes as per instructions stapled to the anteroom door, then enter the room where Mrs. Witherspoon tells her fortunes. The fire in the stove burns low and since the walls are made from stone, the tiny space is getting cold. Rose pulls the cord that raises the flag to announce our arrival.

"If we could, would you want to talk to Mom?" I ask.

"If it were possible, which it's not," she says, "talking to Mom might be ok. As long as she didn't tell me I'm not helping you keep our room clean enough or I should wear dresses more often." She lifts her green eyes to me. "Do you want to hear from her?"

"It would be kind of cool. We could find out why she didn't go to the doctor when she knew she was sick. That's something that's always bothered me."

"I already know."

"You know why Mom didn't go to the doctor? Are you a clairvoyant too?" I hug myself, trying to keep warm.

"No. I'm logical."

"So, why didn't Mom go to the doctor?"

Instead of answering, Rose says, "Remember the day last summer when I talked Dad into looking after Cole while Mom took us shopping for clothes."

"I do," I say.

"And Mom resisted? Like she didn't want Dad to look after his own children?"

"She didn't want to bother him," I say. "You know how Dad is about looking after his kids."

"That's what I thought too," Rose says, "because that was usually the reason. But not that time."

"How do you know?"

"When I was negotiating a deal with Mom for my orange pants, I mentioned that if it hadn't been for me, she would have been looking after Cole the entire time we were shopping. That's when she told me."

"Told you what?"

"At first, I thought I'd overstepped my bounds, because she rolled her eyes like she does when I've asked too many questions. Then, kind of quiet like, as if she was talking to herself, she said she wasn't sure she wanted Dad to look after his kids. When I tried to ask her what she meant, that silly Mrs. Billings trotted up with some ugly dress she thought I might like, you know that one that's been hanging in the closet since Mom bought it for me? I never got a chance to talk to Mom about it again. That's why she didn't go to the doctor; she didn't want Dad to look after us."

The door creaks open and Mrs. Witherspoon enters. Swirls of red, blue and gold, interlace across the bib of her overalls, splashes of black crisscross up the straps, and drips of purple run down the legs. They remind me of a Jackson Pollock painting I saw at the art gallery in the city last year. While Mrs. Olyphant babysat, Mom had taken me with her to the city to buy a new maternity smock, and afterwards, we'd gone out for lunch then toured through the art gallery. It was the last day I had Mom to myself before she died.

"Ladies," Mrs. Witherspoon says.

I hand her five dollars, some in coin, some in bills; the remnants of my allowance and babysitting money, which has all but disappeared in the past six months. I found my share of today's money at the bottom of my sock drawer; how it got there I haven't a clue. Without counting it, Mrs. Witherspoon drops the cash into a pocket in her overalls; I hear the coins jingle against something metal.

She speaks first. "Before we get started, know that your mom loves you. Our souls live long after our bodies are gone and love never fades. Now," she says, "I've been wondering how long it would take you to come and see me."

"How did you....?" I begin to say.

"I notice things, Miss Murphy, past and present. That's the only way one can see the future. You've come to find out if something happened in this town twenty years ago that could have led to the deaths of the Tremblay's and Mr. Drummond. If the friendship between your dad, Carl, Stanley, and Marjorie had something to do with their deaths. Am I right?"

"You are," Rose says.

"Just to be clear," she says. "I only know what I see, I do not interpret what it means. You'll have to draw your own conclusions from what I tell you. Do you understand?"

Rose and I look at each other. "Yes," we say.

"And you're positive you want to know? Once you hear, you can't unhear." The large woman still hasn't sat down, waiting to learn if we're sincere about our visit.

Rose does not check with me but answers for both of us. "We're sure." She pulls a new notebook out of her pocket and flips to the first page.

Mrs. Witherspoon opens the stove door and throws a log onto the fire. Her red fingernails flash in the glow. "All of them," she says over her shoulder, "but Carl came from well-to-do families." She sits down and laces her hands on the table in front of us. "Drummond, Murphy, Pendergrass and Hampton, the four musketeers. But we can't talk about them without first speaking of their parents.

"Your Grandpa Murphy," she points at us, "he had the largest farming operation around, ten thousand acres with many employees. The man had a reputation for being tough on his employees; didn't hand out money for nothing. Treated his children the same way. Both of your grandparents died within months of each other; no discernible disease, they simply passed away, the life gone from them.

"Mr. Hampton, Marjorie's dad, owned the ladies' wear store, as I'm sure you already know. They brought in the latest styles, good quality items and were very successful. Women from all the small towns around here shopped at Hampton's. They sold the shop and moved away the week after Marjorie married.

"And Mr. Drummond, Stanley's dad, he was in farm machinery. That empty lot on the edge of town with rusting skeletons of combines and tractors sinking into the weeds, that was his place. It was a big business twenty-five years ago; family had more money than they could spend. Then the New Holland dealership opened and they closed. Gave Stanley money from the sale of the business and left him on his own.

"Mr. Pendergrass, Carl's dad, farmed like your grandpa but he didn't own as much land. He made enough money to support his family, but he had no employees. Carl and his dad worked those acres, until his dad died in a horrible farming accident. After she lost her husband, Ester sold the farm and bought the two houses in town, one for her and one for Carl."

I glance at Rose; her pencil is flying across the page.

"In high school, the four of them were inseparable," Mrs. Witherspoon says. "You never saw one without the other. At Gas-n-Go, at the Twin-plex Theatre, at Woolworths. Where there was one, there were the others." She taps the table with her fingernail. "It was odd to have a lone girl in that group of boys, even though they seemed happy, joking and laughing all the time. But even children are never as innocent as they pretended to be.

"Carl was different, wasn't like the others. He was studious, more of a bookworm than the other three. They were wilder. Money can do that to a person. Gave the kids the freedom to do what they wanted. Made them think they were better than others, think they were invincible.

"They all had a crush on Marjorie, and she knew it too. But she was flirty and coy, liked being the only girl in a group of boys. Didn't want to drive a wedge between herself and the others by declaring her love for just one.

"Carl, he loved her the most. It hurt him, her not returning his love for her. The other two, at least in the beginning, knew it was all part of the game.

"It was shortly after Carl's dad died when I began to see Marjorie more and more with only your dad and I thought, *I wonder what came between her and the others for her to not worry about losing the others as friends.* She and your dad stayed a couple until graduation when everyone went their separate ways.

"Carl, instead of going to university, got his job with the township right out of high school. He's spent the last twenty years emptying garbage cans and becoming a hermit in that little house his mom bought for him.

"And Stanley, he married the summer after grade twelve. An unpopular girl from his graduating class, Abigale Swanson. Not someone I'd have ever pegged him to marry, sort of an out-of-the-blue relationship. She may have been pregnant when she and Stanley married, can't say for sure because she had Gail about eight months later. He began to drink, or he may have began drinking that last year of high school.

"Marjorie broke up with your dad and went to teacher's college.

From what I heard at the time, she lived a wild life in the city and never graduated. Moved back here to marry Henry. He was ten years older than her. Her parents had arranged the marriage.

"The rest you already know. Your dad farmed with his dad for a few years. Then when your grandparents died, he sold the farm and opened Murphy's Hardware."

"What do you mean by," Rose flips back a few pages, *"Even children are never as innocent as they pretended to be."*

"Everyone has secrets. They were keeping a secret and that's what eventually drove them apart."

"What was the secret?" Rose asks.

"I've no idea, child. And they've kept their mouths closed all these years." She looks at her watch. "Have I answered all your questions?"

* * *

Rose and I say our goodbyes as Mrs. Witherspoon lowers the flag then throws another log into her little fireplace.

"That was certainly informative," Rose says as we pass a lion with hubcap eyes and emerge into the alley.

"You think so?" I say. "Seems like high school theatrics to me."

A whistle sounds and Rose and I turn to watch a train rumble behind Mrs. Witherspoon's house. I count the cars while Rose rustles the pages of her notebook back and forth, moving her lips to the words she's silently reading. When the caboose has passed, we leave the tracks to walk home. Rose turns to the first page and taps her mitten to the paper.

"Why do you think Grandpa and Grandma died so close together?"

"I don't know," I say. "I have heard Mrs. Fogg say she hopes her and her husband die close together because she couldn't live without him. Maybe that's what happened with Grandma and Grandpa. Plus, they were older when they had kids. Older than our parents were."

"From what we've been told, they were both strong, independent people," Rose says. "I'm sure one could have lived without the other. It's like," she pauses, tapping her notebook to her chin, "like they were tired of facing the truth so simply quit. Didn't want to do it anymore." She turns the page. "Why would Mr. Pendergrass's mom buy him his own house? Why didn't she want to live under the same roof with her own son? And Mrs. Tremblay's parents. Why did they arrange a marriage for their daughter then move away?"

I say nothing, knowing she won't hear me when she's on a roll.

"Stanley Drummond's parents did the exact same thing. As soon as another farm equipment dealership moved to town, they closed up shop and skedaddled, left him behind." A gust of wind lifts the page and Rose plasters it back down. "It's as if the kids did something in high school that their parents couldn't face and as a consequence, turned their backs on them. One of them, my guess is Mrs. Tremblay, couldn't live with her conscience and threatened to tell, and that got her and her family killed and her tongue cut out."

"But that would mean Dad knows what they did. Maybe even who the killer is," I say. We've arrived at our house and walk down the flagstone path to the back door. We stop at the bottom of the steps.

"I'm sure among the four of them there were secrets within the group, things not all of them knew," Rose says. "I mean, you know nothing about your friend anymore. Could be Dad wasn't even involved. But I'm positive whatever it was that they did, whatever the secret is, that's what ended their friendship."

CHAPTER TWENTY-NINE

Gail Drummond is standing in our front porch. I saw her walk up the sidewalk, open the porch door and step inside, then I heard nothing.

Unable to decide what to do, I stay sprawled on the couch. If she's changed her mind about coming here, I don't want to embarrass her by opening the door, but I also don't want to leave her standing in the porch. Rose thumps down the stairs in her bare feet.

"What are you doing?" she asks. "Didn't you hear the screen door bang shut?"

I stand and, along with Rose, approach the front door. Gail, who apparently has changed her mind and has her hand on the screen door ready to leave, turns when Rose flings open the inside door. Gail extends her arm, the yearbook clutched in her hand. "Here," she says.

"The yearbook?" Rose says as she takes it from her.

"Found it on our driveway," Gail says. "Your dad came by the day after the fire. Figure it fell out of his truck since he's the only one who's been to the house."

"Dad was at your place?" Rose says. "The day *after* the fire?"

"Gave me some money." She pulls a wad of cash out of her pocket and again extends her arm. "I got a job cleaning houses. Want to pay him back."

Rose reaches for the bills; I push her hand away. Gail's eyes meet mine. "I know what it's like looking after kids," I say. "They always need something."

Gail hesitates, then stuffs the money in her pocket. "Thanks," she mumbles.

"I'm sorry about your dad," I say.

"You're lucky you have your father," Gail says. "My dad, he tried, but life ate him up."

"Yeah, well," Rose says. "Things aren't always as they appear."

CHAPTER THIRTY

The weather has finally warmed up, or at least what prairie people refer to as warming up, and the temperature the past few days has been climbing to the mid-fifties by noon. Rose, Fran and I are taking our time walking back to school after lunch, happy to be outside in the milder weather as we talk about the spring carnival that's happening tonight. The event is a joint effort by both elementary schools and alternates from school to school each year. This year it's at the Catholic school.

Rose jumps in a puddle; the water rises inches from the tops of her hand-me-down rubber boots. "I can't wait for tonight," she says.

"What time can we go, Liz?" Fran asks.

"As soon as supper's done," I say.

"I'm eating at the school," Rose says. "They're going to have barbeques set up out back to cook hot dogs and hamburgers. And there's going to be popcorn, and snow cones, and candy floss, and...."

"Dad doesn't like it when we eat junk food."

"He doesn't care. He's too busy getting the store rebuilt." She jumps in another puddle; the muddy water splashes up the legs of her orange pants.

"I'm glad Dad has something to think about other than Mom dying and the store burning down," I say. "He's not grieving as much as he was a few months ago."

"The only thing Dad grieved about when Mom died, was having to raise a family. And then he didn't even do that, he hired someone to do it for him."

"Shush," I say. Fran has skipped ahead of us, eager to get to school.

"I don't hold it against him." Rose holds up her palm. "I know I was angry those first few months, but I've matured since then."

We walk in silence for a few moments.

"I mentioned the carnival to Dad this morning," Rose continues. "I told him we were taking the girls and since Mrs. Gillespie can't stay until we get home, you'd arranged for her to drop Cole off with Mrs. Henderson around seven. I asked him if he was interested in attending with us, sure he'd say he had to work, but he said he'd like to see what we're up to. Said he wanted to look at my classroom, talk to my teacher."

I open the school door for Fran who runs to her classroom without looking back. A nun walks past and Rose whispers, "I'll believe it when I see it." Then she too runs down the hall.

* * *

After waving goodbye to Cole and Mrs. Gillespie standing in the front porch, Dad, me, Rose, Fran, Robin, and Alex, walk to the school. We've all worn our shoes and spring jackets tonight and it feels wonderful to not be so bundled up. I was getting tired of helping Mrs. Gillespie get the girls dressed in so much gear that all you could see is their eyes. I'm hoping by next winter they'll be more self-sufficient.

Sunset isn't until two hours after supper, not like during the deepest winter months when the sun was already setting by the time we walked home from school. On those days, Mrs. Gillespie couldn't send the girls outside to play and when Rose, Fran and I got home from school, they'd cling to us, pressing their hot little hands against our cold cheeks. I'm happy for summer to be just around the corner, but not looking forward to the anniversary of Mom's death.

We cross The Park and circle the school to the front door. Dad seems excited, as if he's glad to be going someplace with his family; not his usual demeanour. The little girls notice the difference in him and cling to me, looking up at their father with wide eyes.

No cash exchanges hands once you're inside the school, so the line-up to buy tickets for food and games is long, and stretches out the propped open doors of the school, all the way down to the sidewalk. The six of us stop at the end of the line and I dig in my pocket for our money. Rose and I scrounged around in our drawers and found eight dollars worth of quarters, nickels and dimes. Rose even managed to find a two-dollar bill. I'm hoping ten dollars is enough for us all to have something to eat and Fran and the girls to play a couple of games. We inch our way forward, then into the foyer and to the front of the line where, to Rose's and my surprise, Dad buys us a whole roll of tickets, peeling off a few for himself.

"I've neglected your allowance for a few months," he says as he hands me the tickets. "Will this be enough for all of you?"

"Well," Rose says, taking the roll from me.

"Do you need more?" He turns to the woman selling tickets.

"No, Dad," I say. "This is plenty. Thank-you."

"I've arranged to meet some friends I haven't seen for a while, then I'm going to try one of those barbequed hamburgers Rose is always raving about. Have fun, and I'll come and find you before I leave. We can walk home together." Having said more to us at one time than he's said in months, Dad steps into the throng of people and greets old friends with a big voice and a slap on the back.

"Dad's changed," Rose says from behind me as we lose sight of him in the crowd.

"All the parents around here are more relaxed now that the murderer is dead," I say.

The little girls peer around at the school Fran and Rose go to every day.

"There's my classroom," Fran says pointing down the hall. "Number one stands for grade one."

"No it doesn't," Rose says. "I'm in grade eight and my room is number eleven. The broom closet is number eight."

"Look, Robin," I say as I tap a picture hanging on the wall. "Fran coloured this. She signed her name at the bottom. The teacher hung it on the wall because it's so good."

Robin looks impressed by her bigger sister's talent. "Will I have pictures on the wall when I go to school too?" she asks.

"Keep practicing your colouring everyday and you will." We stop beside another group of drawings. "There's one of Rose's. That's actually pretty good. I thought you didn't like drawing?"

"Don't sound so surprised," Rose says. "I am capable of doing stuff other than annoying you, you know."

"I didn't mean that," I say.

"Actually, you're not far off," Rose says. "I had one of my frozen mud photographs enlarged. You know, the ones I took the day we talked to Sister Veronica? Then I traced it." She looks at the drawing. "Kind of turned out like abstract art. I asked my teacher if I could use the actual photo as my contribution to art class and she said no. I did take a picture of the mud puddle, so I thought that should count for something. She's not the most inspired teacher in the world," Rose whispers.

We squeeze our way into the gymnasium. Noise and mayhem abound while kids and adults mill about eating, laughing, and shouting across the room to each other. Games of chance are lined up along the walls, and out the open back doors, kids are bouncing on a trampoline. A row of barbeques stands smoking in the evening light and in one of the line-ups for food, is Jen. She's by herself and I wonder where Holly and the other girls are.

Rose sees me looking at my friend. "Come on," she tugs at my sleeve. "You don't need her. We have to spend some of these tickets Dad bought us. Show our sisters how to have a good time."

I stare at the roll of tickets in Rose's hand. "How are we going to spend all of these?"

"Food," Rose says. "I'm starving."

For the next two hours, the four of us watch in amazement as Fran wins not once, not twice, but three times shooting the toy gun at the tin ducks that march buy. She pumps her fist and says *gotcha*, each time a duck falls over.

We watch in awe as Rose eats one paper plate full of hamburgers and another one filled with hot dogs, then ends her meal with two snow cones and the largest candy floss she could afford.

We tell Robin and Alex they're cute when they get their faces painted respectively as Jiminy Cricket and Cinderella, then laugh as they jump on the trampoline, smearing the paint into their hair.

Three times we see Dad. Once he's talking to Rose's teacher, his head cocked as he listens attentively. Another, he's eating a hamburger seemingly enjoying the taste as he licks ketchup off his fingers and mops his face with a napkin. The last time we see him, Mr. Pendergrass and him are talking. Mr. Pendergrass is agitated and poking his finger in Dad's face, while Dad appears to be trying to calm the man down. The two separate when other friends draw near.

It's the end of the night and Rose and I are bending over putting the little one's jackets on them, and trying to squeeze all the prizes Fran and the girls won into the bag I brought to carry stuff home. I stand abruptly and bump into Jen.

"Hi," she says.

"Hi," I say.

"What do you want?" Rose asks over top of a stuffed elephant.

"Nothing," Jen says. She scratches her elbow. "Just wondered if you're going home?"

"What business is that of yours?" Rose presses the stuffed toy into the menagerie in the bag; its trunk sticks out the top.

"Rose," I say.

"Well, why does she need to know that?"

"I thought maybe I could come over for a Coke or something?"

"Where's your new friends?" Rose says. "This too babyish for them?"

"Never mind," Jen says. "I'll go home. By myself. All alone in the dark." She walks away, glancing over her shoulder, a hang-dog expression on her face.

"Wait," I say.

Rose crosses her arms. "Her Mom's here someplace, you know. She's only playing games, trying to make you feel sorry for her."

"You can come over," I say to Jen. "As soon as we find Dad." I look around, hopeful Dad will walk around the corner.

"It's ok?" Jen says. "For me to come over?"

"Sure," I say.

"I'll go find Mom and ask her. I'll find your dad too; tell him we're going to your house." She takes two steps away, then comes back. "Don't leave this spot, ok?"

"Ok," I say.

We stand by the back door to wait. Rose has a large wad of Double Bubble in her mouth and blows bubble after bubble as she discreetly watches the people come and go.

Jen returns. She's breathless as if she ran both directions. "Mom said ok, I can come over. She was in the coffee room having a cup of tea and a cookie with some of the neighbours. I saw Mr. Pendergrass and your dad. I told them that we were going to your house and your dad said fine, he'd catch up to us later. Mr. Pendergrass said he'd be over in an hour to pick me up and walk me home. Your dad told him not to bother, that he could walk me home, but Mr. Pendergrass insisted."

Rose, Jen and I herd the little girls out the back door. After being in the hot, stifling school all evening, the cool night air feels good.

"I don't want to leave yet," Robin whines, as she sucks the last of her candy floss off the cardboard tube. Her cheeks are pink with the spun sugar.

"It's ten o'clock," I say. "Way past your bedtime. All that's left to do is the adult things. Coffee and tea rooms, stacking chairs." We pass the spot where barbeques and trampolines were standing earlier in the evening. "See," I say. "Everything's been loaded onto trucks. You missed nothing for kids."

"Did you see my teacher?" Fran says excitedly as she runs ahead, her hand bouncing off the posts of the bicycle rack. "She was wearing slacks! I've never seen her wear slacks before. She looked weird. And she was with a man. I saw them holding hands." She giggles.

"Teachers have their own lives," I say. "You only see them in the classroom, but they do other things besides teach you."

Fran is quiet. "I want to be a teacher when I grow up," she announces. "Then when school's done for the day, I want to go home to my very own house where I'll have a garden and make supper for my husband."

Rose runs backwards in front of us. Light from the school turns her face from pale to dark as the backdoor opens and closes. "Guess how many hot dogs I ate?" she asks.

"A hundred million," Robin says.

"A hundred million?" Rose says. "Do you know how many a hundred million is?"

"A lot!" Alex exclaims. "Your tummy must be full."

"I ate four hot dogs, which is a lot considering I also ate two hamburgers." She rubs her belly. "They were so good I could eat another four right now."

"I wonder if Dad liked the barbequed hamburger?" I say. "He looked like he was enjoying himself."

"It was nice of Dad to give us our allowance," Rose says. "Which he missed giving to us for months even though we were doing everything around the house. And to make an appearance at our school and talk to our teacher's like a real parent."

"He's trying, Rose," I say.

"What?" she says, feigning innocence. "Just saying."

The path becomes dim as we walk away from the ambient light of the school and I'm able to see a cigarette glowing from under the slide. At first, I think it must be Mr. Pendergrass, but then I remember Jen saw him talking to Dad. Robin is in the lead and I give her a nudge on the back to move faster.

"What, you're not scared of us are you?" a voice says. "We wouldn't hurt a fly." Three people step forward and block our path. It's Holly and her gang. "We only want to say hi, that's all." She looks at me, a patronizing smile on her face; I lift my chin and match her stare. "Isn't this sweet," she says. "The Murphy girls going home with painted faces and candy floss after the spring carnival. Looks like a real family, even if they don't have a mother." She turns to Robin. "Did you have a good time, little girl?"

Robin nods.

"Come on, Alex, let's go," I say when she's about to tell them she had a good time too.

"So, Jennifer," Holly says. "What are you doing out here with these kids? We won't wait around forever, you know." Holly snorts. "Fourteen going on four."

Rose shifts her gum to her other cheek; it bulges out as big as an egg. "It's time for you to get out of the way so we can take our sisters home," she says.

"You let this kid," Holly says to Jen, "stick up for you?"

Even in the dark I can see Rose's temper flare. She steps closer to the girls.

"No, Rose," I say.

She ignores me. "I may be younger than you," she says, "but I'm smarter and my maturity level is leaps and bounds ahead of yours. You're nothing but a bully who has to make people do what you want so you can tell yourself you're better than everyone else. I believe," Rose continues, "the psychological diagnosis would be *low self-esteem causing narcissism*. You should read a book or two, you might learn something. If you can read, that is."

I doubt anyone has ever stood up to Holly before and it takes a few moments to dawn on her that she's been insulted. "You won't think I'm scared when I push one of your sisters to the ground." She steps towards Robin; I pull the little girl closer to me.

"You touch my sister and I'll beat you to a pulp." Rose puts up her fists and spits her wad of gum to the ground. It sits there, a pale pink blob sagging slowly into the mud.

Jen steps beside Rose. "And so will I," she says. "Lay one finger on this little girl and you'll regret it."

Eventually Holly spits out, "Oh yeah?"

"Yeah," Rose says. "Try it. I haven't beat anyone up since Tuesday."

Holly pauses, appearing to contemplate whether or not Rose means business. After a few moments of hesitation, she takes a step backwards, as do her friends. "Time to go," she says to her gang. "Lots of other kids out here. I don't want to work up a sweat with these babies." They turn to cross The Park.

"And don't come back," Rose yells after them. "Or you'll know how it feels to get punched in the face. I doubt your boyfriend will want to kiss you with no front teeth."

"It'll be a cold day in hell before any boy even wants to go out with you," Holly calls from a distance. "You're the ugliest person I've ever seen."

"Look at the brave girl running halfway across the playground before she comes up with an insult. Come and say that to my face," Rose says. Holly keeps moving in the opposite direction. "And look in a mirror once in a while," Rose continues. "You've got a goober as big as a ping pong ball hanging out of your nose."

Holly stops. She faces one of her friends and points at her nose. "Just look for God's sake," we hear her shriek. Her friend peers up Holly's nose then nods. Holly grabs her friend's arm and furiously wipes her face with the sleeve of the girl's coat, then gives her a push and stomps away.

"Thanks, Rose," Jen says.

"Listen, Olsen." Rose unwraps a piece of gum and pushes it into her mouth. "The only reason I stood up to those punks was because I wanted to show my sisters that bullies are all talk. I wanted them to know that you can't let people walk all over you. I didn't stand up to them for you, I did it for them." She points at Alex, Robin, and Fran, then unwraps a second piece of gum and wedges it beside the first. "If you ever get yourself into something you can't get out of again," she says as she chews around the pink mass, "don't count on me to help."

"I don't know about the rest of you," I say, my heart pounding, "but I've had enough for one night. Time to get home and put the girls to bed."

"I'm tired, Liz," Alex says. She holds her arms out. "Carry me."

"I'm not going to carry you. You can walk as well as the rest of us. You're a big girl now. Just about as big as Robin."

"No she's not," Robin says. "When I have a birthday, so does she. She'll never catch up."

"Well, she's as old as you were when Mom died," I say." And you were a big girl then, right?"

"But she'll never be the same age as me."

"No. And Rose will never be the same age as me, and Fran will never be the same age as Rose, and I'll never be the same age as Jen."

"Jen's older than you?"

"She is."

"Jen's the oldest," Alex states. "She's in charge. Who's older, Mommy or Daddy?"

"Mom," I say.

Our house looms in the distance. Mrs. Gillespie has left the outside light on, but since she dropped Cole off before the sun went down, she forgot to leave a light on inside and instead of a welcoming glow, the windows are black. I told Mrs. Henderson I'd pick Cole up when we were finished at the carnival, but she said there was no sense in waking the child just to carry him across the street and we could pick him up in the morning. So, leaving our brother with the neighbour, we tromp down the flagstone path to the back door. I pull out my key and we pile inside the mud room, kick off our shoes and hang up our coats.

The house feels empty without Dad, Mrs. Gillespie, and Cole here. It felt empty for months after Mom died, but I hadn't realized how much Mrs. Gillespie has filled that void and I feel like a traitor to Mom.

"I want a bedtime snack," Fran says.

"No snack. You ate so much at the carnival, your stomach's going to explode." I clap my hands. "Ok, everyone. Into your pj's. Then brush your teeth, and wash your hands and faces. Rose and I will come and tuck you in when you're in your beds."

"Aw," Robin groans as she climbs the stairs.

"Want a root beer?" I ask my friend.

"Why do you still have root beer in your fridge?" Jen asks. "I thought you were an Orange Crush fan."

"Don't flatter yourself," Rose says. "No one else likes it. That's why it's in the back of the fridge behind the sardines and the pickled onions. We didn't go and buy some just in case you decided to grace us with your presence."

I smile and pull the Hires out from behind a bottle of ketchup, then grab myself an Orange Crush. "Want something, Rose?"

"You're kidding. You never offer to get me a drink."

"Do you want something or not? Last chance."

"I'll take a Coke," Rose says.

The three of us enter the living room. Jen and I sit on the couch while Rose slumps into Dad's chair. "Why didn't you shoplift?" she asks Jennifer as she pulls the tab off her Coke can.

"I don't know," Jen says.

"If you expect me to apologize for accusing you," Rose says, "you'll be waiting until hell freezes over."

"I don't expect...."

"Because you still had those matches in my sister's drawer. And you did dump her for those losers."

"Rose," I say.

"Guess I'm not a very good friend," Jen says.

"It's ok," I say quietly then smile shyly at her.

The mud room door bursts open causing the three of us jump. Dad races into the house. "Time for your friend to leave." He parts the kitchen curtains and peers into the darkness. "I'll walk her home. Lock the door and put on the chain when I leave," he says to me.

"Dad?" I join him in the kitchen. "What's the matter?"

"Did you hear me, Liz? Put the chain on when I leave."

"I heard you, Dad."

"Do not let anyone inside, no matter who it is or what they say."

There's a pounding on the front door.

Jen stands. "That's probably Mr. Pendergrass. He can walk me home, Mr. Murphy."

In four long strides, Dad is at the door. He has the gold chain in his hand and is about to slide it into place when Mr. Pendergrass pushes the door open, knocking Dad onto his back. Rose and Jen run into the kitchen to stand beside me.

Mr. Pendergrass steps over Dad, kicking Dad's hand when he

attempts to grab his leg. Dad presses his knuckles to his mouth and the tall man stops in the kitchen doorway.

"Are you kids alright?" he asks as he stares at Dad.

CHAPTER THIRTY-ONE

Dad rolls to his knees then climbs to his feet. I reach for my sister's and friend's hands. I feel Jen shaking. Alex and Robin giggling in their room, sounds surreal in the quiet.

Mr. Pendergrass looks behind him towards the stairs. "Are your sisters in bed?" he asks.

"Yes," I say.

He nods his approval.

"My children are no business of yours," Dad says, pulling Mr. Pendergrass's attention away from us. He attempts to shoulder his way into the kitchen but Mr. Pendergrass pushes him and Dad stumbles back into the living room.

Jen, Rose and I back up, stopping near the kitchen sink.

"Why did you have to think you're above the law?" Mr. Pendergrass says.

Dad steps closer to the man then snakes out his arm.

Mr. Pendergrass backs up, avoiding his grasp. "Ruined everything."

"It's not me," Dad says. "You and your big mouth, that's what ruined everything. How did your dad know where we were, Pendergrass? How the hell did he know what we were doing?"

"You still think you're above the law," Mr. Pendergrass says. "If she'd only kept her thoughts to herself, she'd be alive today. Couldn't carry the guilt any longer, I suppose."

"Dad?" I say.

"Go upstairs," Dad says.

None of us leave.

"You and I both know that Stan was innocent," Mr. Pendergrass says. "We both know who killed Marj."

Again, Dad moves towards Mr. Pendergrass, and again Mr. Pendergrass avoids his reach by backing up. The two of them are gradually edging their way into the kitchen as they move closer to us. Rose, Jen, and I, back into the office.

"That's true, Carl," Dad says. "Stan was innocent. I only wish my store hadn't been involved. One of my daughters just about died in that fire. Is that why you're here tonight? To kill me and my family too? To keep me quiet like you did to him?"

"Quit it," Mr. Pendergrass blusters. "Don't say such things. You coerced him to the store and you know it."

"Who do you think the police are going to believe; the odd man who lives alone in the house his mother bought him, or a well-respected businessman raising his family after the tragic loss of his wife? You're the one who had a breakdown, you're the one standing in my house threatening my children."

Mr. Pendergrass shoves his hand into his jacket pocket and pulls out a gun. "We're going to the police," he says. "This has gone on long enough. It's time the right person was charged."

I pull Jen and Rose to the bottom of the steps, then the three of us race upstairs and pound down the hall. Rose runs into Fran's bedroom while Jen and I push open the door of the girls' room. From the floor below, we hear a lamp breaking and thuds and grunts as the two men fight. The sound of a gun firing reverberates through the wooden floors. With the girls in our arms, Jen and I follow Rose and Fran into my bedroom where Rose has popped out the screen. One by one I lift the girls over the ledge and whisper to them to go to the treehouse. Rose picks up her camera and a flashcube off the dresser then follows the girls out the window.

When it comes to Jen's turn she balks. "I'm not going out there," she says.

"For God's sake, Jen. Do you want to die? This is not the time to be afraid of heights. Don't look down, that's all. Just don't look down. It's like walking on a sidewalk, only twenty feet in the air."

From the end of the hall, footsteps thump up the stairs. Jen swings her legs out the window and stands at the edge, unable to move.

"You need to move, Jen. I can't get out."

"I can't. I'm going to fall."

Rose leaves the treehouse and makes her way towards Jennifer. "Grab my hand, Jen. I won't let you fall."

Jen shakes her head.

"Move your ass! If you don't, something terrible is going to happen!"

Jen takes Rose's outstretched hand. I climb over the window frame. Then with Jennifer sandwiched between us, we run as fast we are able in this six-legged race, to the treehouse. Fran, Alex, and Robin are huddled on the bench, their faces white with fear. I sit beside them, pulling Alex onto my lap. Instead of Dad, Mr. Pendergrass appears in the bedroom window and my heart drops. He folds his thin frame through the narrow opening and onto the roof.

"That's good," he says. "Stay there. I won't let him get you there."

Out of the corner of my eye, I see Rose lift up her camera. She reaches into a pocket of her overalls and pulls out the flashcube.

Dad's voice yells, "Pendergrass." Mr. Pendergrass turns. "Leave my kids alone." He's shouting loud enough to be heard blocks away.

"It's not me they need to be afraid of, Murphy," Mr. Pendergrass says.

"For God's sake, Pendergrass, I'm not going to hurt my kids."

Dad, who must have wrenched the gun from Mr. Pendergrass, now points the weapon at the man's head. I pull Alex to the floor of the treehouse, Jen, Fran and Robin follow. From my knees, I glance at Rose; she's kneeling and has her camera pressed to her face. A shot rings out and the treehouse briefly glows with the light from the flashcube. Mr. Pendergrass falls backwards. His body drapes over the waist high railing, slips to the roof then drops over the edge. The last thing I see are his long legs as they disappear into the night. Dad appears at the window.

"Liz, are you alright?" he asks, his hand pressing his shoulder.

"Yes," I say.

"Is everyone there with you?"

"Yes," I say again. "Everyone is here with me."

Mr. Krieger's voice shouts from his backyard. "What's going on? Are you up there Jim?"

CHAPTER THIRTY-TWO

Rose and I have been in bed for an hour but neither of us is sleeping. My back is to her and I've heard her sigh multiple times, but so far, she hasn't said anything. From past experience with my analytical sister, I know I'm going to be listening to what's on her mind very soon.

It's been one week since Dad shot and killed Mr. Pendergrass and we are all feeling the effects. Fran reads from the moment she gets up to the moment she goes to bed, lost in a fictitious world where nothing bad happens. Rose, who normally would be roaming the town snapping pictures, has stayed in the front porch, flipping the pages in her notebook, rereading her deductions or simply staring at the street while watching the world go by. I've been trying to distract myself by digging the garden. I have plans to plant vegetables, like Mom did, though not sure if I'll have the energy to get that far. Dad is spending most of his time, as usual, at the store. When he is at home, he seems more content than he's been in months. Alex and Robin went outside for the first time today to play on their swings. For the past week they've clung to Rose and me as if we're going to abandon them, and tonight is the first night they haven't slept in our bed. Rose tosses and turns for five more minutes before rolling to her side and tapping me on the shoulder. I turn over to face my sister. She smells like Ivory Soap.

"How are you managing to buy your soap?" I ask.

"I could tell you, but you're not going to like it," she says.

"What?" I say. "Are you doing something illegal?"

"No, I'm not doing anything illegal. I found some money."

"Where?"

"In Mom's purse."

"In Mom's purse!"

"Don't get all bent out of shape. Dad always gave Mom money on Friday for grocery shopping on Saturday. She would put it in her purse then hang the purse in the closet under her coat. She died on a Friday so I took it before Dad gave all Mom's belongings away. There was a hundred dollars inside. I gave some to you. Little bits here and there so you wouldn't suspect. Say," she says. "You haven't seen a roll of film kicking around, have you?"

"I haven't," I say. "Why?"

"Lost one. I've searched everywhere. Someone must have tossed it out."

"It has been crazy around here these past few days. Wouldn't surprise me," I say.

She's quiet for a few minutes and I think she's fallen asleep. "What did Dad say when he came home from the funeral?" she asks with a yawn.

"Not too much; you know Dad. He said there weren't many people in attendance. A few high school friends, a couple of neighbours. Mrs. Olsen was there but not Jen. Said Father didn't have a lot to say other than to pray for the man's soul."

"I suppose everyone is finding it hard to have sympathy for the man since he was going to let Mr. Drummond take the fall for something the RCMP have now determined he did. And then trying to kill Dad and potentially even us. It's like Mrs. Witherspoon said; he became famous after he died. Or rather infamous." Her voice is quiet in the dark room.

"I didn't know you could charge someone with a crime after they died," I say.

"I did," Rose says. "As long as there's enough evidence. They must consider his coming to the house with a gun, and chasing us across the roof, as enough evidence. I would think they'd need something more concrete, like Mrs. Tremblay's tongue stashed in a jar under his bed, or in a plastic bag in the freezer." She breathes deeply. "Did you notice Dad was shouting?"

"When?" I say.

"When he was yelling at Mr. Pendergrass on the roof to leave us alone. He yelled loud enough for the whole town to hear. Said, *Leave my kids alone.*"

"We were sitting ducks. What was he supposed to do, let him kill us? If Mr. Pendergrass had made it across the catwalk to the treehouse, he'd have dropped us over the side like rag dolls. Can you imagine? There's still a dent in the lawn where he hit the ground. The girls avoided that spot all morning. Why? You think Dad shouldn't have been yelling?"

"I dunno," Rose says. She lifts her head, picks up her pillow, plumps it, then drops it back down. She rubs her nose with the palm of her hand, muffling her words. "It was like he wanted everyone to hear that Mr. Pendergrass was going to hurt us."

"He was going to hurt us."

"But Dad also said, *I'm not going to hurt my kids,* as if Mr. Pendergrass thought Dad was going to hurt us. And remember in the living room when they were fighting? It sounded like each was accusing the other of the Tremblay murders."

"You sound like you're defending Mr. Pendergrass. You were the one who told me last winter that he could be the killer. I was the one who said he wasn't. Now you think otherwise?"

I feel the bed move as she shrugs.

"I think," I say, "when everyone had made it up the stairs and Mr. Pendergrass was at the bedroom window, Dad was shouting to distract him from crossing the catwalk towards us."

Again, she's quiet.

"You don't agree?" I ask.

"I don't think I have any choice. If I want to grow up to become a normal, well-adjusted adult, it's what I have to believe."

CHAPTER THIRTY-THREE

It's Christmas Eve and the manager of Willowsbend Home for Seniors wants Dad's room cleared out so someone new can move in over the holiday season. His funeral was six days ago and I've been procrastinating doing the job. Today, with Rose behind me wrestling boxes down the hall, I push open the door to room 212, Dad's place of residence for the last ten years. I think back to the number of times I've visited him here, how many times I've walked these halls. More than I can count. We celebrated his eighty-fifth birthday in the dining room just last week.

"Seems funny without him sitting in his chair by the window." Rose looks over my shoulder at the work we have to do.

"Yeah," I say.

"He lived a lot of years in here by himself."

"He did."

"I've always thought it odd Dad never remarried. For a while, after everything settled down and the hardware store was rebuilt, I wondered if he might marry Mrs. Gillespie. I suppose that would have been too weird, even for Dad."

"I'm not surprised he didn't remarry," I say. "I don't think anyone could replace Mom."

"Sweet Liz," Rose says. "Still seeing the world through rose coloured glasses. Anyone who would have looked after his kids, made his meals and kept his house clean would have done as his wife." She sits in Dad's chair, rubbing her hands on the thread bare arms. "I wonder what went through his mind while he sat here day after day. Do you think he had fond memories about us, about Mom, about the hardware store?"

"Of course he did. Dad's never been effusive, that's all. He keeps his emotions beneath the surface. I think the only one who knew him well was Mom."

"Did he talk to you about Mr. Pendergrass, Mr. Drummond, the Tremblays?" she asks. "He sure wouldn't talk about it with me. And you know me; I tried for years."

"Never did. Every time I brought up the subject, he'd dismiss it. Said it was history and he wasn't about to dredge up the past. He'd lost his friends, his wife, and his store all within an eight-month span. That's a lot for one person to endure. I think he wanted to forget about it and move on."

I stand behind Rose and stare out Dad's window to look across the street at the apartment block where Mrs. Witherspoon's house once stood. Fifteen years ago, when she died at the ripe old age of ninety-nine, her daughter had the house demolished and the yard art, which had grown immensely in the years after Mom died, dismantled and hauled to the dump. Many of the neighbours were happy to see it cleaned up, but I was sad. I thought it added an element of eccentricity to our town, which is one reason I chose to marry a farmer and stay here.

"Do you remember when we went to the grand opening of this place?" I say.

"I remember everything about growing up here," Rose says. "Mom forced me to attend. I complained the whole time and sat without paying attention through the entire ceremony until the sign was unveiled. I was kind of a smart aleck when I was a kid."

I put my hand on her shoulder. She rests her head, the red hair now streaked with grey, on my hand. "We sat in chairs on the front lawn and listened to the mayor make a speech about what a grand place this was." I look at the walls that need a coat of paint and the flooring, now chipped and cracked.

Rose laughs. "I even took a picture of the mayor when he saw the Willowsbend Cemetery sign. He was elected for a second term on that mistake. Everyone thought he was a good sport about it when he announced, *Welcome to Willowsbend, where our seniors come to rest in peace.*"

"When I went to that opening, I never thought Dad would be living here. But then, when you're a kid you don't imagine your parents growing old or even dying."

"You and I grew up that summer, there's no doubt about that," Rose says as she stands and places empty boxes around the room. "Jen too, though at the time I didn't have much hope for her. She packed a lot of life into a few years, that girl. Guess I shouldn't have told her I hoped she'd get cancer and die."

"Cigarettes killed her, Rose, not what you said. Do you ever wonder if things would have turned out differently if Mom hadn't died?"

"I'm sure lots of things would have been different," Rose says. She pulls some shoes out of the closet and drops them into a box. "One event can alter the course of events for many years. And something as traumatic as your mom dying, well, there's no telling how much that affected everything."

"Maybe Jen wouldn't have been at the house. Maybe Dad wouldn't have chased Mr. Pendergrass up the stairs and through the window. Maybe...."

"Maybe Mr. Pendergrass wouldn't have been found guilty. It's funny they never found the tongue," Rose says. "Those things are taken as trophies; they are not tossed out with the garbage."

"He was the garbage man," I say. "Probably dropped it at the dump, never to be seen again." I laugh. "Remember when you theorized that Mr. Pendergrass was the murderer because the Tremblay's yard was messy and he was such a fuss-pot that the clutter drove him crazy?"

"Yeah, well, not my best hypothesis."

"From child crime scene investigator to most sought after criminal defence lawyer in the province. You had the right person even though the reason he did it was never established."

"I wish I'd been old enough to work that case. So many suspects, so many deaths, never any motives for any of the accused." She reaches into the closet and pulls some shirts off the hangers.

The door swings open and Fran steps into the room.

"Fran," I say. "Glad you made it." I give her a hug. "Driving isn't too bad today?"

"Not bad at all. They keep the road between here and the city perfectly clear, not like when we were kids and the highway was ploughed only a couple times a winter."

"Have you seen Cole? Is he coming to help?"

"I left him at the hardware store. He'll be by as soon as he closes up for the day. I'm so glad it's Christmas break. I love my grade one kids, but it's good to have time off."

"You'd have made a great mother, Franny," I say.

"Not as good as Mom." She tosses her purse on the bed. "I stopped at Cole's house to drop off my suitcase and gifts. Place looks like it did when Mom was alive. I still remember the tree in the corner in the living room, baking covering the counters." She blinks behind her glasses. "When do the girls arrive?"

"They fly in tonight. We'll all go to midnight Mass together. I wish Dad were here to celebrate with us. I guess we can't choose the time of our demise. Don't you think it's funny we still call Robin and Alex the girls. Like they're twins."

"They may as well be," Rose says. "Both doctors and married with two kids. Both big city dwellers with houses in the suburbs. You'd think they were in competition with each other. I myself have never competed with anyone." She sits on the edge of Dad's bed and opens a drawer. A comb and brush set, inlaid with abalone shell, rests on top of a matching mirror. "It's Mom's dresser set. I don't remember Dad keeping this."

"That's because he wouldn't let us help him pack up their bedroom when he moved here. He wanted to do it by himself. He still missed Mom."

Rose lifts out a pair of glasses with yellow frames. "Look at these," she says.

"Hey, those are mine," Fran says. "My first pair of glasses. You took me to the eye doctor, Liz." She takes them from Rose. "I can't believe he saved these."

Rose puts her hand in the drawer and pulls out a pair of blue sleepers.

"Those had to have been Cole's," I say. "Other than the few things the neighbours gave him as baby gifts, that boy wore nothing but pink for the first year of his life. I bought him a pair of blue-jeans when he was twelve. He wore them until the cuffs were up to his knees. Then I cut them off and made shorts out of them."

"You were a good sister," Fran says.

"Who's a good sister?" Cole says from the doorway.

"Liz," Rose says.

"You got that right," he says.

Being as how Cole was only two months old when Mom died, he's never had to grieve her loss like the rest of us. As far as he's concerned, I'm like a mother to him. Unlike his five sisters, his resemblance to Mom is uncanny with his dark hair and blue eyes. But every once in a while, I see our dad in him when he walks with his confident gait or gives us one of his rare smiles the same way Dad did.

Rose opens the bottom drawer and pulls out a pink dress. "Oh my God. It's Alex's pink fairy costume." She gives it a shake; sequins fly across the room. "She looked so cute in this." She reaches in the drawer again and takes out a ghost costume, then a cowboy shirt. She waves the shirt at me. "Remember these? We wore them the night Jen talked us into going to the Tremblay's that first Halloween after they died. We took off our costumes and stuffed them in our candy bags. Then when the ghost chased us, we dropped the bags by the hedge and ran."

"A ghost chased you?" Cole says.

"Not really a ghost, Jen's ghost," Rose says. "And he wasn't a ghost, he was...." She waves her hand at her brother. "Too hard to explain."

"It was Stevie Drummond," I say to Cole. "Your sister punched him in the nose. He was hiding by the porch waiting to scare us."

"You punched a boy in the nose?" Cole says. "Why am I not surprised?"

"I still maintain someone else was there," Rose says. "The next day I went back to the Tremblay's to get the pillowcases but they were gone." She fingers the yellowed costumes. "I wonder how Dad got these." She reaches in the drawer and pulls out a stack of papers held together with paper clips. *Through Children's Eyes*, is written in red marker on the cardboard cover.

I take the pages from her. "That's my grade nine paper. We had to do a ten-thousand-word story by the end of the year. The teacher, I can't remember her name."

"Mrs. Cooper," Rose says.

"Yes, that's right. Mrs. Cooper," I say. "She told us to write about anything we were interested in."

"What's it about?" Cole asks.

"Everything that happened from the day you were born until Mr. Pendergrass tried to follow us across the cat-walk."

"Must have been pretty good." He points to the A+ on the cover.

"There's something else in here," Rose says. She slides her hand to the back of the drawer and pulls out a photo album. On the out-side in black marker is written: **Summer 71 Through Spring 72**. "Oh my goodness," she says.

"That looks like one of your photo albums," I say.

"Dad seemed bored sitting here by himself and I figured it was high-time he took an interest in his family so I gave him this years ago to look through." She taps the album.

"Open it," Cole says. "Let's see what you took pictures of that summer."

The first picture is of Mom standing in her garden, seed packets in hand. She has Alex in her arms and is very pregnant with Cole.

"Oh my God," Fran says. "I remember that garden." She wipes a finger under her glasses.

"I remember how much work it was," Rose says. "Picking beans, helping Mom make relish."

"Helping Mom make relish!" I say. "You never helped. It was me who picked and scrubbed cucumbers for hours on end." I poke my sister in the back.

Rose turns the page. We look at a picture of me sitting on the ground, my hand in mid-air as I attempt to block Rose from taking my picture. "What the heck am I doing?" I say.

Rose taps the word, *eavesdropping* that she's printed and stuck at the bottom of the picture. "Dad had the neighbourhood men over to toast the birth of Cole. You were listening by the front porch."

"It was hot and I was waiting for Jen. The three of us walked to The Park," I say, the picture jogging my memory.

The opposite page has a picture of Jen sitting on the slide at the playground.

"Were we talking about the murders?" I say to Rose.

"That's all we talked about back then."

"By the time my kids got to that playground everything had been modernized. No more merry-go-round that makes you so nauseous you can barely walk," I say. "And no more swings that you could pump so high, you could just about swing over the top bar."

"Thank God," Rose says. "I'd have killed my kids if I ever saw them doing that."

She turns the page to a picture of a house with a gravel road in the foreground. One person is on the road, one in the ditch. I look more closely. "This is the Drummond's street. You thought this person, who is most likely Mr. Drummond," I point at the blurry figure in the ditch, "was the killer."

On the opposite page we laugh at Sister Veronica sailing past on her bike. When she died, her obituary said she was sixty-nine years old and I was surprised. That made her only eight years older than me. The day Rose and I talked to her in front of Mr. Pendergrass's house, she seemed older and wiser than I do now. The next picture is of Mr. Pendergrass, his hat in his hands, looking right at the camera. None of us say anything.

She flips another page. A picture of Mom holding Cole in his blue sleepers while we stand around the rocking chair, looks back at us. "This is the day Mom brought you home from the hospital. She was in the office, sitting in the rocking chair holding you while the five of us stood around her. We'd just come back from swimming."

"I remember that day," I say. "Seems like a lifetime ago."

"That's because it was," Rose says.

"We were all worried our brother was going to take over. We thought we weren't wanted anymore," Fran says.

"Remember when you told Alex that Mom loves all of us, not only our new baby brother." Rose says. "You tried to make everything ok. Always the peacemaker." She turns to her brother. "You were the cause of a lot of stress to us. We thought Mom and Dad would love you more because you're a boy, the only boy. They obviously tried five times to have a son."

"I've heard this story for forty-six years," he says.

The next page has two pictures of me tucked under its plastic cover. "What's in my mouth?" I ask as I point at the first picture.

"Peanut butter." Rose points to the words, *at the pool*. "You took a bite of the wrong sandwich."

"And this one?" I point at the other snapshot. "I look like I've seen a ghost."

"That one I remember clearly. Mom asked you to accompany Father to the Drummond's to take the family some clothes and food. Everyone thought Mr. Drummond was the killer. That's why I titled it *Scaredsville*. Guess that was kind of mean."

"Father was the only adult who would talk to me about the murders. He was a nice man, said nice things at Mom's funeral."

Rose turns the plastic sheet and the women from our childhood fill the page. "Mom had the neighbour women over for iced tea to thank them for their help after Cole was born." We look at our neighbours, most of them dead and gone.

Rose continues to flip through the album. Some of the pictures I remember, most I don't. Rose, of course, remembers them all.

A picture of the five of us standing from tallest to shortest against the side of the house, brings tears to my eyes.

"I loved those orange overalls," Rose says. "First day of school for you, Fran."

On the opposite page, the picture of Halloween after Mom died is tucked under the plastic. Me as a ghost, Rose as a cowgirl, Fran as a clown, Robin as a princess and Alex as a fairy. "Mrs. Olyphant took that," I say.

A baby in a pink snowsuit under a Christmas tree is in the next shot.

"Who's this?" I ask. "I thought you didn't get any pictures of Cole as a pink Baby Jesus."

"On Boxing Day, I dressed him in the snowsuit when you were busy with the girls. I put him under the tree and took his picture."

"You used to try and get me to wear pink shirts to school," Cole says. "You'd say things like, *they aren't that pink!* or, *maybe you'll start a new trend.* I'd stuff the shirt I wore the day before in my school bag and change behind the garage."

When we get to the end of the book, a small bundle of pictures falls to the floor. They have an elastic band wrapped around them.

"What the heck?" Rose takes the elastic off the stack.

The first picture is of our house. Mom's handwriting on the white border says, *Our first home, 1956.* Mom is standing on the front step, pointing at the address, 106 Pine. She's smiling. I reach out and rub my thumb over the words.

"That's Mom." Cole says.

"It sure is," Rose says. "She must have been about twenty-five in that shot. You look a lot like her."

Dad's in the next shot, same step, same pose.

"They were both so young," Fran says. "Innocent."

The next picture is of the treehouse when it was new. Mom stands below, very pregnant.

Rose taps the picture. "There you are, Liz. First baby picture. Mom looks happy."

The last picture is one I've never seen. "What's this?" I ask. "Did you take this, Rose?"

"Oh my God," Rose says. "This is the night Dad shot Mr. Pendergrass. I snapped a shot as he fired the gun."

The four of us stare at the picture. Mr. Pendergrass is on the catwalk, his back to the camera and his arms extended as if blocking Dad from getting to the treehouse. Under his outstretched arm, an image of Dad peering from inside the bedroom window stares back at us frozen in time. He's pointing a gun at Mr. Pendergrass and a flash is coming out of the muzzle.

"Why haven't we seen this before?" I ask.

"Lost the roll of film," Rose says. "Figured in all the commotion of Dad killing someone, I set it down somewhere other than the to be developed box and it got tossed. I can't imagine I'd do such a thing, but reasoned that when your dad kills someone, it's a traumatic experience for a kid. And there were lots of people in our house for a few days after; cops, neighbours, reporters. I tore the house apart but never found it. I wonder why Dad didn't tell me he found the film and had it developed. Wouldn't he be proud for saving the lives of his family?" Rose asks.

"He probably didn't want to traumatize us any further." I take the picture from her. "It is rather an upsetting picture for a child to see; her dad killing someone."

"This is unbelievable," Rose says. "Award winning photography.

Rose and I glance at each other, remembering Mrs. Witherspoon's prophecy.

"Why does Dad look happy?" Cole asks.

"What?" I say.

"Why is he smiling?"

Instead of grimacing as most people would when they're shooting someone, Dad has a broad smile on his face. "I suppose it's because he's got Mr. Pendergrass in his crosshairs," I say.

Fran takes the picture from me and holds it close to her glasses. "He was stopping a killer from throwing his children out of the tree. Wouldn't that make him happy?" She squints at the photograph. "Wouldn't that make anyone happy?"

We stare at the picture in Fran's hand, lost in our thoughts.

"There was never any suspicion placed on Dad, was there?" Cole asks. "In the nine months or so of the investigation, did the cops ever consider Dad as a suspect?"

"Never," Rose says. "The cops suspected Mr. Drummond from the very beginning, then of course, Mr. Pendergrass was charged post-mortem after he came to the house waving a gun. Dad was never on their radar."

"I can't believe I'm asking this," Cole says to Rose, "but in your educated opinion, would someone be happy if the person he was killing had knowledge of something they did? Something that could change their life?"

Rose stares at Cole, her green eyes unblinking as she thinks. "You're right." She repeats her brother's question. "Why *is* he smiling?" She takes the picture from Fran. "You know," she says, "I was the only one not lying on the treehouse floor that night. You," she says to me, "pulled the kids down to keep them safe. But I knelt because I wanted to get the proper angle for the picture." She looks at the three of us. "I remember Dad smiling. I remember him smiling and saying something as he fired the gun."

"What? I ask. "What did Dad say?"

"*I win*," she says. "As Dad fired the gun, he smiled and said, *I win*."

"Oh, come on, Rose," I say. "You've never told me that before."

"Everyone was so upset; I didn't see any reason to cause any more problems. And I couldn't say for sure because it was such a crazy situation in the first place. With the treehouse swaying, the girls crying and Dad and Mr. Pendergrass yelling, it was difficult to hear. So, I pushed it out of my thoughts." She shrugs. "This," she shakes the picture, "brought it back."

Suddenly, Cole grabs the photograph and tears it in two.

"Hey," Rose says. "That's mine!"

"I've changed my mind," he says. "I wish we'd never seen this stupid picture." He hands the pieces to his sister. "I know you pride yourself on your memory, Rose, and I have to agree, it is amazing the things you can recall. But you can't remember what happened that long ago, no one could." He waves his hand at the photograph. "I don't want to see any more pictures. Dad is not," he moves to the door and pushes it closed, "a murderer. Especially when he can't be here to defend himself!"

"I kind of feel the same way," Fran says. "We shouldn't be speaking ill of the dead when the one who we're speaking ill of is our own father."

I shrug my shoulders. "Too late to change anything. Everyone involved is dead and buried," I say.

I look at Rose, she raises her eyebrows. "Ok then, that's settled," she says. "Mr. Pendergrass killed the Tremblays, then killed Mr. Drummond because he was going to turn him in for the murders. He came to the house that night to kill Dad and maybe even us. He'd suffered a severe mental breakdown. That's what was decided in a court of law and we should leave it at that." She straightens the stack of photographs, stretches the elastic around them, then drops the pictures into her purse.

Fran walks to the closet and tosses a few more items into the box Rose had already begun to fill. "Time to clean this room up and go to Cole's for Christmas Eve. I'm excited to see Robin and Alex." She closes the flap with tape and drags the box to the hall for Good-will to pick up.

For an hour the four of us empty Dad's dresser and closet, strip the bed and gather his toiletries. We take what mementos we want, then put the rest of his belongings into boxes to be given away. Memories all gone in the blink of an eye.

"Bye, Cole," I say. "See you at home."

He gives me a kiss on the cheek. "See you at home," he says cautiously. "Are my nieces coming over too?"

"They are. And their spouses, and my granddaughters," I say.

Fran rushes out the door. "Just a couple of last-minute gifts to pick up. See you later," she says from the hallway.

After our siblings are gone, Rose and I pull Dad's dresser away from the wall to leave in the hall along with the other donations to Good-will. As we're dragging the heavy piece of furniture across the floor, tape peels away from the back of the old wood, and an envelope drops to the linoleum.

Rose picks it up and easily opens the glued flap. "Oh my God," she says as she peers inside.

CHAPTER THIRTY-FOUR

She pulls a writing pad out of the envelope.

"It's your notebook," I say. "The one you lost."

"I didn't lose it; it went missing." She flips a few pages, rereading what she wrote all those years ago. "I was reading this to you the day we saw the fire. I never saw it again. I wonder how Dad got hold of it?"

"He probably found it and forgot to give it back to you, I say.

"And secretly taped it to the back of his dresser?" She turns to the first page and looks up at me with excited eyes.

"You want to read it to me now, don't you?" I say.

"I wouldn't mind."

"Ok. But make it quick. I want to get to Cole's. I'm feeling the need for a glass of wine, or maybe even two."

"Remember," she says. "This was written by a twelve-year-old." She peruses her notes from long ago. "Well, this page has the names of the people I thought could be guilty." She turns the writing pad around so I can see.

"That is vaguely familiar," I say.

She flips the page. "This is the part I never got a chance to read." She begins to pace the room as if addressing a jury. "Clue number one. On the day of the murders, why was Dad late picking Liz and me up at the Olyphant's farm when he went into the city to visit Mom? He told Liz that Mom didn't want him to leave but Mom said he'd left in plenty of time." She slides her finger down. "Clue number two. In my photographs, is the man standing in the ditch outside the Drummond's house the same man who's standing behind Mr. Pendergrass? Is he the killer? Clue number three. Why did Mrs.

Witherspoon tell Liz that the killer walks among us? Is she right?"

"That's not really a clue," I say.

"Give me a break, I was a kid," Rose says. "Clue number four. What was Dad doing at the Tremblay's the day we had the wiener roast? He was kicking at the stones on the driveway like he was looking for something. Was he looking for clues? Clue number five," she says. "Why does Mr. Pendergrass keep going back to the Tremblay's? Is he looking for clues too? Is he the killer?"

"That was pretty good deducting for a kid," I say.

She flips the page. "Clue number six. Dad lost his cufflink while Mom was in the hospital. Yet he had it on the night Liz asked him to make an optometrist's appointment for Fran. It was on his sleeve when he pushed his supper to the floor. Where did he find it?" She looks up from the page. "Not sure if that's a clue, just something I noticed at the time, thought I'd jot it down."

"It's funny the things you remember," I say. "Dad was so angry at me for bugging him about that appointment, and all I could think was, *I'm glad you found your cufflink, Dad.* They were emeralds and I knew he was upset to have lost one. His mom gave them to him."

Rose paces across the room. "Clue number seven. How did Dad get so dirty the day he came home and scared Mrs. Gillespie so bad she cut off her finger? Clue number eight. Did Dad go to Gail Drummond's to give her money the night Liz and I saw him when we hid by the step, or was there some other reason?" She closes the book. "That's as far as I got because after that, the list went missing."

"You were always an astute child." I stand and tape the last box closed.

"Why did Dad take his truck to the fire?" she asks as she tucks the notebook into her purse. "That's been on my mind for years. I asked Dad once. He said he always took his truck on Sundays, but he didn't."

"Took his truck to the fire?" I open the door and stack a few of the boxes in the hall, anxious to get to my brother's house.

"Before you went inside the hardware store to rescue Fran, you told me to run to the firehall. Dad drove up in his truck at the same time as the firemen arrived in their firetruck. He never, in all the years he owned the store, took his truck to work. Why would he take his truck on the exact same day of the fire unless he was taking something out of the store?"

"Maybe he wanted to get home early that night. It was a Sunday; Mrs. Gillespie cooked a big meal on Sundays."

"But where was he? He wasn't at home because we were there and we didn't see him. He wasn't at the store because Fran was there and she couldn't find him. Did you see him on your way to the store?"

"I don't remember. Though I doubt it. He'd have come with me the moment I told him we'd seen smoke at the store."

"As I was running around the side of the house to go to The Park, I glanced at the garage. I have a vague recollection of the interior light being on. It's something that sticks out in my memory because you know how mad Dad would get when I left a light on. Maybe he was in there?"

"What does it matter?"

She shrugs. "I don't know, just something that sticks out in my mind. Do you remember Mac?" she asks.

"I do not," I say.

"He was hitchhiking across Canada. Mom gave him biscuits and coffee. You had a crush on him."

"Oh yeah!" I say.

She flips open her notebook and rifles through the pages. "It was after Dad said it was the perfect crime when Mac said, and I quote, *sooner or later something will turn up to incriminate him, something left behind at the crime scene.* That's when Dad started going to the Tremblay's. It just occurred to me that perhaps he was looking for his cufflink."

"His cufflink? He could have lost it anywhere."

"You're right, it's conjecture based on a slight degree of credibility. Dad lost the cufflink, and Dad kept going to the Tremblay's. The two could be connected but there's no way to prove that's what happened."

"Now you sound like a lawyer."

"It was the day after the murders when he couldn't find it. We heard him grumbling about it the morning after Mom brought Cole home. That means he lost it the day before, the day of the murders. The same day he was late picking you and me up at the farm."

Our eyes meet but we say nothing.

"Likely a weird coincidence," Rose says. She peers into the envelope. "There's something else in here."

"We've come this far," I say.

Rose pulls out a blue box. We sit on the edge of Dad's bed and I take the box from my sister. It's weighted and about the size and shape of a pound of butter. I hold it in my hand, some lost memory flitting through my brain.

"Well," Rose says, "are we going to open it, see what else our father saved?"

"Are you sure you want to? Like Mrs. Witherspoon said, once you see you can't unsee."

"I believe that was once you hear, you can't unhear. And I thought you couldn't remember that far back?"

"For some reason I remember everything about visiting her that day. So, I ask again, are you sure?"

"I am positive."

I set the box in my lap.

"This is familiar," I say. "I've seen it someplace." I think for a moment then tap the cardboard. "This is what Dad found at the fire. You and I were looking around at items we recognized and he was kicking at the ice like he was searching for something."

"I remember," Rose says.

"I found our family picture and Dad found this. He used his jackknife and dug it out then stuffed it in his pocket, I'm sure of it."

I slide the lid off. It makes a sucking sound as if it's been closed for decades. Inside is a half pint sealer, the kind Mom used for canning relish and crab-apple jelly. Inside the sealer is a murky liquid with a perfectly preserved human tongue lying on the bottom.

EPILOGUE - SPRING 1950

It's quiet in Gas-n-Go this afternoon with only three booths occupied. One booth has a family crowded onto the seats and the parents, with school out for another year, are trying unsuccessfully to keep their three youngsters from bouncing around like ping-pong balls. Another booth holds an older couple. They're from out of town and point at the farmland in the distance where the earth is being churned by machinery they don't know the names of. The third booth has four youths seated around its table. Many of the high school kids are farm kids who had to leave right after final bell to help their parents—spring is a busy time on the farm—so the rest of the booths are empty. Celebrating graduation will have to wait for those kids. But Marj told Jim, Carl, and Stan she needed to talk to them after last bell. Said it was urgent.

Afraid of getting in trouble with his dad, as he was expected to drive the tractor as soon as school was done, but also eager to do as Marjorie asked, Jim phoned home first to explain to his parents that he had to help the teacher close up the classroom for the year. His dad gave him an hour to finish the task then get to the farm. Because of this, he's the last to arrive. Carl and Stan sit on one side of the bench, and Jim slides in beside Marjorie who sits alone on the other side. The waitress, with a cigarette hanging from the corner of her mouth, wanders over. Smoke wafts into her eyes as she places the Cokes Marjorie already ordered, in front of each of them.

"So, we made it," Marj says when the waitress is gone.

The three boys are quiet. Jim takes a sip then shifts his eyes to Marjorie.

"It was an eventful year," she continues. "More eventful than we imagined it would be when it started."

Carl snorts and shakes his head. "Eventful," he says. "That's an understatement."

"You have something to say, Carl?" Marj asks.

Carl lifts his eyes to Jim. "Why did you have to kick the jack out?" His voice is hostile, angry. "You shouldn't have done that. You shouldn't have kicked the jack out."

"Be quiet," Marj says as she looks around the restaurant.

They haven't hung out together much in the past seven months, the happenings last fall, having torn them apart. Only Jim and Marjorie have been seen together lately, and that's as a couple, not as the friends they were at the beginning of grade twelve.

Marjorie hisses through her teeth. "Your dad would have dragged our good names through the mud. Jim only did what was best for all of us." She smiles. "I don't know about you, Carl Pendergrass, but I have important things to do with my life, and being accused of shoplifting would have ruined any chances I have."

Carl turns his head to hide the tears welling up in his eyes. "Dad told me he wouldn't say anything as long as I stopped hanging around with you guys. You didn't even give him a chance to explain, just kicked out the jack before he could get up off the ground." He and his dad were close and Carl misses him.

"We've been over it a hundred times, a thousand times," Marjorie says. "How could we trust him? I'd never be able to hold my head up around here again if he decided to turn us in. How could I get a job, go to school, do anything with a criminal record, how could any of us? And look at the bright side; your mom wouldn't have been given all that money if Jim hadn't done what he did. That little farm you and your dad worked barely made a living. Now you have enough money to live the rest of your life without having to work."

"You think money can replace my dad?"

"And how did your dad find out what we were doing, Carl?" Marjorie says sweetly. "You couldn't keep your big mouth closed, had to confess to Daddy. So don't harass Jim. He only did what he did to protect us."

"You said you had something urgent to talk to us about." Stanley stands to go. "I've better things to do than sit here and rehash everything. Isn't it enough that you," he looks at Jim, "made us all accomplices? God," he shakes his head, "I should have gone home, talked to my parents, confessed, not gone to your farm to try and talk your dad out of turning us in." He sways on his feet having drank a half mickey of whiskey before he arrived.

"Are you done, Stanley?" Marjorie says. "Sit down before you fall down. I have something to tell you." She puts the straw in her mouth and sips, leaving a smear of red lipstick on the paper tube. The boys wait without complaining. "I've been accepted to teachers' college. I leave next week."

"You what?" Jim says. "You're leaving? But I thought...."

"I know what you thought, Jimmy," she pats his hand, "but I don't plan on settling down. At least not yet and certainly not with you."

"You told me if I joined your little band of thieves," Carl says, "that you'd..." He stops, embarrassed talking about something that should be private between a man and a woman.

"I'd what, Carl? Go to bed with you?"

"I thought you knew I loved you," Carl whispers.

"Ah, Carl. Don't you understand? It's lust, not love."

"No, it's not!" Carl shouts. The older couple look at the booth with the four young people and Carl becomes quiet.

Stan laughs. "I could say the same thing about you, couldn't I, Jim? Lust, not love?"

"Stan's right, Jimmy. Were you trying to make me jealous?" Marjorie says.

Jim looks surprised.

"Do you think I didn't know about Abigale?" She laughs then strokes Jim's cheek. "You've always been a bit naïve about women, haven't you? All Abigale wanted out of you was marriage." She touches Stan's hand. "My sweet Stan. Such a kind boy. If I was going to pick one, it would have been you. You are a sweet and simple man. But you got sidetracked. Tying myself to a drunk for the rest of my life is not something I'd ever do."

Jim stands. His voice is quiet. "I've had enough of this bullshit. I may have been the one who kicked the jack, but all of us are guilty. Deep down none of you wanted to get caught. Deep down you're glad I was the one man enough to step up to the plate. And just so you know," he looks from face to face, "if any of you blab about what I did, if any of you tell anyone, threaten to tell anyone, you'll be sorrier than you can imagine. I'll do whatever it takes to protect my reputation. Whatever it takes. Remember that." He leaves Gas-n-Go without another word.

THE END

ABOUT THE AUTHOR

A Snake in the Raspberry Patch is Joanne Jackson's second novel. She lives in Saskatoon, Saskatchewan with her husband and a border collie named Mick. If you keep your eyes peeled you will see the three of them walking every morning; come rain, or shine, snow, or whatever weather Saskatchewan might throw at them.

ACKNOWLEDGMENTS

I would like to thank Heather Macdonald for reading the first and final drafts.

Thanks to Kathy Seamer for reading the final draft.

Thanks to Netta who suggested the first draft needed to be paired down considerably.

Thanks to Shelly Gregg for reading the rewrite then encouraging me to send the MS in again.

Many thanks to Lisa for her edits and advice, for without her, there truly would be no book.

Thanks to my husband for his encouragement, and thanks to my son, daughter and son-in-law for being my tech experts.